THE GIRL IN THE PHOTO

Sam Carrington lives in Devon with her husband, two border terriers and a cat. She has three adult children and two grandchildren. She worked for the NHS for 15 years, during which time she qualified as a nurse. Following the completion of a psychology degree she went to work for the prison service as an Offending Behaviour Programme Facilitator. Her experiences within this field inspired her writing. She left the service to spend time with her family and to follow her dream of being a novelist.

Readers can find out more at samcarringtonauthor.com and can follow Sam on Twitter @sam_carrington1 and on Facebook samcarringtonauthor.

THE
GIRL
IN THE
PHOTO

SAM CARRINGTON

avon.

Published by AVON
A division of HarperCollins*Publishers*
1 London Bridge Street
London SE1 9GF

www.harpercollins.co.uk

HarperCollins*Publishers*
Macken House, 39/40 Mayor Street Upper,
Dublin 1, D01 C9W8
Ireland

A Paperback Original 2023
2
First published in Great Britain by HarperCollins*Publishers* 2023

A catalogue copy of this book is available from the British Library.

ISBN: 978-0-00-843641-4

This novel is entirely a work of fiction. The names, characters
and incidents portrayed in it are the work of the author's
imagination. Any resemblance to actual persons, living or
dead, events or localities is entirely coincidental.

Typeset in Minion by Palimpsest Book Production Ltd, Falkirk, Stirlingshire

Printed and Bound in the UK using 100% Renewable Electricity
at CPI Group (UK) Ltd

MIX
Paper | Supporting
responsible forestry
FSC™ C007454

This book is produced from independently certified FSC™ paper
to ensure responsible forest management.

For more information visit: www.harpercollins.co.uk/green

For Shirley Cogan
(Sorry about the cursing!)

THE GIRL IN THE PHOTO, although fictional, contains discussions of mental illness that are frank and frequent throughout. Please read safely and responsibly. If you'd like to find out more, please read the author note at the back of the book but be warned it does contain spoilers.

Prologue

'Would you run through what we can see here, please?' Detective Sergeant Harris says as he pulls his chair up to the table and stares at the wall of monitors in the windowless room.

Wesley, the supermarket's on-duty security guard, quickly swipes the back of his hand over his forehead, then leans forward. He reaches across the table and points at the images on the first screen, revealing a damp patch beneath the armpit of his white short-sleeved shirt.

'A group of male teenagers enter, obscuring clear observation of the . . . erm . . . female in the blue coat, who's just visible and—'

'The actual colours of the clothing here aren't necessarily accurate,' Simon Tyne, the manager of the store, butts in. 'When used for these purposes, we have to inform you of that. We only use colours to facilitate identification on the CCTV but they might appear differently in real life.'

'Okay, thank you – that's helpful,' DS Harris says, scribbling in his notebook. 'Carry on, Wesley.'

'There's possibly a child walking behind – but it's difficult to confirm that because of the large group of males

1

obscuring the view.' Wesley takes a deep breath, then skips the footage ahead a few frames. The detective asks him to stop and go back.

'This female, seen standing beside the vegetable aisle, picking apples, may well be a witness. We'll need to speak with her,' DS Harris says. He turns to Simon. 'Can you have her brought to the staffroom please?'

'Yes, will do.' Simon gives Wesley a tight smile before backing out of the security room, leaving him alone with the detective.

'Are you the only security on duty?' DS Harris asks.

'No, but my colleague was on his break at the time.' He avoids eye contact with the detective and resumes playing the CCTV.

'That must be you, then?' Harris points to the screen – at the man in the white short-sleeved shirt and black trousers. 'Assuming the colours are correct,' he adds, wryly.

Wesley gives a silent nod.

'So, she's talking to you here?'

'Well . . . not exactly talking . . . as such.'

'What then?'

'I don't recall, if I'm honest.'

DS Harris frowns. 'Right,' he says, making another note in his book. Wesley stretches his back, a cracking noise sounding, then runs his hand over his cropped black hair as he side-eyes the detective. 'The group of males there,' Harris says, pointing. 'They the same ones that were at the entrance too?'

'Yeah, I guess.' Wesley shrugs, then seeing the detective's expression adds: 'They appear to be the same group, yes.'

DS Harris lets out a long hiss of air, frustration beginning to show. 'Are there any other angles – because those lads are partially obscuring the scene here and this is a critical moment.'

'No, sorry, that's it in this aisle.'

'And they'd left the supermarket before it was locked down. Great.' He shakes his head. 'No one monitors these cameras live?'

'No. Usually only look at it if something's happened, or we suspect someone of shoplifting.'

'Okay. What's next?'

Wesley plays the footage and they both watch as one witness stops to speak with a member of staff as the female in question rounds the corner – her back to the camera.

'Now she's in aisle two,' Wesley says. His attention shifts to another screen on the wall.

'And you're where?' DS Harris says.

'Er . . .' Wesley screws up his face. 'I must've gone back towards the desk. Close to the entrance.'

'And you didn't see the girl?'

Wesley scratches the stubble along his square jawline, then gives a cough before answering. 'No, sir.'

'That same group of males walk by her as she's ducking to the lower shelf,' DS Harris says, making another note before looking up. 'Now what's she doing?' He moves his head closer to the monitor, tilting as if to try and see around her. 'Looks like she's on her mobile phone.'

'Oh, I'm not sure. Difficult to say. Could be she's holding an item she's just picked off the shelf.' Wesley raises his eyebrows, then crosses his arms – the muscles in his forearms are so large he can barely complete the manoeuvre. DS Harris makes him rewind a few frames and watches it again. Seemingly satisfied, he gestures for Wesley to carry on.

'You can see the female looks around, then she drops an item to the floor and goes back up the aisle, leaving the trolley.' Wesley's narrative is monotone, like he's spoken the same sentence a million times before. Yet, this is the first time he's been involved in anything of this nature. He hopes it's the last.

'So this is where she finally realises.'

The two men watch in silence as the woman is seen to run back down aisle one, towards the entrance to the supermarket.

She falls to the floor and, even though there's no sound, you can practically hear her hysterical cries.

A member of staff approaches her.

'In the blink of an eye,' DS Harris says, almost in a whisper. Then he turns and glares at Wesley. 'And apparently, you didn't even see it happen.'

Wesley hangs his head.

'We'll need to review all available CCTV. Especially the entrance, exit, and outside footage. Do you go outside at all?'

Wesley's eyes widen. 'What do you mean?'

'You said you went back to the security desk close to the entrance – which also acts as the exit – so, did you step outside during any point?'

'Uh . . . maybe. I – I can't remember now.' Wesley stammers, shifting uncomfortably. 'It's all been very stressful.'

'Well.' DS Harris stands and walks up to Wesley. He's at least a foot smaller than the security guard but he squares up to him, nonetheless. 'I guess we'll find out soon enough, eh?'

*

'It took two and a half minutes for me to lose my child.'

The woman sits on a cream-coloured sofa, her eyes downcast, watching her fingertips as they absently twirl the corners of a crinkled tissue, forming it into a long, thin spike.

'I'd like you to reframe that sentence, if you could,' Dr Connie Summers says, her words spoken softly, yet with authority. The woman looks up, a curious expression on her face. As if expecting this, Connie immediately adds, 'Say that sentence again, removing yourself as the one doing the losing.'

The woman lets out a juddering sigh. 'It took two and a half minutes for someone to snatch my child.'

'Good, good.' Connie nods as she scribbles in her notebook.

Client presents with persistent complex grief disorder following the trauma of losing her daughter*. She is currently resisting change and continues to hope that her daughter will return.

*All references to the abduction are made by the client and have not been substantiated. Currently in the process of gathering evidence from the various authorities to enable best practice.

MEETING 1

Chapter 1

Erica

It's not something I'm doing lightly. I've thought of nothing else for months. I've tried everything . . .

No, that's not right. Too much focus on 'I'.

We love each other, but it's not enough anymore, is it. We've done everything in our power to keep going, keep trying . . .

I pick up an avocado, twisting it in my hand and pressing my thumb against the green, bumpy skin.

Even you have to admit defeat, surely? Sometimes it's not about staying together, it's about how to part amicably.

A child's crying pierces through my mind – interrupting the conversation I'm attempting to plan. Now I'll have to start over; it's the fifth false start. How am I going to be able to say this to Jamie's face?

I place the avocado in my shopping basket and look around to see a little girl, about four years old, her tearstained face red and bloated. She's wearing a pink coat buttoned up high, with a belt fastened tightly around her middle – the poor thing looks like she's parcelled up ready to be shipped off somewhere.

'Hey, sweetie. Can't you find your mummy?' I bend down to be on a level with the girl. She cries even harder. 'It's okay, shush, shush,' I say, frantically casting my eyes around the store for a member of staff. The child's wailing increases, and my heart rate picks up. Should I walk away? I'm clearly distressing her further and, in a minute, everyone will be staring at me and assuming I'm the one causing the girl's distress. They might think I'm trying to harm her, or worse, abduct her.

But I can't leave her like this, she needs me. A griping pain in my stomach steals my breath; I gasp, struggling to regain my composure. How can a simple act of kindness, concern for a child's welfare, be misconstrued?

Don't be so silly, Erica – just do something.

'I'll help you find your mummy,' I say, softly, and hold out my hand for her to take. I'll head straight to the customer services desk, and they'll put out an announcement. It'll be fine. The child and mother will be reunited within minutes.

Other shoppers stare at me as I pull the girl through them, half-dragging her up the aisle, her cries rising in pitch. I feel my face burn and I mumble, 'She's lost' as we pass by, just to make sure they know I'm helping.

'This little girl's become separated from her mother,' I say when I reach the counter, beads of sweat prickling my forehead. I leave the crying girl with the customer service assistant and immediately my stomach unknots, relief flooding my body. I wipe my damp hands down the legs of my skinny white jeans. I'm so pleased to have handed her to a member of staff. Now I can get on with my shopping in peace and finish the conversation I was having in my head. My mind, though, drifts instead to what I'm going to post on my Instagram page later. It's been two days since I updated my grid and my followers will be eager to learn what I've been up to. Engaging with my audience is a key attribute for a successful account, and sharing my IVF journey with them, the struggles, the highs and lows, is what keeps them interested and helps them and me to navigate this sometimes traumatic procedure.

My basket is still where I abandoned it, the avocado the lone occupant. I pick up the shopping where I left off, but the conversation with Jamie is, for now, lost. The desire to get back home and immerse myself in my Instagram life is enough to propel me around the store, popping the dinner items in my basket with speed. Just when I think I'll be done and home within the next half-hour, I clock the queues. Shuffling through the tightly lined-up customers, garnering tuts along the way, I head to the self-checkout only to be faced with a line snaking around towards the exit. I give an exasperated sigh and scan the tills for any potential gaps. I've only got one basket; it's overflowing, but I should be able to get away with the aisle for ten items or less. No one will care. With confidence, I join the line and position my basket so it's not so obvious I have at least twenty things.

As I move forward, my gaze wanders to the customer service desk. I hope the little girl was safely reunited with her mum. Heat flushes my cheeks; it's really warm in here. Christ, do they have some form of heating on? It's only autumn, not winter. I lay my basket on the conveyor, then shrug my jacket off, hanging it over the crook of my arm as I begin unpacking my basket. The woman behind the till lends me a sideways glance, glares at my growing line of groceries and gives a condemning shake of the head.

Her lips press together, forming a thin line, and her nostrils flare, so I flash a wide smile in return. You have to be confident if you're going to knowingly break the rules.

When the person in front of me has paid, the stern-looking till woman – Karen, her badge states below the Bateman's logo – snatches the 'next customer' bar and rams it up against the others to the edge of the conveyor, the loud clacking sound making me flinch.

'Morning,' I say brightly when it's my turn.

Karen's thick, black pencilled-on eyebrows rise but I avoid eye contact as she begins swiping my items through with exaggerated arm movements and a speed which makes my head spin. I struggle to keep up, practically throwing my things in the large 'bag for life'. I briefly wonder about the honesty of that statement. Whose life are they referring to? Because *this* bag won't last for the entirety of mine. It'll break at some point, then if I bring it back, they'll replace it for free. However, that will be a *different* bag. Karen barks the total at me before sitting back, arms crossed as she waits. I've gone through the ten items or less with more than that, but it's not as though I've committed a crime. Now, if I were to have walked out with said items without paying, that's a different matter. I'm about to point this out, when a tap on my shoulder startles me, and I turn sharply. I half expect it to be someone I know who's spotted me and is just saying hi. But it's no one I recognise. Distress is etched on the woman's face; her eyes are wide and imploring.

'Yes?' I ask.

'Have you seen her?' The single sentence sends a sliver of ice trickling down my back. I look down to her hand, where she grasps a photo. She pushes it in front of my face, too close for me to focus on it, but I can tell it's an image of a young girl.

'Er . . . have you lost your little girl?' My mind flounders for a moment, before settling on the assumption this woman must be the mother of the child I took to customer services. 'I found her and took—'

'You found her. Where? Where did you find her? Take me to her!' The woman grabs my arm, shaking it wildly. I take a step back, pulling away from her panicked grip.

I anxiously point across the supermarket. 'I . . . I took her to the customer—'

'Hang on!' Karen booms from behind the till. She extricates herself from her seat and shuffles towards us. 'Come on, love,' Karen says. 'Not again, okay?' She tries to guide her away from me and the till.

'Don't touch me.' The woman shirks her arm away and comes at me again with her outstretched hand. With my attention fully on her, I note her face is drawn, her skin dull, the crow's-feet spanning from her eyes look more like spiders' legs and her irises are so dark, it's as if the light's gone out in them. Her hair is wispy – I can see a patch where a clump of it has either fallen out or been torn from the follicles. It's pitiful, and something deep inside me breaks. 'You've seen her, haven't you?' she demands. 'You know where she is.'

My heart squeezes in my chest as she thrusts the photo into my hand. This poor woman, she must be distraught. For a long time I've been desperately trying to have a baby; I can visualise holding the tiny bundle in my arms, imagine the overwhelming love that will rush from me like a burst dam, but I don't ever want to think about the sheer hell of losing a child. As Karen talks to her, asking her to leave

13

the customers alone, I'm able to take in the details in the image. It's a head and shoulders shot of a girl in a stripey top, around the age of three. Her round blue eyes are edged with long pale lashes; she has bow-shaped lips that are slightly parted as though she's about to speak and her pretty freckled face is framed by strawberry-blonde curls. She's been captured while her attention is only half on the person snapping the photo, like she's in a world of her own. I smile.

But it's not the girl I found wandering the store earlier.

I push between Karen and the woman to hand back her photo. It must be precious to her. 'Where did you last see your daughter?' I ask.

'Here, at this supermarket,' the woman says, her breaths coming short and fast.

Karen puts her hands up in defeat. 'Look, I'm going to have to get security. You can't keep harassing the customers.'

I take a step back, shocked by Karen's attitude.

'This woman has lost her child. Are you listening?' My cheeks burn. 'Why aren't you *helping* her?' Karen lets out a long, deep sigh. She's not even looking at me, she's waving a security guard over.

'I'm sorry she's bothered you.' Karen returns her gaze to me, our eyes meeting in a hard glare. 'And there you were trying to be quick to get out of here. Bundling all your twenty items on the conveyor hoping no one would notice.'

I fluster, but then anger rises inside me. How dare she treat me, but more importantly this woman, with such disrespect? 'Well, I don't think something as critical as finding a missing child is a bother. Why aren't you doing something?'

A burly security man, young and brimming with

attitude, strides up to us but I instinctively stand in front of the woman, like somehow that'll protect her. He hesitates, shooting Karen a look that makes me think he doesn't much care for her attitude either.

'Yes, yes – I'm aware how it looks,' Karen says to the onlookers as she shimmies back around the till to take her seat. 'This isn't the first time. It won't be the last.' She rolls her eyes at the security guard. 'Can you do the honours again?' she says.

My expression must still be one of incredulity, as she gives a little shake of her head, some long silver-grey strands of hair escaping the band she's had it scraped up in. The queue has reached epic proportions and there's an air of restlessness as those who've been waiting patiently now huff and complain.

'This happens every bloody Friday,' Karen says in a hushed whisper. Like *now* she's being discreet. 'Poor thing. She's deluded . . .' I'm curious to learn more, but my attention is taken with the security guard attempting to remove the woman. I catch some of what's being said though – the customers in the queue suddenly keen to pipe in with their own opinions.

'Really? Has anyone even checked?'

'Trust me, the first time she came in here crying and distraught, it was taken very seriously. Full search of the supermarket, police called, CCTV checked and all. But nothing.'

'So, she didn't lose her child here?'

'I don't think there even was a child. Let alone a lost one,' she says.

'Why would she keep coming here to ask if anyone has seen her then? And who is the girl in the photo?'

Karen shrugs and begins swiping items through the checkout, the bleeping getting quicker as she speeds up. I'm gently nudged out of the way. As I leave the store with my two bags of shopping and head to where my car is parked, I scan the area.

But the woman is nowhere to be seen.

Chapter 2

Erica

With the food for tonight's meal put away in the fridge, I sit on the silver chenille cuddle chair with a mug of coffee in one hand while I scroll through my phone gallery with the other. I find the best image of my face that depicts 'exhaustion' but with eyes that show 'hope'. It's good to keep it real, but it's also important to show something positive. I took this selfie in bed a couple of weeks ago – my satin pyjamas shimmering in the soft lighting, my chocolate-caramel ombre hair cascading over my shoulders in an I-just-woke-up, messy look that took an hour to create – but following my opening caption, I describe it as if it were this morning. I detail how having another round of IVF treatment and the fear of failure fills me with such anxiety I can't sleep; the bags under my eyes are testament to this. I add how I'm 'manifesting success', though. That this will be the cycle that works. I *will* hold our joyous bundle in my arms, feel the baby's delicate soft skin against me, breathe in the intoxicating new-born scent.

After careful rereading to make sure it sounds right, I

tap the tick to upload the post to my grid. This is my hundredth post since embarking on my journey.

Erica_IVF_Journal This is what day 100 feels like . . .

Within minutes I've had thirty likes and my notifications are pinging.

My_IVF_journey_dani Thank you for sharing the reality, Erica – you're such an inspiration. 😊

ForeverHopeful So important to envisage the end goal. It WILL happen. Keep the faith. Hugs.

HopeSpringsEternal You look great Erica – don't forget some self-love. I found hypnosis helps too. Have you tried that?

Ivf_mummy_Jo I've experienced so much disappointment it's hard to keep going sometimes. Reading about other people's journeys reminds me I'm not alone. Thank you, Erica. We've got this!

A warm sensation radiates through me while I read some of the comments. So many women are yearning for a baby to love, going through painful and challenging experiences, many suffering with depression following failed attempts – if sharing my posts helps just one of them through the process, then I've done some good.

After spending my allotted time responding and commenting on others' images, I rub my eyes, pocket my phone and make a fresh brew to take upstairs. We made the spare room of our three-bedroomed, terraced house into my office – before that it'd been a dumping ground for anything we deemed 'useful but not needed', which turned out to be quite a lot. It's amazing what you can collect in a relatively short space of time – we've only been here for four years. We moved here, to the South Devon coast, from Bath, even though it's further away from any of our support network. I can't remember now whose idea it was to relocate to Kingskerswell, but I was the one to spot this place and was excited by the prospect of an extra bedroom. It was never meant to be an office. But after a few trips to the recycling centre that's what it became. I popped in a desk, chair and some shelving bought from IKEA, which I painstakingly put together myself, and Jamie had been both amazed and impressed when he saw how much bigger the room seemed when I'd finished.

I can't help but pause now, though, before passing by the second bedroom. The nursery. With one hand on the doorframe, I gaze longingly at the pastel aqua walls, the jungle mural, the crisp white furniture, the polka-dot and star-print rug. My breath snags in my chest and I pull the door closed before the tears start.

The house is too quiet. When it's like this, my thoughts become even louder. 'Hey, Siri,' I say to my Apple HomePod. 'Play Hans Zimmer film scores.' Firing up the computer, I find the document I was last working on and begin tapping away at the keyboard as 'No Time for Caution' from *Interstellar* plays. My latest article is taking shape. Just as well, really, seeing as it's due to be sent to the editor tomorrow. When I decided to leave my full-time journalist role at the *Mid-Devon Advertiser* and do freelance writing, it was so I could be flexible, more able to fit in around the lifestyle we'd chosen. To enable me to spend more time focusing on our goals.

I sit back in my chair for a moment, a fleeting memory of being in a busy office setting off a twinge of regret. There's something to be said for being surrounded by colleagues. Friends. I barely see anyone socially these days. Bea is one of the only friends I'm still in contact with, and even that's sporadic. In fact, now I think of it, I can't even remember when I saw her last. Being your own boss, working from home, isn't always what it's cracked up to be.

But, Jamie likes me being here when he gets back from work. Working with offenders in prison all day is demanding – he often comes home with a drawn face and short temper. Last night it had taken him several hours to wind down. I inhale slowly as his face snaps into my mind – his clenched jaw, narrowed eyes and lips pressed in a harsh line inches from my face. Lately, it hasn't taken much to push him into an angry rant.

Maybe I'll suggest a getaway – we haven't been away for ages. It doesn't have to be abroad, we've got a couple of favourite places locally, and there's nothing stopping us using our own holiday home – we haven't rented it out the past three years, so it's empty all the time. If we're in a different environment, we'll find it easier to relax, and there's a stronger likelihood I'll be able to transfer the serious conversation that I've been practising from my head to my mouth. Ending our marriage on more neutral territory will at least make the process slightly less heartbreaking. This idea spurs me on, and I quickly finish and send the article, then check my diary for commitments. If he's in a good mood, I'll broach the subject.

The rhythmic clacking of metal on wood as I chop the veg for the casserole takes my mind away from my thoughts. I get lost in its sound, until it somehow muffles. Sharp pain shoots through my finger. 'Damn!' I drop the knife as I retract my hand, quickly sucking on my bleeding fingertip. I grab a tea cloth and wrap it tightly around the wound. It's just superficial. Lucky I didn't lose the end of my finger.

'Careful! Clumsy you.'

I spin around, startled by Jamie's voice. 'I didn't hear you come in,' I say.

'Looks like you were too busy giving Freddy Krueger a run for his money.'

I offer a weak smile, but quickly flip into my usual bright and breezy self – the one I know is expected of me. 'How was your day?'

'Stressful.' Jamie's hazel-green eyes avoid mine.

'Oh?' A niggling feeling pulls at my stomach. I'm used to this line because he describes every day as stressful, but this evening it's as if the light has faded – even his skin looks dulled. 'Any particular reason?'

He runs a hand over his close-cropped hair, pushing his lips downwards. 'Just not getting anywhere with my latest client. It's been weeks and I'm failing to make headway.'

Jamie always refers to the criminals he works with as clients; I find it quite endearing. Of course, I'm sure I wouldn't feel the same if I knew what offences they'd committed, but he never tells me stuff like that. Protecting me from the horrors of the world is important, he often says, but more than that, it's because he takes his forensic psychologist role and patient confidentiality extremely seriously.

'Massage later?' I offer, knowing this usually improves his mood.

His smile doesn't quite reach his eyes. 'Yeah. Sure.'

I feel my forehead furrow as I stare at him, concerned by his lacklustre response. Does he know the conversation I'm planning in my head, or has he simply sensed the underlying current of disquiet that's been running within me for the last few months? The fact there've been occasions when I've had to drag myself out of bed in the morning, taken extended showers because my body ached with exhaustion and refused to move from underneath the jets of water battering my skin, or stared into space while eating, my attention taken by rehearsed conversations in my head. Maybe I've not been hiding any of it as well as I'd thought. It's not easy to go through what we are and remain the happy couple we once were. It takes its toll – numerous medical visits, mounting fees. It's the emotional impact that's the worst. At times, I've felt like everything is building up inside me like a pressure cooker. I have an outlet, at least. I know it's only Instagram, but I have a whole network of people I 'talk' to. I can escape into it; it's a distraction, of sorts. Jamie has prisoners, colleagues he doesn't see much outside of work – or so he says – and only a handful of mates. None of whom are in our position.

'I've done a casserole,' I say, as if this is going to melt away his tension.

'So I smell.' He moves in close, giving me a feeble kiss on the cheek. 'I'll go change.'

I watch him as he leaves, a heavy stone lying in the pit of my stomach.

The scent of ylang-ylang wafts up as I pour drops of oil onto Jamie's back; he flinches as the cool liquid hits his skin.

'Sorry, should've warmed it first,' I say, jiggling to get myself into a comfortable position, my legs straddling him. He groans when I press my palms into his lower back and push them up towards his shoulders, the knots of tension making my hands bump like a car going over speed humps. 'Wow, you really are uptight.'

'Yep. Months of stress will do that.' He says it lightly, but I immediately stiffen. He means because of me. I'm the one causing the most stress. I bite my lip, and continue massaging, my hands now gliding effortlessly across his smooth skin. No point me choosing this moment to get all defensive as he'll go off on one and the night will be a car crash. 'Pick your battles' my mum used to tell me. A confrontation now, while he's in this mood, won't serve me well. The idea of a mini-break will also need to be put on hold; he'll see straight through my suggestion if I bring it up now.

The Split comes on the telly and Jamie raises his head from the floor, reaching for the remote and switching channels without asking if I was watching. I know why. A programme about divorce lawyers is something to be avoided. It might force us to confront our own marriage, and while I'm ready for that, it seems he is not. As I rub more oil on, my attention drifts to the woman at the supermarket.

'I had a really odd experience at Bateman's today,' I say. Partly because I want to fill the void of silence, but mostly because I want to share what happened so I can get it out of my head.

'What kind of odd?'

'A little girl was lost, crying for her mummy, and so I took her to the customer service desk—'

'Well, that's what most people would do. I assume she was reunited.'

I stop massaging, balling my hands into fists. I hate it when he butts in before I've even finished speaking.

'Let me finish . . .' I say, calmly. He mutters an apology and I continue without further interruption. Once I finish describing the incident with the lost girl, I then tell Jamie about my encounter with the woman with the photo.

'They were so nonchalant about it all. Like she didn't matter. It was awful.'

I feel Jamie's muscles tense against my inner thighs.

'Really? And no one did anything? That doesn't sound right.'

'Meaning? You don't think my interpretation of the event is correct?'

'No, Erica. The way they dealt with it wasn't. Anyway, don't worry yourself over it. There are some troubled souls out there – that's life.'

'That's harsh,' I say. 'Coming from someone who's meant to care about people.'

'I *do* care. But those I'm closest to come before strangers.'

'Well, you're no better than them, then. How can you say they didn't deal with her in the right way when you're now saying, "That's life"?'

'Obviously, I mean had I been there myself, observing such a situation, I'd have acted differently to the staff at Bateman's. But you're not staff and it's not your problem.'

'But I can't stop thinking about her. About the little girl in the photo.'

Jamie's body bucks beneath me. I slide off him as he sits up and turns sharply to face me. His eyes seem to spark as the light from the lamp catches his irises.

'You give her an inch, she'll take a mile,' he says. I'm taken aback by the force of this statement; the way his eyebrows knit together making his features hard. Angry. It's as though I'm being told off by my father for directly disobeying him – the way I used to when I'd sneak out in the dead of night to meet up with my boyfriend after being grounded. I shake my head, bewilderment clouding it.

'What do you *mean*?'

Jamie's brow unfurrows, his face settling into a more concerned expression. 'She's probably unwell, Erica. Trying her luck, latching on to anyone who gives her the time of day. I've seen similar behaviour, don't forget.'

'I don't think you can compare her to those you work with, Jamie.'

'But if there really was a missing child, we'd know about it. It'd be all over the news, wouldn't it? Honestly, don't give it any more thought, okay?'

How can he be so flippant? It's like water off a duck's back with him. I'm not sure why I'm shocked by his reaction though. I always wondered why he went into psychology as a profession because he has an amazing ability to brush aside emotions, pack them into a suitcase and hide it away in a closet. It's one of the reasons I want to leave.

Or that's what I tell myself.

'Sure,' I say. 'I'll forget about it like it didn't even happen. If that's what will make you happy.'

'Don't be like that,' he says, coming in closer and laying an arm over my shoulders. 'It's nothing to do with what'll make me happy. I'm thinking of you. What's best for you. There's so much going on already, we're trying to relieve stress, not add more. It's not good for you, you know that.'

It's not good for either of us. The way Jamie talks makes it sound like it's just me who's affected by the IVF process and it's me who needs protecting, to be wrapped up in cotton wool. He seems to have conveniently forgotten how low his mood was last year. I recall the first evening I realised. We'd found out in the morning, and I'd thought he was okay, but when I came home from Bea's to find him curled up on the cuddle chair, the room in darkness, I knew he wasn't. I hadn't even known he was home, had come bursting into the lounge, whacking the main light on and jumping when I saw him sitting there pale and still like a stone statue.

'Are you sick?' I'd asked, going to him and laying the flat of my palm against his forehead. He'd silently brushed it away. Seeing the blank expression on his face made my heart pound. I was used to him being the strong one, the one to push on through whatever life threw at him. At us. All of a sudden it was him who needed my strength. 'I'm sorry, babe,' I said, nudging him up so I could fit in beside him. 'We can try again.' We'd stayed that way for hours, had fallen asleep like it. When I'd woken, he wasn't there – a blanket had been placed over me; he'd gone to bed. Days had passed during which he'd barely spoken. He'd just trudged along, pretending everything was fine, but his drawn features had told a different story.

I look at him now and resist the urge to mention it; I'm too tired to bring any of that up.

It's gone midnight and I lie in bed watching the steady rise and fall of Jamie's shoulders, listening to the gentle hiss of air escaping his parted lips. He always seems to sleep soundly these days, no matter what's going on in his head, however stressed or worried he is. It's like he has a switch he can flick off the second his head touches the pillow. Sometimes, the fact he's capable of it causes a twinge of jealousy to creep under my skin. Other times, I just despise him for it. Right now, my eyes sting with tiredness but they refuse to stay closed. I can't stop running over the day in my mind – can't think of anything but the woman and her photo. It niggles at me, like a woodpecker tapping at my skull.

When I eventually fall asleep, it's short-lived. My mind is riddled with nightmares. I see the little girl from the photo, her stripey top torn and bloodied, her tiny body pale and motionless, dumped beside a river in a forest. A scream rips me away from the dream into reality and I sit up, sweat dampening my skin, a deep ache in my stomach. I get up to go to the loo, half expecting to see blood on my pyjama bottoms – another failure – but there's none. I sit on the cold toilet seat, the echo of the disturbing dream reverberating inside my brain.

That poor woman, she must feel so alone. How would I feel if people didn't take me seriously? If they swept my fears and anxiety, the longing for a child, under the carpet? The woman in the supermarket *must've* lost someone to be there every week, as Karen said. Surely she wouldn't waste her time like that if it wasn't true? What on earth would she gain by doing that? She's genuine. Not for one second did I disbelieve her; I saw the honesty in her eyes. Maybe meeting her – her choosing me to approach – was some kind of sign.

Buoyed by this thought, I climb back into bed. A strange calmness washes over me and I suddenly feel like I could sleep soundly. I've made up my mind. I don't care what Jamie says, I'm going to look for the woman, Karen said she was at Bateman's every Friday. If I ask her for more detail, I might be able to help in some way. The woman clearly just wants someone to take her seriously. I can be that person. *I'm* meant to help her. Perhaps it's a test. To be worthy of having a child, I must show I deserve one. It's good to help others. It'll ensure good karma. And Lord knows I could do with that.

Chapter 3

Erica

My bulging gym bag sits in the hallway by the front door, ready for me to throw into the car. I sit on the bottom stair trying to gear myself up as I pop my trainers on. When having IVF treatment, it's advised not to do strenuous exercise – among a list of other things, like vetoing alcohol – so I swapped my usual high-intensity workouts in favour of yoga. Mentally, it's supposed to be good for reducing anxiety and improving mood. Win–win.

So, why am I struggling with motivation? I stare at the bag, the rolled-up mat looped through the handles, and sigh. As I heave myself up, pulling on the banister, my entire body feels sluggish, like it's moving five times slower than its surroundings.

'You'll feel better once you're there, and definitely when it's finished and you're back home with a cuppa,' Jamie's words repeat in my head. When I was perching on the edge of the bed this morning, head in hands, he'd attempted to offer encouraging words. 'You'll have a sense of accomplishment,' he said, kissing the top of my head.

I beg to differ. I'm thinking of skipping the middle part – the bit that's going to take the most effort – and going straight for the cuppa. A relaxing hot drink with a sweet treat is as equally beneficial to my mental health as an hour of twisting into poses and deep breathing along with a bunch of strangers.

But you promised yourself. And Jamie.

I groan at my irritating inner voice. To get the desired results, you need to put in the required effort. I slap my cheeks to liven myself up. It's one hour out of my life. I can do this.

'It's just a yoga session, Erica,' I tell myself as I lift the bag onto my shoulder and open the door. I smell someone's fry-up wafting on the breeze and stick my nose in the air to breathe it in. Can't remember the last time I had a full English brekkie – it's not classed as eating healthily in Jamie's book. I throw the bag on the back seat and walk around to the driver's side, my attention catching on the house opposite. Over the last few months, it's gone from being pristine, perfectly painted and with a neatly manicured garden, to a house looking a little unloved and in need of attention, with a garden I'd describe as more wild than tamed. The lady who lives there with all the cats is currently manoeuvring herself into the armchair in the centre of the front window, the cats darting about like blobs of flying fur, waiting for her to settle so they can. I never see the cats outside, so I assume they're indoor ones. Place must stink; I can't imagine how much litter they must go through. Thinking of it now, I don't see deliveries being made to the house either and the woman doesn't seem to get out much, not even for a walk. She certainly doesn't look capable of lugging around bags of cat litter.

She must have family to do stuff for her. But then, if that's the case, why don't they tend to the garden, or maintain the exterior of the house, or at least organise someone else to do it? A good neighbour would offer to help in some way, wouldn't they? A twinge of guilt makes me drag my gaze away. I know what my subconscious is doing – trying to get me to focus on someone else's life so I don't have to think about mine. But as I reverse out the drive, I can't help but look at her, and as I pass by, I give a wave. That could be me, I think, in thirty years' time. No husband, no human contact at all – just a load of cats. Does she talk to them, I wonder. Like, full-on conversations as if they were her human friends. A dull ache resonates within my gut. It's a sad thought, really.

She gives a slow nod of her head and I swear I feel the weight of her dark eyes on me as her gaze follows my car's progression. A strange sense of unease creeps through me and I shudder. There was a woman just like her in the village I lived in when I was around eight years old. The old spinster had managed to gain the reputation of being a witch among the younger generation – she had a single cat, not even a black one, but that, together with living alone in a run-down house with an overgrown garden and a penchant for shouting at kids, was enough for the nickname to stick and the rumours to grow.

But, as far as I know, there are no such rumours about the cat lady around here. Then again, there aren't a lot of kids in this older part of Kingskerswell. Plus, nowadays I suspect they've moved on from village folklore, exchanging real-life antics for TikTok videos.

I push my strange sense of unease back down. She's my neighbour and although I might not know her, the fact

I'm even allowing such thoughts to germinate in my mind goes to show I'm taking the principle of focusing on others too far.

The devil makes work for idle hands.

Chapter 4

Dr Connie Summers

Connie Summers sits back, crosses her legs, then pushes her glasses up, resting them atop her shoulder-length, sleek black hair. Her green eyes are intense as she focuses her gaze on the woman opposite her. She's so petite that the huge, six-foot-long cream sofa which dominates the room almost engulfs her. Connie has slept on the same sofa on more than one occasion, her client's notes slipping from her stomach to the lush beige carpet with hardly a sound. Since the passing of her wife, Lindsay, Connie has committed more time to her therapy sessions, more time to thinking about other people's broken lives. Less time in what was the marital bed. This has been her job for over eight years, since leaving the forensic field and retraining, gaining a PhD in psychotherapy. Running her practice from home was always her goal and, thanks to Lindsay's support and encouragement, last year it was realised.

This client, she reflects now as she offers the woman a gentle smile, is by far her most challenging. She has tested Connie's skills, demanded more exploration and research than anyone. She's stretched her capabilities and pushed her to her limits. She's one session away from passing her to a colleague to see if they can break the barrier. Because Connie is struggling. With such lack of progress, it seems unprofessional to keep taking the fee week on week. The whole point of her work is to guide people through psychological issues. Not get stuck in the middle, forever doomed to go around in circles like a merry-go-round. It's a sticking point and, no matter how Connie tries to steer the woman around it, it always comes back to this.

'No one helps. No one listens.' She chews on a fingernail, the chipped polish flaking even more. Connie follows the path of the flakes as they flitter to the carpet – bright red dots scattering like minute droplets of blood. Last week, Connie had taken the painted nails as a good sign. Their state this week cancels that out.

Connie returns her attention to the woman's tearstained face. 'I'm listening,' Connie says. She's uttered those words so many times before.

'How can people be so filled with their own self-importance, consumed by only their stupid lives? Even to the point people photograph their food and post on social media. How preoccupied and self-indulgent are they? All the while, my daughter is gone. I put it on social media, of course I did – it's the only way to get noticed these days. But after a while, they lost interest. It's just online – they're not real people. I need reality.'

'What is your reality? Describe it.'

'*My* reality is daily fear, anxiety. Longing. Each morning I wake up, it's like a fresh day for a second, before the crushing realisation she's not here. Then I wish I hadn't opened my eyes. Darkness descends but I have to live it

– and I've tried to make friends, find someone to share my innermost thoughts with, but I'm ignored. I'm alone. I can't sleep through every second of each day, which would be preferable.'

'And how might you change that?'

'Are you kidding me? Don't ask such stupid questions. I want my daughter back of course.'

'For now. In the short term – how can you change the feelings you're currently experiencing?'

'By reaching out. Getting help.' The words trip off the woman's tongue in a rehearsed way, but Connie takes them and rolls with them.

'Good. And you've taken that first step with me.' Connie holds in a sigh. That first step was months ago, but each time feels like the first. She blinks, slowly. 'It's a moment-by-moment recovery—'

'It's not recovery I want. It's my daughter.'

'Perhaps you need one, before you can have the other.'

The woman shakes her head. 'Are you saying I can't have my baby back unless I recover?'

'No. That's not what I'm saying. The road you're on is a long one, it's not going to be a straightforward journey. If you manage some of the most challenging aspects – the ones you can realistically change, say – then you'll be in a better position to move forwards.'

'I don't know where to start.'

'At the beginning.'

'When I let her go?'

'I think we need to go further back than that.'

MEETING 2

Chapter 5

Erica

I've half a mind on my shopping, the other on the bustling people, some more speedy than others as they pile items into their trolleys. I'm knocked by an impatient man as he reaches above my head to the highest shelf – he then proceeds to elbow me out of the way. On any other day, I'd be quick to trot out a pass-agg comment, but I'm too keen to pick out the woman from last week among the shoppers to waste time with him. Karen had said the woman with the photograph was here every week 'harassing the customers', so I'm hopeful I'll catch her as I made sure to be here at the exact same time.

Jamie said I should go shopping on a different day. I told him not to be so ridiculous, that I'm not changing my habits. I'll easily be able to avoid her if she's there, I'd assured him. Of course, I'm trying for the opposite. He doesn't need to know what I'm planning. I'm capable of making my own decisions. I haven't been able to rid the woman's desperate face from my mind, much less the photo of her little girl, so I've no choice but to ignore his negative take anyway. Besides, just because he's a psychologist doesn't mean he knows about every person, their motives for what they do or why. He's been wrong before.

I slip my mobile from my pocket and see I've been here an hour already and there's been no sign. Hovering near the tills, I scan the area the woman was in last week. She's not there. The security guard, with muscles straining beneath his white shirt, offers a cautious glance in my direction. I stare at him until his focus shifts to someone else. Disappointment swoops over me as I check the customers packing their bags and don't spot anyone brandishing a photo, nor do I see Karen. I can't remember now whether Karen said the woman is here the same *time* every Friday, or just that it's every Friday. It's now a good half an hour past the time I was approached last week. Either I've missed her, or she's going to be in later today. How long can I get away with loitering here? I've parked close to the entrance, so maybe I'd be better off sitting in my car and keeping watch from there. Less suspicious, at any rate. I see Mr Muscles is eyeing me again. It's the same man from last week, I realise, and I'm tempted to ask him if he's seen the woman with the photo today. He takes his radio, all the while watching me. I tilt my chin in the air as I move towards the checkouts, hoping my indignation is obvious. I don't need his help.

After packing my few items and paying with no interruptions from anyone asking me to look at a photo, I go to the exit. I catch sight of a familiar-looking woman trussed up in a heavy raincoat coming in the store and stop dead. I ignore the annoyed muttering of the person who bangs into me from behind and retrace my steps, pushing the exit barrier to get back inside and follow the woman. A whirring noise blares and people turn to look at me. I lift my shoulders in a shrug, and carry on, scooting around the end of an aisle to see if I can catch the woman up.

As I come level with her, I see it's not her. With a deep sigh, I turn and push through the self-checkout line to leave the shop. I sense Mr Muscles' eyes on me again and half expect a tap on the shoulder once I've left the premises. No one follows me.

I sit in the car, shoulders slumped. Deflated.

Never mind. She may still turn up. I rummage in a carrier for the pasta pot I bought. I'll eat that while I stake the place out. A knock on the driver side window makes me jump; I drop the pot in the footwell as my hand flies to my chest.

'Jesus!' I'm ready to give whoever it is a piece of my mind, but as I snap my head around to face the window, my words freeze in my mouth.

It's her.

She's wearing a dark grey oversized raincoat; it's old fashioned like something my nan would've worn. There are patchy areas of paler grey where it's been bleached by the sun. It could've even been blue once upon a time. Last week when she approached me, I'd have put her age at forty-ish. But dressed like this she appears older.

I fumble in the footwell to retrieve my pasta pot, which luckily didn't spill its contents, then turn the key in the ignition so I can lower the window.

'Hi,' I say. 'I was looking for you.'

'Yes, I know. I was watching.'

I sit up straighter, my eyebrows shooting up. She was *watching* me? How come I didn't spot her?

'Oh, right . . .'

'I was keeping a low profile. Wes had already had a word.'

'Wes?' I narrow my eyes.

'Security.'

So, she's on first-name terms. I guess if she's here every week, that makes sense.

'Low on shoplifters, I suppose. Probably bored if he's targeting you like that,' I say. It must be the same bloke who was just keeping a watchful eye on me, too. Unless his interest goes beyond catching people shoplifting and is more about staring at females for his own pleasure. I remember a case in the news not long ago, where a man employed in a public-facing role had kept his head down for years, not attracting the wrong kind of attention from his employer or those he worked with, and all the while he'd been abusing his position to acquire contacts of lonely women. He'd gone on to obtain intimate images of them which he'd claimed were for his own use, but further evidence had found he'd sold them on the dark web. I'd hope that kind of thing is rare, but no doubt Jamie would inform me otherwise if I asked.

'He thinks he's something special, that one,' she says, rolling her eyes. 'Bet he's a failed cop. But all he has to do is flex those muscles and all the sad, pretty women fall for it.'

I raise an eyebrow, the bitterness in her voice clear. At least I have a name for Mr Muscles. *Wes*. The name fills my mind, but now all I can think of is the director guy, Wes Craven, who did all those horror films my friends love.

'I didn't even clock him before last week,' I say, snapping back to the moment.

'That surprises me,' she says. I don't think she means it in a bad way, but I blush, slightly affronted by her assumption. Before I can think any more about it, she carries on. 'It's as if he's waiting for me and ready to pounce the second I walk through the entrance. Creeps me out.' She gives a little shudder.

This close, I can see dark circles under her eyes. Her straggly hair whips around her face with a gust of wind and she brushes it back, tucking it behind her ears. 'I knew you'd come back,' she says, the corners of her mouth hitching into an ever-so-slight smile.

Her words make my stomach knot, and tears I wasn't aware were close spring to my eyes. How could she know that? Is my own pain obvious – like a tattoo etched on my skin for all to see? I swallow hard.

'Do you want to talk?' I say, not really having a plan beyond this moment. I've spent the best part of a week imagining what I'm going to say to her, but now those carefully thought-out words abandon me. I don't know why I bother rehearsing what I want to say. I never can manage to articulate it when the time comes.

'Yeah, please. I could really do with a friend.'

Jamie's words of warning scream in my head. *She's probably unwell, Erica. Trying her luck, latching on to anyone who gives her the time of day.*

Pushing them away, I smile at the woman. 'Get in.'

My heart batters against my ribs as I let her into my car. Her coat flaps open as she climbs in. Underneath, I can see a woolly jumper – scruffy and bobbly. I wonder where she lives, if she has a house.

'Thanks, Erica.' She extends her hand towards me, and I take it. Her hand is soft, warm to the touch despite the nip in the air today. 'I'm Mercy Hamilton,' she says.

My lips part, ready to respond with my name. But the words catch as I realise she already said it.

Chapter 6

Erica

'Oh,' I say, blinking at Mercy as I try to recall if we'd exchanged names last week – the first time I'd set eyes on her.

'You don't remember me?' Mercy frowns, and confusion floods my mind.

'Well, yes, from last Friday, but . . .'

She gives a little huff. 'Apparently, I'm easily forgotten.'

A shot of embarrassment floods my face with heat. 'Oh, um . . .' I'm flailing around in the dark. I've invited this woman into my car, and now she seems to think I must know her. Remember her. I assume from when her daughter went missing? I want to ask, but her expression is stony and a sudden apprehension paralyses my vocal cords. Mercy's eyes don't leave my face and right now, with her here, sitting next to me, I don't know what I'm doing. I shift uncomfortably in my seat. Jamie's voice is clear in my ears, loudly saying, *I told you so.*

'You're different from the others, though,' she says, thoughtfully. She lowers her head, staring into her lap, her focus now on her wringing hands. 'At least you were bothered enough to seek me out today.'

My muscles relax – my unease lessening. I offer an apologetic smile, on behalf of everyone who's ignored her or treated her with disrespect. I can't believe people are so selfish, that they can't even take a minute out of their day to listen to her. Look at a photo. What harm is there in that?

'Yes, I was most certainly bothered. The way you were dismissed, it's awful.' I pause, taking a breath before speaking again. 'I wanted to ask you about your daughter,' I manage, more confidently than I feel. 'I haven't stopped thinking about her all week.'

'You believe me then?' She nods, smiling. Her face lights up when she smiles, taking years off her appearance. Any brightness vanishes, though, the second it settles back into its resting position. It's as if it was a figment of my imagination.

'Yes, of course.' And I do. Because not for one minute can I comprehend why someone would put themselves through this otherwise – why she'd turn up here week on week unless it was in the hope of finding that first crumb in the trail that might lead to her daughter. Mercy has nothing to gain by lying. And if Jamie thinks she's doing it for attention, then he's mistaken. Because let's face it, she isn't *getting* much.

'You have no idea what that means. Thank you.'

My stomach flutters, and I look away. The windows are beginning to huff up with our hot breath; the people passing by to go into the supermarket or back to their cars appear as blurry blobs each going about their own business.

A car horn blares from somewhere behind me and I

turn sharply to see a bloke in a people carrier gesticulating madly.

'What's his problem?' I say, looking at Mercy as though she can give me the answer.

'Everyone's always so rude and impatient here,' she says with a knowing sigh.

He honks again, so I fling my door open to find out what the hell he's playing at. Other shoppers turn and gawp in our direction. Great. Just what I need – more attention. With a heavy scowl and my mouth open ready to give him a piece of my mind, I face him. I refrain from verbalising my angry outburst as I see a little boy in a car seat behind him. I won't be rude back, not in front of his son. The man jabs his finger towards something behind me, and I turn to see the sign. A parent and child parking space. I suck in air and hold it in my lungs. My eyes prickle and I have to remind myself to breathe. Does my mind and body crave a baby so much that I unconsciously chose this space? The intensity of my desire wells inside me and I have to mentally push it down. I mutter an apology that seems to fall on deaf ears.

'I said, I'm sorry,' I repeat. 'It was a mistake. I'll move now.'

I climb back in the car, my face burning. Mercy gives me a sympathetic smile.

'Wanker,' she says, and it offers the light relief needed to balance the situation. I smile.

'Right,' I say. 'I'd better hurry before he bursts a vein.' My eyes dart to my rear-view mirror – the father is still waving his arms. Anyone would think I've been caught committing a crime, not simply parking in the wrong space. His child's face is now pressed against the glass, his squashed features resembling those of a Cabbage Patch doll.

'Yeah. I need to get going anyway,' Mercy says, and her head lolls as she reaches for the door handle. It's taken a few hours to find Mercy again and now thanks to the aggressive man's interruption, our chat has been cut short. We've managed a snatched conversation – but I sense she wants more. 'Perhaps we could do this again next Friday?' she says, her voice hopeful. 'It would be really nice to have someone to talk to about my girl.' Mercy's bloodshot eyes bore into me. 'But we should do this in comfort next time,' she says.

The mention of a next time stalls me, and my jaw moves without my lips forming words. I hadn't gone as far as to think past this one meeting. But what else had I been expecting? It's not as though I can simply ask about her missing daughter then say goodbye, good luck finding her. In my gut, I must've known this wouldn't be a one-off. By purposely seeking her out today, I must've *wanted* it to be more. The revving engine behind me forces me to make a quick decision.

'Erm . . . Yes, sure.'

Mercy smiles and gets out of my car. By the time I've moved out of the space for Mr Dad of the Year, she's gone.

I drive home, the sets of traffic lights, the other vehicles on the road, all unattended and filtered out of my mind, my attention fully on thoughts of Mercy and her child instead.

It's not until later, when I'm looking through my Instagram grid, that I remember Mercy had called me by my name. I was flustered when she first got in the car, and then side-tracked by the man blaring his horn at me, so forgot about it. At the time, she'd seemed more concerned that I didn't remember her. There's probably a simple explanation of course. But I find myself wondering just how *did* she know my name?

I guess I'll have to wait another week now to find out.

Chapter 7

Erica

Once home, I make a hot drink and head straight to my office. Clicking on my work folder to take my mind off Mercy, I bury myself in the lifestyle article I'm meant to be writing for *OK!* magazine.

I speed through, my fingers furiously tapping on the keys, then hit the send button, emailing my article to the editor, before immersing myself in Instagram. My activity is rammed with notifications of likes and comments, and there are a load of messages. Some are from my regular followers, the ones I've built a connection with, but there are a whole bunch in the 'request' file. Spam no doubt. I hit 'delete all' without reading them, then move on to the comments. I mostly respond with a hug emoji, so they know I've seen it, but the odd one requires an actual reply. I try to keep them succinct – a 'Thank you for commenting', or 'I appreciate you reaching out'. Many are of the 'I'm so sorry to hear that' responses as women share their losses and their unfortunate failed IVF attempts. It's heartbreaking – so many women in the same boat, desperate and on their last hope.

But not me. I'm not like them. Not really.

Mercy's face flashes in my mind. A loss in terms of failed IVF is gutting, but the loss of a child. The little girl must've only been around three years old . . . I don't ever want to know that pain. I take in a slow, deep breath and hold it for a few seconds before releasing it, the exhalation whispering through my lips. I need to see what I can find out about the case. I type 'Bateman's' and 'missing child' into the search bar to see what the internet yields. My eyes scan the list of hits, including those from true crime magazines, but none are immediately obvious as being linked to Mercy's daughter's disappearance.

As I'm about to type in Mercy's name, a new message pings in my inbox. I open the tab and my stomach drops as I see it's from the editor. Such a rapid response from her is unusual and the negative thought that it's because my article isn't up to standard is the first to push into my mind. I give my shoulders a shrug to release the tension, open the email and screw my eyes up. Not looking at it straight away isn't going to alter her response of course, but I feel the need to build up to it, nonetheless. I open one eye. The first line is thanking me for the submission but that's where the positives end. The rest is basically pulling my work apart and ends with a request to resubmit. Shit. I slouch back, all energy draining from me.

This is how it starts.

Jamie's voice is loud in my head: 'Suck it up, try again – only giving up is classed as failure.' With a sense of surrender, I sit forward, open my article, and begin rereading it.

*

A shiver ripples through my body and, looking up from my keyboard, I realise the light is fading and the evening is beginning to draw in. I stretch, pulling my cardigan over my shoulders, and get up to close the window. I stand and stare outside for a while. The cat lady opposite is looking out as she usually does. The lamp behind her lends a sinister vibe – illuminating her motionless body. I watch intently, wondering if I'll see a flicker of movement. Maybe she's passed away like that – posed with her knitting needles in her hands, her hungry cats jumping all over her, feeding on her withering body. I give myself a shake. Why do my thoughts turn to the macabre all the time?

As I stare, she looks up and waves, and I feel my muscles relax. I raise my hand in response, offering a weak smile I know she can't see from this distance. Although she sits in that position every day, looking out, I don't think she actually *sees* much. It's like she's lost in her own little world.

I envy her.

MEETING 3

Chapter 8

Erica

This time as I swing into a parking space in Bateman's car park, I double check that it's not a parent and child bay and, once I'm certain, I sit back in the driver's seat and start people watching. I debate whether I should go inside the supermarket as that way Mercy will spot me first and it won't look quite as desperate as me sitting here like a stalker awaiting my prey. Not that I'm doing that, I tell myself. I'm here because she asked me to be.

'And because you think this will help *you*, too,' I whisper, as I catch my reflection in the visor mirror. When I return my gaze, Mercy's face is at the passenger side window, and I start.

'Christ!' I say, throwing my head back and slapping my palm to my chest. 'Creeping up like that,' I mutter as I beckon her inside.

'Sorry, didn't mean to scare you,' Mercy says, settling herself on the leather seat. She has on the same grey coat as last week and we survey each other in the same way we did then too. I wonder if she's just got here, or if she's already been inside the store. 'I'm glad you're here.'

My lips shake as I attempt a smile. I flick my thumbnail with my forefinger as the silence becomes too much.

'Did you drive?' I blurt. When the words leave my mouth, I'm not certain what I've even said – I just know I had to say something. Mercy gives me a cautious look.

'I don't have a car,' she says. 'I cycle or get the bus. A taxi sometimes.'

'Oh, okay. Well, do you need a lift back home after . . .' *After what?* I think. 'I mean, I can—'

'Oh, you mustn't go out of your way. It's fine. Really. I live in the sticks. I'll treat myself to a taxi once I've finished here.'

'Finished here?'

Mercy checks her watch – a Timex with a yellow strap. It's old; I'm pretty sure I had one just like it when I was a teenager. 'It's almost time. I have to go in again now.'

Again? The thought must show on my face, because Mercy nods then says: 'I went in just before you got here – I was trying something out.'

'Oh?' I raise an eyebrow.

'If I've been thrown out once today hopefully it'll mean I've fooled Wes and he won't be on high alert for a reappearance.' She taps her forefinger to her temple. 'I have to be sneakier than him.' She takes the photo of the little girl. A plastic sleeve covers it, to protect it I assume, but it's bent from being inside her coat pocket. I'm curious as to why she doesn't carry a handbag; it'd be safer.

'Can I?' I ask, reaching for the photo. I'd only held it for a minute or so that first time she thrust it into my hand and, with all the fuss last week, there was no time to ask to see it again. I'm keen to study it for longer in the privacy of my car. Mercy allows me to take it.

'My angel. My Tia,' she says. It shakes in my grasp, like I've a trapped nerve in my hand. I inhale deeply to steady myself. I can feel Mercy's eyes boring into me as I look at the image. *Have* I seen this little girl before? I vaguely recall a similar-looking girl, but I can't be sure because I see children here every week. And when you're longing for a child yourself, you're suddenly so much more *aware* of babies and children – it's like I see them absolutely everywhere. Though I do wonder if it's a possibility I recognise her face from when she went missing. I continue to stare at her. At Tia. I speak her name, but it comes out as a hoarse whisper. I sense Mercy stiffen beside me, and I look up.

'She's beautiful,' I say, tears clouding my vision as I imagine the anguish of losing such a precious child. I blink rapidly. 'This must be destroying you.'

'Each and every day without her, a little bit more of me dies. This past year has been a living hell and if I don't find her, I'll lose myself completely. I was, *am*, Tia's mum. If I can't be that, there's no point to my existence.' Her voice is clogged with tears, her face ashen. My pulse quickens as I not only see, but feel, Mercy's pain like a deep ache inside me. I reach for wise words, something I can offer this woman as a comfort. But there's nothing I can say, so I lay my hand over hers and give it a squeeze. We sit for a few seconds in silence, then Mercy takes the photo and thanks me for listening.

'See you next week, maybe?' she asks, her tone hopeful, before opening the car door.

I contemplate her question and decide in this instant that I don't want to wait a whole week. 'I could wait,' I say. 'If you like?'

Mercy narrows her eyes. 'Wait here for a week?'

I laugh. 'No . . . for you to come back out. We could grab a coffee in there?' I tilt my head towards the supermarket café.

'Oh – that would be nice. Thank you.' Mercy smiles and gratefulness exudes from her.

'Great. I'll see you in a bit, then.' A warm sensation spreads inside me. Kindness matters.

Chapter 9

Erica

Twenty minutes crawl by. I've done all I can on my phone – answered some emails and made notes on possible future articles I could write – and now I'm playing Wordle to pass the time. There's still no sign of Mercy. I guess that's a good thing, in that Wes hasn't yet found her, or at least hasn't decided she's causing enough of a nuisance to warrant frogmarching her out again. It might also mean she's gaining valuable information from shoppers, although I do find myself questioning just what will be helpful after all this time. Would people remember anything significant after a year? And, now I think of it, the likelihood of her finding any of the same customers who'd been shopping here the day of Tia's disappearance must be really slim. Perhaps, though, it helps Mercy mentally, to be in the same spot; it might give her the sense she's still doing something. Not giving up on her little girl.

I wonder how long I should wait for her return. I've said I'll be here and we'll go for a coffee, so I'll have to keep to that; it's not like I can just drive off because I'm bored with waiting. If she's not back in another ten minutes, I'll go inside to find her. I don't want her to think I'm impatient because doing this is clearly important to her, so I'll offer moral support while she approaches people.

When I fail to guess the word in the game, I toss my phone onto the passenger seat and drum my fingernails on the steering wheel, transfixed by the flashes of colour. It's been a few weeks since my gel manicure, it must be coming up for my next appointment. Despite not being seen out much, I like to maintain my appearance. I pick my phone up again and open the calendar app. There's nothing scheduled. Did I forget to pop it in when I was last at The Beauty Cabin? As I begin tapping out a message to Emily asking her if I'm booked in, the car door opens.

'Well, that was a waste of time,' Mercy says, breathlessly, as she ducks her head down to my level. Then without getting in, or any explanation, she slams the door closed and strides towards the supermarket entrance. I assume I should follow, and quickly get out and run after her. A brief 'what am I doing?' thought goes through my mind, which I shake away as I slow to a walk inside the supermarket foyer. I give a cautious glance around to see if Wes is about – hoping he hasn't immediately apprehended Mercy when she entered for a third attempt. The coast is clear.

As I turn into the café, I'm relieved to see Mercy already seated at a table by the window, clutching the photo of Tia to her chest and staring at the other people at nearby tables. Tension hangs in the air and I tentatively pull out the chair opposite her, waiting for her to scream at me to leave her alone because that's what I feel is going to happen – her face is contorted with anger and her body is trembling.

'What happened?' I ask.

'I don't know why I think it'll be any different,' she says, her nostrils flaring. 'Each week I come here with fresh hope. But no. People are too wrapped up in their own self-importance to give me the time of day.'

'It must feel that way, Mercy. I'm sorry.'

'Yet, they're happy to stare.' She accentuates the last word, her head snapping around to take in each person in the café. 'And talk shit about me behind my back. They'll take the time to do *that*.'

I watch as other customers' gazes drop away. 'Ignore those people, Mercy. Unfortunately, there are always those who'll judge, and those who are too busy to even take a few seconds to look at your photo – but you only need one person to stop and look. One person to recall Tia, or something vital from that day.'

Mercy lays the photo flat on the table and sits back. 'Yes, you're right. And *you* did. *You* stopped. Shame you can't remember anything though.'

My pulse jumps. Poor Mercy, she's right. The only person who's been bothered enough to give her the time of day is useless to her. I don't remember the case, have no recollection of it on the news or anything like that. The one person who listened is the one person unable to help. Unless, of course, there is something in the back of my mind maybe, something tucked away, something I didn't realise was important. Whenever you watch appeals, or see crime shows on the TV, the police always reiterate that any information, however insignificant you feel it is, might be something that triggers another line of enquiry.

'Tell me from the beginning, Mercy,' I say. And as Mercy relives the experience and the days following Tia's abduction,

I purse my lips together tightly in an attempt to prevent the tears.

'I'm sorry,' she says, her brow furrowed. 'I forget sometimes.'

'What do you mean?'

'I forget that hearing about something sad can affect those listening, too.' She reaches across the table and puts her hand on my arm, giving me a pitiful look. I'm confused at first, why is she offering me sympathy? Then I realise I've been crying. I snatch a serviette and dab my eyes.

'Goodness. I'm the one who's sorry. Look at me; such a state.'

'No need to apologise,' Mercy says. 'If I'm honest, it's kind of comforting, you know? Seeing that reaction from you gives me hope. Shows you care, and there's not much of that around.'

'What was your life like before?' I ask. Mercy looks beyond me, out of the window, like she's struggling to recall anything prior to her trauma.

'I took a lot for granted, that's for sure.'

'We're all guilty of that,' I say, a little too emphatically.

'When I look back, I realise my time with Tia was usually quite rushed. Like one moment we'd be playing in the sandpit, or baking, walking through the woods collecting treasure, as she called it – she loved picking random things up: sticks, stones, leaves and feathers, then popping them in her special bag.' Mercy's eyes glaze over, and her smile makes me smile too. 'Then the next, I'd be bundling her in the pushchair racing off because I had to be somewhere for an appointment, or to take her to her father's – we weren't together you see . . . There always seemed to be something that had to be done. I wish I'd refused to go anywhere, just made others come to us.'

'Modern life – most people are the same, Mercy. Juggling a million things is what mums do, isn't it?' I drop my gaze. What I'd give to need to juggle my life and a child.

'I guess it is. If only we could see what's right in front of us, though. Appreciate what we have without always striving for more.'

We walk out of the café, passing Wes at the security desk. He stares at us, his distaste evident. I feel his eyes on me until I'm outside. What's his problem? When we get to my car, I hover with my key fob outstretched. Mercy declined my offer of a lift before, but should I mention it again now? Before I can ponder further, she asks,

'Same time next week?' Her eyes sparkle with anticipation as I hesitate, taking a few seconds to think my response through.

I *can't* say no now. I've already met with her twice since she first approached me and have now extended the hand of friendship.

'Same time, same place,' I say, giving a firm nod. With what looks to be a grateful smile, Mercy turns on her heel and walks off and I climb into the car.

There's no going back now. And besides, it's giving me something to think about other than my own preoccupations. It was quite nice to sit and talk with someone – socialising has become such a rarity for me this past year. And while it would be fair to say that Mercy wouldn't usually be my first choice of friend due to us having little in common, it would also be fair to say the selection is lacking. My only 'friends' these days are those on Instagram, and while they offer a lot of virtual support, nothing quite beats real-life interaction.

Chapter 10

Erica

I awake on the cuddle chair, stiff from the curled-up position I've been asleep in. As I stretch to reach my phone, a series of soft clunks sound from my joints. When I got home from Bateman's, weary from the bombardment of emotions, I fully intended to go upstairs and lie on the bed to rest – but my eyes had been so heavy with exhaustion, I hadn't made it past the lounge. Checking my phone, I realise it's been several hours, and Jamie will be home any minute. With exaggerated effort, I climb the stairs, but manage to swiftly pass by the nursery, the thought of it too much to contemplate after the chat with Mercy.

I fire up the computer, low-level anxiety gripping me as I think about my unfinished articles. My motivation seems to be higher for non-work projects – like helping Mercy. I toggle to Google, type in 'Websleuths'. I heard they focus on crime and missing person cases, so they could well offer an alternative to the standard internet searches.

A car draws my attention and, standing, I spot Jamie's

BMW rounding the corner. Slowly, he manoeuvres into the drive and parks. Doesn't get out. I crane my neck to try and see what he's doing. He's taking a call. It's strange, watching someone talk without hearing the words – his body is stiff, his hands jerking in a manner that implies he's not happy with whatever discussion he's having. Or with whom he's having it. I sigh, a sinking feeling overwhelming me. More stress. I'm not sure I can be bothered to offer my usual calming words, give another sensual massage to unknot Jamie's tense muscles. What about me? What about what I need? I can't recall the last time he asked me how I was doing, offered me a massage.

I rub my eyes, stepping back from the window slightly as he opens the driver's door before slamming it dramatically. A twinge of worry begins in the pit of my stomach. There's something in his sluggish, hesitant walk towards the house that bothers me.

It's as though he doesn't want to come inside.

I try and push away the intrusive thought that he's been distant lately because he's busy paying someone else more attention – seeking comfort for the stress of failed IVF attempts in the arms of another woman – but it niggles away in my gut. Who was on the other end of that phone call?

'I'm home,' he shouts from the hallway a few minutes later. What took him so long? He tears his coat off, then flings it over the banister. I tut as I reach the bottom of the stairs and take it, hanging it on one of the hooks. I see him slide his mobile into his trouser pocket.

'Are you all right?' I ask as I follow him into the kitchen.

'What's for dinner?' He opens the fridge, closes it again with a huff, then grabs a bottle of cabernet and opens it.

The ruby-coloured liquid glugs as he pours himself a large glass. He tilts the glass towards me. 'I don't suppose you'll be wanting one,' he says.

My throat constricts. 'Obviously not,' I say, my tone sharp. He's spoiling for an argument. I must make sure not to become hooked by the bait. 'And dinner is a takeaway. I've not had time—'

'Really? What've you been doing all day?'

'Jamie,' I say, lowering my voice to an almost-whisper. 'I work too, don't forget. And we're not living in the 1950s. Feel free to cook if you wish.' I leave the kitchen shaking my head, my fists clenched at my sides. I hear the unscrewing of the bottle cap again behind me and turn to see him topping up his glass. When he drinks immediately upon coming home from work, it's usually because something bad has happened. Given his obvious annoyance while on the phone in the car, the two are linked. Dare I ask? No. I'll wait for him to tell me.

I pull the cuddle chair out from the edge of the room, positioning it so I can see the telly. Then, I tuck my legs up and switch on *Richard Osman's House of Games*. Jamie comes in, but doesn't sit down – he stands behind my chair, one hand on the back. The air expelling from his nostrils is loud. For Christ's sake, I wish he'd get this over with. I pause the telly on the 'Richard's Junk' round.

'What do you reckon? I think it's the butterfly,' I say, hoping to relieve the tense atmosphere.

'I think it's the wool.'

'But the question is—'

'I don't care what the question is, Erica.' He takes a gulp of wine.

'What is the *matter* with you?'

69

'It's the wool. You know, as in the saying "Pulling the wool over someone's eyes."'

I look to the screen, then back at Jamie. 'But that doesn't make sense.'

'God's sake. Doesn't it, Erica?' he snaps.

Confusion fogs my mind – why's he being argumentative over a quiz show question?

'Look, you've had a bad day. I get it. But don't take it out on me. Either talk to me, like an *adult*, Jamie – or don't bother at all. Choice is yours.' My cheeks burn.

Then he laughs. 'Always so dramatic. You really should've gone into acting.' He swivels the chair around with one hand so I'm facing him. He towers above me, his eyes ablaze. 'Why don't you ever listen to me?'

'I do listen. God, that's all I've been doing for months.'

'But you don't take my professional opinion seriously, do you? You never have, it's like you don't think I'm good at my job or something.'

'That's not true.' But with a jolt of realisation, I know he's right. Any time he's offered some kind of psych evaluation or advice, I've disagreed with it, batted it away. Ignored it. And now, looking at his tense jaw, his tight-lipped smile, I also have the uncomfortable feeling he knows where I've been today. I'm not sure how, but he knows I've been to the same supermarket. After he warned me not to go on Fridays again – to avoid getting embroiled with the woman and her missing daughter. He was adamant I shouldn't get involved; that it would only spell trouble. I've done the opposite – and not just the once – and now he's pissed off with me. I start to panic. Was the call he took earlier from someone who saw me at Bateman's today, I wonder. I brush off the absurdity of that.

Jamie's shoulders slump and he puts his glass on the table and squeezes in beside me on the cuddle chair. I let out my held breath.

'I've been a shit to live with lately, I am aware of that. And I'm really sorry. The pressure of work, on top of everything else. I'm not coping.'

My pulse thrums in my throat. This is the first time he's admitted such a thing. I place my hand on his thigh. 'You need to say when things are tough. You tell me not to bottle things up, you should take your own advice sometimes.'

'I know. And I am talking about it. At work. I've been chatting with a colleague who's been extremely supportive.'

'That's good. I'm glad. They're best placed to help relieve some of the pressure, too. They must realise you're being landed with too many cases to effectively deal with. The targets aren't being met for a number of reasons, and none are down to you.'

He shrugs. 'Maybe. There are a few high-profile inmates at the moment, all coming up for parole hearings. Each needs a psych evaluation and none of them are easy to work with. It all takes time and things have been piling up a bit.'

'I'm pleased you're telling me. Half the battles we have are down to lack of communication, you know?' I quickly lower my gaze from his. It's a bit 'pot calling the kettle black'. I've not been communicating how I feel, either. I've only been brave enough to have the much-needed conversations about our future in my head. And even now, with the perfect opportunity arising, I'm unable to allow the words to leave my mouth.

'Yeah. On that note, Erica . . .'

My stomach lurches as my mind leaps to an irrational

place. What's coming? Is he about to tell me he's been having an affair? Possibly with his super-supportive work colleague. Or maybe his ex who still works at the prison? That would explain his behaviour this past few months. I stare at him, open-mouthed. Waiting. My legs tingle; my heart races.

'Do you want to tell me about your day?' he says.

For a second, I'm stumped. He's tricking me. Asking me to tell him what I've done to catch me out in a lie. Then he can come down hard, saying I'm not only going against his professional opinion, but I'm lying to him too. Hiding things from him. As I look into his eyes, I try to find the Jamie I first met and fell in love with. It's a long time ago, but I remember the buzz of adrenaline when we collided in a corridor at Bath University. I was immediately attracted to him and for a while we were inseparable, spending all our spare time together. Our mates called us 'Jamica', a play on Bennifer – the nickname of celebrity couple Ben Affleck and Jennifer Lopez. Thankfully that died a death.

As did our teenage romance.

It was years later that we bumped into each other again, quite literally, in Bath. Believing it to be fate because it was how we'd met the first time, we picked things up pretty much how we left off. Except this time, we fell in love. The real, all-consuming, powerful kind.

His hazel-green eyes aren't as sparkly now; they've dulled, I think, as tears come to mine. I don't see the passion in his that was once there. There's still love, of course – but it's been stripped down to its bare bones. Other things consume our marriage now and wanting a baby despite all our troubles seems to have been the final nail in the coffin.

'Well?' Jamie gives me a nudge. 'I'm always harping on about my day, you must be fed up with hearing about it. I want to know about yours.'

So I tell him. It doesn't take long.

But I miss out the crucial part about befriending Mercy.

Chapter 11

Dr Connie Summers

FACEBOOK

Spotted Newton Abbot

2h. 🌐

MISSING GIRL – please post anonymously

A 3-year-old girl went missing while at Bateman's with her mother on Friday at around 11 am. If you were shopping at that time, did you see her? Or anyone strange lurking around? Was teeming with police – the place came to a standstill while they searched the whole area. Didn't find her. Anyone see anything?

Alisha Garner

I was bloody stuck with my shopping on the conveyor. Told to leave! I do enjoy wasting my time.

Andy Wethers

Woman was attention-seeking. I don't even think she had a kid with her. NO ONE saw her with a girl.

Kaycee Smith

I've seen her before, I don't think she's all there, if you get me.

Abbi Hope

So rude. What's wrong with people? A child is lost, missing – could be abducted and you're all worried about your precious shopping, or saying the poor woman is delusional? God help you if you ever need help.

Shaun Pollard

Abbi Hope Get a life, love.

Lou Thomas

Typical Newton Scabbot – place is a shithole.

Emily Hellyer

Has anyone got anything HELPFUL to offer? What if this were your child?

Francis Colby

With all the paedos being released from prison, wouldn't surprise me if one of them had her.

Sammi Peters

Jesus.

Carmen Allan

I think I saw the mother. She had a lovely turquoise coat on, I remember cos I almost asked her where she got it from. Don't remember seeing a girl with her though. Maybe she'd already gone wandering off by then.

Ki-Ki Fellows

Did they check the playpark beside the store?

Pam Llewellyn

Police were everywhere, so yeah.

Kaycee Smith

Sure the woman didn't leave the kid at home? Lol.

Carmen Allan

I think she'd have realised that, don't you?

Raj Antony

Don't joke *Kaycee Smith*. Remember that full-scale search, police, helicopter, groups of villagers out in force, looking for that boy in Dainton? After all that fuss, he was found hiding under his bloody bed! Stranger things have happened.

Connie flicks through the many papers littering her desk, moving piles of notes to one side as she spreads the collection of evidence in front of her. Her client has been shown some of these before, in carefully considered moments during her treatment plan. Connie's experimented with the timings, occasionally showing a newspaper article or police report after the same topic has been discussed in a session. At other times, she's randomly selected a document at the start of a session in the hope it will guide her client to talk about the desired subject. But Connie must be careful. One push in the wrong direction could see them right back at the beginning.

Additional insight has been gained through discussions with a colleague, and now, she wants to try something a little different. Connie's knee bobs under the desk. She doesn't often experience nerves, but today her skin is alive with tiny prickles of electricity. She reaches for the framed photo beside the computer and runs her fingertips over the smiling face of her wife. She knows loss. How deep it runs, how endless it seems. She also knows hope. What Connie does is a careful balancing act. Becoming too enmeshed could spell disaster. For everyone involved.

The doorbell rings and Connie gathers the documents, shoving all bar one of them into the thick, cardboard file.

'Come in,' Connie says, opening the door wide.

The woman smiles and takes her seat on the cream sofa, the same spot she always chooses. There's a lightness to her today, Connie thinks as she sits down opposite. Connie returns the gesture, her head slightly cocked, curious as to what's brought on this change.

'Tell me what's been good about your week?' They always begin their session with this question – it allows her to focus on the positive achievements, not dwell on what hasn't happened, what she didn't do.

'I've finally made progress,' she says. Her back is straight, her unclenched hands lightly laid in her lap.

'Oh, that's excellent,' Connie says. 'Great to hear you've worked on your goals from last session. How did you—'

'I found someone who said they saw her. Isn't that great? I think I should go to the police station straight after this session to get them to look into it.'

Connie's smile slips from her face and she closes her eyes.

Chapter 12

Wes

A quick flick of the hair, a flutter of the eyelids, a fleeting glance before coyly turning away again – those are the signs Wesley Little looks out for. Working security has its benefits and he usually has a better hit rate than when he goes out clubbing, or even at the gym. But the pickings have been slim for a while now. Or, maybe it's because he's been off his game since The Incident. His heart hasn't been in it; playing Xbox has been a safer pastime than playing the field. He needs to get back on form, though, to take his mind off the more serious stuff.

He's running late this morning, shoehorning his gym session in before work. He's the most senior security guard at Bateman's, which should offer him some leeway, but the boss decided to take a hard line after what happened and so Wes hasn't been able to get away with much lately. And he can't afford to lose this job because it pays for his memberships and the computer and gaming set-up – and his mother's carers. He's lucky he wasn't fired, and although it would suit him better to leave his store job – leave town, even – he can't uproot his mum, it wouldn't be fair to her. And given his wages, he can't afford a place without her. He tries not to tell people he's living with his mum; he's almost thirty – it's embarrassing. She mostly stays in her bedroom, though, so it's not like she disturbs him, but it's not ideal.

Every now and then he partakes in a 'side-job' – stuff that's not always above board. He's always on the lookout to make a quick buck, anything to enable him to escape the restrictions of his current situation. He often fantasises about becoming a private investigator – he could make a tidy sum from that because there's always some gullible person to take advantage of.

He side-eyes the women doing the downward dog as he walks past the yoga group to reach the weights. He smiles at the row of bottoms in the air – such a weird practice, he thinks. His gaze meets with one of the women just as they flip over and he gives her a swift appraisal. Her long hair is plaited and hangs down the centre of her back. She's wearing Lycra and there's a sheen of sweat on her lean arms. She's pretty hot, he concludes. She quickly looks away, but he hovers for a while longer, waiting for her to check him out again, because he absolutely knows she will.

And there it is.

He knew it. They can't resist his physique, his obvious good looks. Wes gives her a wink, then struts into the gym. He does some stretches – poses – in front of the mirror before hitting the weights. Wednesday is chest and triceps day. He showers after he's done his required reps, then shoves his gym bag over his shoulder. He walks past the yoga group as they're finishing, but the woman he picked out isn't there any longer.

No worries. Plenty more to choose from.

Chapter 13

Erica

A cold lump sits in the pit of my stomach as I steer the car onto the driveway. The session went as usual – it's not enjoyable, as it should be, it's more of a necessity. I drag my gym bag from the back seat and the yoga mat slips from it and unrolls on the driveway.

'Dammit.' I kneel to get it, then freeze, sensing I'm being watched. I look up and see the cat lady in the window – staring out. There's something about her constant presence there that's unsettling; the way she keeps tabs on people – on me. It's like she's all-knowing, sitting there, silently observing. Judging me? I drop my gaze and bundle my mat up, shoving it under my arm. Out the corner of my eye, I swear I see her beckoning me. A shiver runs the length of my spine and I dart inside and close the door, leaning back against it. How much do I even know about her? All I know is she sits and knits all day, I don't even know her name. My stomach sinks and I shake my head at my rudeness – there's no excuse. The poor woman probably just wants contact with another person. Someone to say hello to, to gossip with. She likely knows far more than I do about the goings-on in this road. She must be incredibly lonely – she appears so isolated. But I've already taken on one new friend, and I can't open my life to another, there's no time.

The image of Mercy's distressed face is etched into my mind. Her pain crouches deep inside me. That's the one thing we have in common. Our lives might be very different, but we both know longing. I long for a child, she longs for hers to come back to her. My chest tightens and I take some deep breaths. The danger of embracing Mercy's plight is that I'll absorb her emotions, drag myself down further than I am already, and it'll affect my chances of pregnancy. Stress isn't good for me. Jamie tells me that almost daily and he won't like it if he finds out what I'm doing.

'You want a cuppa?'

I start at the voice. 'Jamie?'

'Who else would be in our kitchen, Erica?' he calls, giving a mocking laugh.

'Wasn't expecting you to be home,' I say, wandering in as he pours boiling water into two mugs. He frowns, but doesn't respond. He's dressed in one of his work suits, but his tie is missing, his shirt partly unbuttoned, as though he dressed in a rush. My heartbeat stutters. How long has he been home? I give a cautious glance around, not sure what I'm looking for but half expecting something out of place. An extra used glass? A discarded item of unrecognisable clothing? My nerves jump as Jamie eyes me curiously, a tension building between us.

He hands me my 'This is what an awesome wife looks like' mug and, for a split second, the warmth radiates through my palms into my body. Jamie bought me this mug for our second anniversary. It's been in the back of the cupboard, he would've had to really delve into it to retrieve it. He could've easily picked one of the many that are crammed in the front. Has he purposely chosen this one to put me on the back foot? Or because he feels guilty about something? I smile at him and he puts his head on one side.

'You okay?' His eyes shine with tears, which starts me off. My throat thickens and all I can do is nod. 'You're very quiet,' he says. 'What are you thinking about?'

I frantically search for something to say, anything other than what is really on my mind. 'Work, mainly.'

It's all I've got. I'm done talking about our marriage, about what's going on in our lives, and I don't do anything else – I'm sure he wouldn't want to hear about yoga. There's no point telling him anything about my Instagram life, either; he wouldn't understand. It's the thing that helps keep me sane and sharing it with Jamie will take something from it. And I've avoided any mention of the supermarket and Mercy so as not to give him a reason to bring it all up again, so we sit at the kitchen table while I chat instead about my ideas for the next writing project. He nods, uttering a few key words in the right places to show he's listening and to pretend he's interested as I continue to speak with exaggerated enthusiasm.

It feels wrong withholding the truth from Jamie, but I seem to be doing it more and more. For now, keeping Mercy secret seems like the only course of action. Especially given I've agreed to another meeting with her this Friday. What Jamie doesn't know won't hurt him, I guess.

MEETING 4

Chapter 14

Erica

It seemed to take an age for Friday to roll around. I awoke this morning to the sound of birds, then, reaching across to snooze my phone alarm, seeing the date led to a jolt of awareness, and I sprang out the bed with more vigour than I've managed for months. My anticipation caused the first few hours to go at half-speed, though, and I had to force myself to appear nonchalant with Jamie over breakfast. I tried not to let my nerves and impatience show, taking slow bites of my toast, refilling my mug with coffee so it appeared I had all the time in the world. He was engrossed in a file – psychology notes of some kind – he wasn't taking notice of me anyway, but I kept my cool all the same. No need to draw attention to myself and have him question what my plans for the day were. If he'd asked directly about going shopping, I'm not sure I could've hidden the truth from him again.

Now, as I sit and wait in my car in Bateman's car park, I try to still my nerves by listening to a discussion about dealing with menopause in the workplace on BBC Radio 2.

I make a mental note to contact them, it's about time an IVF discussion was aired. It would fit in nicely with the article I've been planning about how the postcode lottery dictates which women can receive the treatment under the NHS. It's appalling how infertility is handled in different areas of the same country and, although it's a topic that's been covered in the past, there's been no recent awareness in the news.

Thinking of news and media, one of the things Jamie said when I told him about Mercy that first week now pops into my mind. A missing child surely would've been big news both locally and nationally – so why didn't I find any mention of it online, and why don't I *remember* it? I tilt my head back against the car seat and close my eyes as I go back over the year, attempting to pinpoint major news stories. My focus has very much been on getting pregnant. A shudder ripples through me as I remember Jamie's accusation that I'd become obsessed, with everything revolving around my desperation for a baby – so maybe I was simply too engrossed in my own life to notice what was going on in the world. No wonder Mercy was a little off when she first got into my car and I didn't remember her – she'd probably been on the telly at the time of the disappearance appealing for information and would expect to be recognised, or at least be familiar to people. But she'd known *my* name; I never did ask her how. I guess I either told her, or she'd overheard me saying it to customer services, or something.

The passenger door flings open, snapping me from my thoughts. Mercy gets in, her face flushed and tear-streaked.

'Oh, no. Are you okay?' I grab a packet of tissues from the door pocket and pull one from it, handing it to her.

Mercy shakes her head, then blows noisily into the paper tissue.

'They're monsters,' she says, screwing the tissue into a ball. 'Called the police on me, saying something about needing to prevent a further breach of the peace. Disturbing the bloody peace? How dare they. I never do that. I make sure of that, so they don't have a reason to throw me out.' I watch her fingers tremble with anger.

'I'm so sorry, Mercy.' Guilt floods through me. Should I have gone in with her to do the rounds? I'd considered it last Friday when I'd been waiting for her to return to my car, and was going to offer to accompany her this week, but something holds me back from taking that step. From getting involved that deeply. This is only the fourth time I've spoken with her; my confidence about fully immersing myself in Mercy's search for her child isn't quite there yet. I still feel I should get to know her a bit more first.

'No need for you to be sorry, Erica. It's not like you're the one telling them to treat me this way.' Tears shine in her eyes and my heart aches for her as she hangs her head, strands of greasy hair falling forwards. Is it her appearance, I wonder. Social class shouldn't come into it, but I fear it does. I remember the conversations about how a missing girl back in the early 2000s had been reported. Her family background, the area she lived, was thought to have impacted on the focus to find her – or lack of – the story apparently being less newsworthy than the missing girl from the middle-class family with professional parents from the previous year that it was compared to. Publicity and public reaction were said not to have been at the same level. My muscles tense as I think this could be what happened to Mercy with Tia – what's still happening – and like a switch, my guilt turns to anger towards the supermarket staff.

'I can't believe they're being so callous. What on earth do they think the police will do in any case? It's really not like you're causing a disruption!'

'Bateman's are apparently seeking some kind of injunction. An order to prevent me entering their premises.' Her words are flat, as though the fight's gone out of her and has been replaced with a sinking sense of inevitability.

'Jesus,' I say, slowly expelling air from my lips. 'Aren't they the ones in the wrong? Standing in the way of justice or something?'

'All they keep saying is there's no evidence. No one saw anything. It didn't happen – none of their CCTV proves anything . . .' Mercy rattles this off; she's clearly heard it all before.

'Why don't they believe you?' It's meant to be a thought but, as Mercy tilts her head to one side, I realise I've asked it out loud.

'The police?' She frowns.

'Well, yes, them . . . and the staff in there.' I gesture towards Bateman's.

Mercy seems to contemplate my question, her mouth twisted in concentration.

'It's some kind of conspiracy,' she says, uttering the words with complete seriousness. I have a sinking feeling in my gut. Up until this moment, Mercy has come across as a distraught mum, doing everything she can to find her child. Someone who somehow has been wronged, let down by people in authority. But now a conspiracy theory has been mentioned, a part of me can't help but acknowledge that Checkout Karen, and Jamie, could well be right. Maybe she *is* suffering with some kind of delusional mental health issue.

'A conspiracy?' I echo, because right now I can't think of what else to say.

'Yes. Like, they know who took Tia, really, and they're in on it. It's a child-trafficking ring or worse – but they're making me out to be crazy to detract attention from them.'

A dozen questions swim through my mind, but I can't add to her distress by asking now.

'You know, some of them are saying I didn't even have a daughter – it's so ridiculous, it's like they're gaslighting me. But they have all the power and I have none. They grind me down, bit by bit. Especially Wes.'

To be fair to Mercy and her conspiracy theory, stranger things have happened and I have to admit to also picking up on some odd vibes from the staff. There's something awry in the way Bateman's is treating Mercy, I can sense it – it makes the hairs on my neck prickle.

'The power needs to be flipped in that case,' I say. 'Not that I know how to make that happen.'

'It's been a struggle, on my own,' Mercy says. 'Having someone else on my side could make all the difference.'

I feel the weight of her gratitude and smile. 'Let's hope so.'

'Look,' Mercy shifts in the passenger seat. 'Can't we go somewhere else? It's cramped in here. No offence.' She glances around my compact Fiesta, then narrows her eyes at me.

'Yes, of course.' I inwardly wince at my eagerness as the words leave my lips. I should suggest somewhere public, maybe the Costa in town. 'How about C—'

'Come to mine,' Mercy butts in. 'I don't get visitors; it would be nice.'

As I hesitantly agree and pull out of Bateman's car park, heading out of town down narrow lanes, I wonder why she doesn't get visitors. In my eagerness to help, have I perhaps overlooked something?

Chapter 15

Wes

With well-practised technique, Wes smacks the bottle cap on the wall-mounted opener in his room before collapsing onto his bed. He shuffles back so he's sitting upright against the pillows, then gulps the lager greedily, swigging half the bottle in just two mouthfuls.

God, what a fucking day that was.

He rolls the ice-cold glass over his forehead, the temperature making him gasp, before glugging down the remainder and launching the empty bottle towards the bin. It misses, landing with a dull thud onto the carpet beneath the desk. Reaching across to his mini fridge beside the bed, he swings the door open to grab another. There are only two left and he'll need them later. With a loud sigh, he slams it shut and sits forward, laying his head on his crossed arms.

The woman's desperate face flashes inside his mind and the usual nausea when he thinks about her makes the liquid in his stomach churn. He couldn't look at her as he escorted her away from Bateman's yet again and tried to block his ears to her anguished cries as she begged him to let her stay so she could ask customers if they'd seen her girl. He delivered his usual lines: *I'm sorry, you can't be here*; *Bateman's will be forced to take out an injunction*; *I'll call the police*. He doesn't think about the words he's saying, they're automatic. He knows he's meant to be handling things differently, but he also needs to preserve his own sanity – he's not sure he can do both. His life, he concludes, is like *Groundhog Day*. Only, unlike Bill Murray's character, Wes isn't learning anything from the constant reliving; he's unable – or too afraid – to try something new to help him escape the perpetual loop. And, unlike Bill, he doesn't have a script.

He can't let guilt take hold. Wes bolts up and turns his computer on, then gets comfy in his gaming chair. But, after ten lacklustre minutes of playing *Forza Horizon*, he throws his controls onto the desk and scoots his chair away from the screen. The images in his head are stubborn tonight. He bangs his palms against his temples and groans.

Taking his mobile and lying back again, he begins to scroll through old text messages from his previous conquests. His heart hammers as his eyes snag on one name in particular. Wes bites hard on his lower lip as he opens the thread of texts. The one that got away, he thinks. He coughs, clearing the growing tickle at the back of his throat.

This isn't helping – why is he doing this to himself?

He clicks on the three dots in the top right of the screen and taps the delete option. For a moment, he stares at the alert message 'This action cannot be undone', his loud breathing the only sound in the room. But before he can dwell too much and change his mind, he confirms the deletion.

Then he grabs his gym bag and barrages down the stairs.

'I'm going for a session, Mum,' he calls over his shoulder. 'You'll be okay for an hour, won't you?'

He doesn't wait for an answer, because even if she says no, he has to go anyway.

He has to release the tension, the regrets and the guilt somehow, because gaming isn't working.

Chapter 16

Erica

My car bumps and grinds along what I can only describe as a dirt track. We jiggle inside, my head banging against the headrest a few times.

'It smooths out in a minute,' Mercy says, one hand grasping the handle above the door, the other gripping the edge of her seat, keeping herself as steady as possible. It's like being in a washing machine. The uneven ground and large stones won't be doing my tyres any good – I'll probably get a puncture. Then I'll be stranded out here. Wherever here is.

'I've lived around here for years but not sure I've ventured this far into the wild,' I say, giving an awkward laugh. No wonder she doesn't get many visitors.

'It's why I chose it. Remote. No one bothers you out here. No phone signal, no internet – I'm practically off-grid.'

Shit. That's perfect. Literally no one knows I'm here and I can't contact a soul. My rash decision might well come back to bite me; I've only met this woman a few times.

What the fuck are you doing, Erica?

'You've lost your colour,' Mercy says, staring at my face. 'Are you going to vomit?'

'I used to get travel sick,' I admit. 'It's been some years since I've puked into a carrier bag in the car though.' The car jerks sharply and veers off to the right. 'But maybe today's the day.'

As I regain control, the track widens slightly and finally levels out. Thank God. I allow myself to relax for a moment before beginning to worry about what I've got myself into. I sneak a sideways glance at Mercy. She's looking dead ahead and she's smiling. Butterflies tingle inside me. I grip the wheel a little tighter. What's the worst that can happen though? She's just a sad, lonely and frustrated woman. Much like myself, now I think of it. She needs someone to believe in her. That's it. And since the first time I set eyes on her I've been strangely drawn to her. I should trust my gut.

The track splits up ahead, and Mercy instructs me to take a left. A few seconds later, a cabin comes into view. Is this where Mercy lives? It looks more like a holiday let than a permanent residence, it reminds me of a place Jamie and I once rented. As I come to a stop, I take it all in. It's well-maintained on the outside – the horizontal dark wood slats neat, no missing ones, and the two windows I can see are intact, clean and framed by pretty green-gingham curtains. I don't know quite what I expected – a ramshackle cottage?

She was right about being 'off-grid'; there don't appear to be any cables running to the one-storey cabin. Does she even have electricity or running water? I can see the attraction of spending time here to get away from the stresses of life because God knows modern living is filled with those, but to be here, alone, twenty-four-seven, is a bit extreme.

Then I realise. She never said she lived alone, that was an assumption I made because she mentioned packing Tia off to see her father – she could have a boyfriend. She said she didn't have *visitors*. What if this is some kind of trap? What if, inside the cabin, a man is lying in wait to kidnap me? These are the types of questions I should've asked prior to leaving the town and driving miles to an unknown, remote rural location. I was so caught up in the moment, thinking of myself as some kind of saviour befriending someone in need, that I hadn't once considered my safety.

I suddenly feel foolish.

As if sensing my unease, Mercy lays a hand on my arm. 'Don't worry,' she says, sweetly. 'I don't bite.'

My smile wobbles. Her assertion doesn't put me at ease at all; it's such a strange thing to say. I can't even think of a fitting comeback. Should I just say I've forgotten something, that I need to be back in town for an appointment? I stay put in the driver's seat as she opens the passenger door and swivels to get out. I could drive off now and never seek Mercy out again. That would be the sensible option.

So why, then, do I reach for the handle and open my door?

It's like I'm compelled to follow her into the cabin. Derren Brown-level hypnosis is making my feet take one step, then another, without my consciousness being able to stop them. Before I fully comprehend it, I'm inside, the door creaking to a close behind me.

Chapter 17

Erica

Stepping inside the cabin, the first thing that hits me is its beautiful simplicity and warmth. If I had my Insta hat on right now, I'd get my phone out and start snapping away, adding a plethora of hashtags like #cosycabinvibe, #cabingoals and #countryliving. The space is separated into 'zones', each with its own colour palette of earthy tones: fern green, chestnut brown and slate grey with richer accents of russet, forest green and aubergine being added through the soft furnishings.

I've been quick to judge Mercy, I realise. Because she's looked a bit scruffy and unkempt on the occasions I've seen her, I'd expected to walk into chaos. Into a house she doesn't care for or keep clean. I've made so many assumptions and, so far, all are proving to be incorrect. My stomach dips a little; is this who I am? Someone who judges others on initial appearances? I've become so used to looking at people's photos on Instagram, making an immediate assessment of them to decide if I should click 'like' or not, I've forgotten how to look beyond the façade. I give myself a mental kick. I should know better.

The single floor is compact, but seems to have everything required. The lounge has a two-seater sofa and leather footstool, a small, round occasional table made from a tree stump and, on the back wall, a wood-burner. The kitchen comprises of a square wooden table and a few units with what looks to be a portable oven. So, maybe there is electric. Mercy is watching my reaction. I shoot her a smile.

'This is lovely, Mercy. I wasn't expecting . . .' I falter, realising how that sounds.

'I know. Don't worry, I'm used to being underestimated.' She shrugs.

'I meant, I wasn't expecting electricity – you said about being off-grid, so . . .' I hope I've pulled it back.

'Solar panels,' she says, simply. I hadn't seen any on the roof, though. 'On the south side.' I feel heat flush my cheeks. Can she read my bloody mind?

'That's good,' I say. 'I've spoken to Jamie about installing them, but he doesn't think we'll stay long enough to benefit.'

'He doesn't think *he'll* be staying there?' She gives me a questioning glance. I swear this woman knows my thoughts.

'He doesn't think *we'll* be staying there,' I repeat carefully, ensuring she can't mishear this time.

She nods. 'I have power, but no internet or anything. And I use the river water for most things – I buy bottled water to drink though.'

'How are you keeping track with the investigation, or recent sightings, with no internet?' I'm not sure I'd cope with such a lack of contact with the outside world. My mobile is never more than a metre's distance from me and

I must check my socials every couple of hours. What does Mercy *do* here on the days she's not in town?

'There is no investigation,' she says, slamming the flats of her hands down on the kitchen table. 'It's been closed. Never really opened, they just keep trying to say she's not missing.' She drags her fingers through her hair now and I wince as I see strands tear from her scalp. It's a quick change as she shifts from calm to anxiety-ridden in a second. Would Jamie say that's a sign of a mental health condition?

'Don't do that,' I say, unable to stop myself. I stride towards her, taking her hands and pulling them away from her head. 'Come on, don't let them do this to you. They can't simply deny she ever existed, Mercy. There's a record of her birth.'

'Well, that's the thing.' Her shoulders slump.

I have a sinking feeling in my stomach. The conspiracy theory talk already rang an alarm bell. If she's about to tell me Tia's birth record has been miraculously wiped from the system, I'm not sure how I'll respond. I bite the inside of my cheek as I prepare myself for what's about to spill from Mercy's lips.

'What is?' My question hesitant.

'There was a fire,' she says, her eyes filling with tears.

Oh, God. Of course. A fire destroyed all recorded evidence of her daughter – that's convenient. I suddenly feel hollowed out. Empty. Jamie's right after all. I've been had. Suckered in. I've fallen for this poor woman's grand delusion.

'Oh. I see,' I say. I do pity her; it must be terrible to believe you're experiencing trauma even when none of it is real.

103

'And when I contacted the register office for a replacement, they said there was no record of my Tia's birth.' Mercy's expression is wild as she tells me. 'I was astounded,' she says. 'More than that. I mean, how could they not have a record of it? I was there, I remember giving birth well enough – you don't just forget that pain, do you?'

'I guess not,' I say. And of course you wouldn't forget. But could you believe in something so much that you have false memories of it? 'Did you visit the hospital you had her in? They also record births.'

She looks at me with a hint of wariness. She's picking up on my suspicion, but for the moment seems to be going along with it. Humouring me. If I carry on with this line of questioning, I doubt that will last. I need to be careful.

'I delivered her here,' she says, her eyes squinted. 'Without a midwife present. Living in a remote place in the middle of nowhere, there was no time. I had her in the bathroom.'

It's the truth in her eyes that gets me. She wholeheartedly believes what she's saying. Why isn't she getting the help she needs?

'Are you . . .' I grasp about in my mind for the right words. 'Under the care of a doctor, Mercy?'

'Why would I be?' she snaps. 'There's nothing wrong with me. Why would you ask me that?'

'Sorry,' I say quickly, realising I've pushed it too far. 'No, no. I know that. I meant for the trauma of what's happened. It's like PTSD, really. And I was just wondering if someone . . . professional . . . was helping you through this.'

'I've seen some people. Bloody do-gooders. Police involved damned social services at one point. They were useless. Hadn't even come to see me during Tia's first years of life.'

'I thought they had to? Like, to do developmental checks and stuff.' It's a genuine question, I'm not trying to catch her out – my thoughts are converting to speech far more quickly than I can control.

'Slipped through the net, didn't I.' And instead of getting more angry, as I assumed she would, she now begins to sob and her frustration fills the room.

'Oh, Mercy. Please don't cry.' A crushing sensation pushes the air from my lungs as though someone is sitting on me. I'm adding to her suffering when I should be helping ease it. 'I'm here to help. Tell me what I can do.'

She brightens at this, beaming at me before abruptly turning away. I stand for a second, stunned. The array of emotions I've been privy to today are head-spinning. Mercy disappears through the door going off the lounge area and I do a three-sixty, taking in the room I'm in. Apart from the door Mercy's just gone through, there are two others. The cabin didn't seem that big from the outside, so I wonder what those rooms are. I can't imagine they're both other bedrooms – maybe a utility-type room? Where the batteries for the solar power system are kept, possibly. Unless she has a basement.

Mercy returns with a small cardboard box.

'What's in here, and the photo, is all I have left,' she says, laying it gently on the wooden table. I sit on the sofa as Mercy pulls the footstool across and places it opposite me. For a few moments, we both stare at the box. Then Mercy takes a deep breath and lifts the lid. The air escapes her lips in a slow hiss – just as I hold my own breath – as she takes a stripey top from the box. It's the same top the girl in the photo is wearing. My heart hammers. Mercy holds the item to her face, inhales the scent. I cough to clear the huge lump in my throat. Even if I had words for this moment, I doubt I'd be able to squeeze them through my vocal cords. She places the top beside the box and puts her hands back in.

'Three things,' Mercy says, her eyes wet with fresh tears. 'That's all I have left of my little girl. The giraffe was one of her favourites.' She holds the well-loved soft toy up for me to see – the once plush fur is flattened and hard. All queries regarding Mercy's claims evaporate as I imagine Tia playing with the giraffe, taking it everywhere with her and refusing that it ever be washed. That's what I used to be like with my special blanket. The times my mum said she'd attempted to steal it from me in the dead of night so she could wash and dry it quickly, and return it without my noticing, ran into the dozens. But it's like I had a sixth sense and each attempt ended in failure because the second she pulled on it, I'd wake up and tell her off, or I'd roll over onto it in my sleep so she couldn't retrieve it. The thing eventually fell to bits. But I won; it never did get washed.

'I can see how loved it was,' I say, choking back tears.

'She wanted her whole room to be filled with them,' Mercy says with a smile. 'Do you want to see?'

Oh, God. My heart drops as my stomach rises. I'm not sure I can cope with more. But, before I can finish my thought, I hear myself saying, 'That would be lovely.' I stand and follow Mercy, my legs as wobbly as a new-born giraffe.

Chapter 18

Erica

My knees give a little as we enter the room and my mouth slackens. The aqua shades and white furniture all too familiar. A mural covers one wall, elephants and giraffes. I snap my head around to look at Mercy. She appears lost, as if seeing her little girl playing in this room, an echo of what once was. I want to ask her how come she chose this pastel colour scheme, why the jungle-type mural. I'd posted images of my room on Instagram – shared how I'd made the perfect nursery in anticipation. But of course, Mercy couldn't have seen it, let alone copied it. She doesn't have internet.

Though she goes into town – there's nothing to say she doesn't go to the library to access theirs.

I inwardly berate myself. I must remember it's not all about me. And plus, if Tia was three, then this room was likely decorated before mine was. It's a coincidence, that's all. Most children's rooms are similar – I don't have the monopoly on pastel shades and jungle murals. Then it hits me.

'You mentioned a fire. That everything was destroyed.'
I cast my eyes around, looking for any evidence such a
thing occurred here, then stare at Mercy. It's like I want to
believe what she tells me, but a part of me is fighting against
it – trying to find the plot holes in her story.

'Yes, that's right. The box I showed you – that's it. All
that was saved. The priority was getting out alive, not saving
material possessions.'

'But everything here is pristine. When was the fire?'

But Mercy isn't listening anymore. She walks to the
window and, with her arms crossed, she gazes out into the
woodland. She's avoiding answering. Is that because there
was no fire? I thought it a convenient explanation for not
having a birth certificate, or any other proof of Tia's
existence. My shoulders slump as I consider the possibility
that I'm being sucked into a delusion. I want to believe
Mercy so desperately because, in a roundabout way, it helps
me too. Inserting myself into a mystery is giving me
something else to focus on. A sadness washes over me now
as I look at Mercy. She must be a very desperate woman,
and quite possibly in need of professional help. She doesn't
need someone who thinks they can help find a non-existent
child.

'I'm so sorry, Mercy,' I say, walking up behind her and
laying a hand on her shoulder. The trees outside seem as
though they're creeping up to the window, closing in on
us and blocking the light. Darkness waits. 'I was wrong . . .
to tell you I could help—'

'What? No!' She swings around to face me, her eyes
blazing. 'You have to. You're the only one who believes me.'
Panic hardens her features and in turn a wave of foreboding
surges through my veins. I stutter an apology as I back

away, my pulse jumping – I can feel every bang. Hear it whooshing in my ears. I've made a huge mistake and I need to get out of here.

'I'm so sorry, Mercy. Maybe I'm just not the right person to help.'

'You *are*, Erica. You're the perfect person. Please.' She strides towards me and I turn, pulling open the door to leave. Something snags my foot and I fall. My outstretched hands fail to stop me crashing onto the floor, and my head makes contact with the tree-stump table with a sickening thud.

Chapter 19

Dr Connie Summers

```
Haytor Ward, Torbay hospital
Emergency admission following incident
at a supermarket. Patient presented
with extreme panic disorder symptoms,
unable to state her name. Obs on
admission were: BP 180/95, pulse
110, resps 22. Admitting consultant
prescribed sedative and, following
initial assessment, a referral was made
to the Liaison Psychiatry service.
At 17.50 following administration
of 10mg Diazepam IM obs stable at
BP 140/75 pulse 80, resps 12.

Police are seeking next of kin.
```

Connie crosses her legs and leans her upper body forward slightly as she focuses on her client.

'We touched upon your earlier life in our last session.

Time got away with us, though, and I'd like to pick up where we left off.'

'I'm not sure I remember where that was,' the woman says.

'You were telling me about a traumatic experience you had, when you were a child. Something to do with losing your mum while on a trip?'

'Oh, that was nothing, really. Just a few moments being lost on a beach.' She shrugs.

'What emotions do you recall while that was happening?'

'Well, fear, obviously. The beach was huge, packed. People and umbrellas, those windbreakers that everyone liked back then all strewn about the place. And I was only small, couldn't see over them.'

'What else do you remember?'

'Frantically gazing around, trying to find something that looked familiar. Mum and her friend were near rocks, they'd set up there to ensure we were sheltered from any strong breezes. But I'd gone to the sea to fill my bucket with water and somehow wandered off-course and when I was heading back I must've taken the wrong trajectory. I started calling for Mum. Everyone stared at me. My breathing was all wrong and I felt light-headed.' The woman shakes her head now, as if experiencing it all over again. 'I walked along the beach, my feet slipping in the hot sand, crying. Praying Mum would call out to me, say, "Over here!"'

'How long was it until you were reunited?'

'Apparently it was about ten minutes, that's all. But it felt like eternity. Not that I knew what eternity even was, but I know I thought that was it – I'd be forever lost on that beach.'

'That must've been horrible. But you were found.'

'Yes. Eventually a woman came up to me, bent down in front of me and asked if I was lost.' Her face screws up, squeezing out the tears in her eyes. 'She was kind, I can still hear her soft, silky voice. She took my hand and walked me up and down the beach until my mum came rushing over.'

'Your mum was frantic, I assume?'

'Yes, she kept saying, "*I thought you'd gone, I thought someone took you.*" She was so relieved and hugged me so tight I struggled to breathe. I hadn't understood what she meant at the time about being fearful someone had taken me. I was just lost. But of course, now I know all too well.

'But there's been no kind woman with a soft, silky-smooth voice to bring my daughter back to me. And sometimes now, I find myself being jealous of my mother. I know that sounds weird.'

'It's how you feel and it's important to recognise and accept everything, no matter how strange you think it is.' Connie pauses, then adds, 'Is a part of you still hoping a woman like the one who found you and returned you to your mother is going to do the same for your daughter?'

'Not a part of me! All of me. It's what's going to happen, I *feel* it.'

Connie suppresses a sigh.

Chapter 20

Erica

Pain shoots through my temple as I open my eyes and try to sit up. I blink rapidly, trying to rid myself of the blurriness and finally focus on my surroundings.

'Don't make any sudden movements.'

My heart drops as I freeze, half sitting, half lying. My mouth is dry, my lips sticking as I go to speak. 'What happened?'

'You tripped on the rug. I'm so sorry. I've been meaning to get those sticky strips to secure it to the wooden floor but never got around to it. Took a nasty tumble. You managed to make it to the sofa, but passed out.' Mercy hands me a mug. 'Here, sip this. I've put sugar in for the shock. And luckily I had some Steri-Strips in my first aid kit, so I've patched you up.' She points to my head. I touch my fingertips to it and wince, then take the proffered mug.

Confusion fogs my mind. The last thing I remember was rushing towards the door to get away. I cast my gaze towards the room – Tia's bedroom – and note the open door; the rucked-up rug. She's right, I must've fallen in my haste to leave. I take a mouthful of the warm, sweet liquid, eyeing Mercy over the rim of the mug. Her face is slack, pale, her mouth downturned – she looks like the sad Pierrot clown I had as a child and my gut twists. I don't want to add to her sadness.

'Why did you come here, Erica?' Mercy asks. She's on the footstool beside the sofa, watching me as intently as I'm looking at her.

'Because you asked me,' I say.

'That's not what I mean,' she says, her eyebrows raised. 'Why did you agree? It's like you were dangling the carrot – saying you'll help me, then when you get here, whipping the carrot up and away from me. It's pretty cruel of you.'

'God, Mercy. I'm sorry. I really didn't mean to give you false hope. I thought, well . . . I believed I could help before. But now I've been here . . .'

'I don't understand.' She takes a juddering intake of air and I do the same.

'Neither do I, really,' I say, honestly. 'There are a few things that, well, don't . . .' I am in a vulnerable position here; do I really think now is the time to question her story? Or should I save this for another time? If there is one.

'Don't what?' she says. 'Add up?'

She's doing it again. Reading my mind. But it's almost a relief, and I let out a long sigh.

'I'm sorry, Mercy. It's just, well, quite hard to take it all in, that's all.'

She nods. 'I know. Trust me, I've doubted my own mind sometimes. It's so exhausting.'

My shoulders sag, my muscles releasing the tension they've been holding for this entire exchange. 'It must be awful living this day in, day out – the mind is a tricky place.'

'Yes,' she says with a slight smile. 'There are days when my memories are clear and everything makes sense, you know? Then, at other times, all of them will be in complete disarray, jumbled up and unclear. Like none of the memories are mine, they belong to someone else. They're messing with my head, Erica. The police, the dumb psychiatrists they've tried to make me see. They're denying my daughter's existence. Have you any idea how that feels?'

'Frustrating. Scary,' I venture. 'You must have moments of anger and despair. Isolation. You're alone here, far away from any support.' I seem to be saying the right things because Mercy seems calm; she's not fidgeting or anxious as far as I can tell. Feeling a bit more confident, I ask: 'Do you think it's time to move on, maybe?'

A flash of anger crosses Mercy's face and I immediately wish I could take back those last words. But then, it's gone again, and her features soften.

'How can I?' Her voice breaks and I look away for a second, unable to witness the pain in her eyes. 'The only way I'll move on is by finding out what happened to Tia. Someone has her, Erica. They took her from me and I won't stop until I get her back. Can't stop.'

I place my mug down on the floor beside me, then look Mercy dead in the eyes.

'However much I want to believe everything you've told me, there's a part of me that is holding back. I don't know you, Mercy. Yet somehow, we've been thrown together, so I saw that as a sign, I guess. But that doesn't mean it's a sign I should help you find Tia.'

Mercy widens her eyes, moves forward. I quickly

continue. 'It might be that I'm here to help you overcome the trauma, not by finding a missing child, but by helping you come to terms with everything.' I swallow hard, afraid my words will throw Mercy into panic mode. What am I doing? 'Maybe, if you saw my husband – he's a psychologist, he'd be able to offer proper help?'

'You want me to trust your husband when you clearly don't?' She laughs. I sit back, like I've been physically struck.

'What?'

'I know why we were brought together,' Mercy says, reaching forwards and taking my hands in hers. I don't pull away, despite that being my instinct. 'We are meant to help each other.'

I narrow my eyes at her, but there's a sense of intrigue that swirls in my gut; I've had the same feeling – that it was fate that brought us together. I'm convinced my role is to help her so I can show the universe I'm worthy of having a child. I wonder what Mercy believes her role to be.

'I've seen you, Erica. I know you hadn't noticed me until I came up to you. But I've been watching you. I heard you rehearsing your little leaving speech to Jamie.'

Jesus Christ. I hadn't ever considered I was talking out loud – my practice conversations were inside my head; I was imagining them, not speaking them, surely? But how else would she know? I pull my hands away and cover my mouth, sighing into them. I can't believe it. I'm often distracted, though, so there's a possibility she overheard. In which case, so might other shoppers. Embarrassment floods my face.

'Don't worry,' Mercy says, her voice soft. 'As I say, I'm going to help you. You obviously need to talk through what's going on for you at home. With Jamie. So, I'll be here for you, and you'll offer your support to me. A quid pro quo, so to speak.'

She pats my knees and gets up. A shudder runs down my spine. The only time I've heard that saying was when I watched *The Silence of the Lambs*. Has Mercy been stalking me?

'I'll be at the same place, same time next week. See you then.'

I've half a mind to ask why we should leave it an entire week before seeing each other. If she's so desperate for my help in finding Tia, I'd have thought she'd suggest seeing me sooner – even every day. As I'm not sure that's necessarily a good idea, though, I don't question her timescale. With some effort, I lift myself up from the sofa. The pressure in my head feels like it's building, so I take it slowly even though my fight-or-flight response is currently encouraging me to run, not walk out of here.

I stare at Mercy as I back out of the cabin, conflicting thoughts jutting up against each other in my aching head, then approach my car and climb in. She stays at the threshold of her cabin as I turn the key. Just as I begin to reverse, she steps down, her arm waving. Shit. The desire to ignore and screech away, tyres throwing up mud in my wake, is overwhelming, but my foot slips from the accelerator. She's at the driver side window before I know it.

'Oh, and Erica?'

I gulp. 'Yes?'

'Be careful driving back. You might be concussed.'

Chapter 21

Erica

Every muscle hurts. They've been in an uncomfortable spasm the entire journey home. Now, as I sit in the car on the drive rotating my neck and pushing my shoulders down, they finally begin to relax. I blow out my cheeks, then get out. My gaze catches on the house opposite. The woman is there again, sitting in her window. She's knitting – I can see the needles moving in and out. She doesn't look down at what she's doing, though. I pause to wave, but then go inside without waiting to see if she responded. I've thought about it a few times now, and I really should do the neighbourly thing and pop over one day. Say hello, ask if she needs anything. She might appreciate having someone to speak to, rather than just watching them from behind glass. And, if I'm being honest, even though I tell myself I don't have time for another friend, I would also welcome some company – someone to talk to who I don't feel a responsibility to help.

My legs are like lead as I trudge upstairs and my bed looks inviting as I pass by the bedroom. I need to do something first, though. My eyes sting as I try and focus on the words on my computer screen. But it's a waste of time. The hits from my numerous searches are still too wide and none match Mercy's missing daughter. The name 'Tia Hamilton' only returns results of social media profiles and Mercy's is much the same – with the addition of finding the Mercy Hamilton hospital in Ohio. After twenty minutes of trawling the internet, I slam back in my chair, huffing loudly at my lack of success. I need more to go on. Or, as the staff at the supermarket and Jamie said, there was no missing girl to begin with and that's why I can't find anything.

I resist the urge to go to bed – I'll never sleep tonight if I pass out now, so instead I flop down on the cuddle chair, arms and legs sprawled out like a starfish. My eyes are heavy, head fuzzy. Perhaps I do have concussion, I think, gently feeling along the Steri-Strips. I'll have to pull them off before Jamie gets home. Maybe my hair will cover the cut. If not, I'll say I've just hit it on an open cupboard door.

A tingling sensation ripples along my skin as fragmented memories of the episode in the cabin come to me. I tripped – probably on the rug. I'd been trying to leave – *escape?* – the room because of Mercy's reaction. She didn't want me to go. Could it have been that during Mercy's frantic attempt to prevent me leaving she pushed me? She's desperate. And that's a dangerous state to be in. People do extreme things when they're running out of options. I sit up, rubbing my face roughly with both palms. Red flags are waving madly, yet I'm compelled to keep going. There's something about Mercy that has sucked me in. Partly it's the desire to unravel the mystery, but more than that it's the fact we're both so intent on finding something to give us purpose. We both just want to be mothers. So, while I'm fighting the urge to believe her because of what Jamie said, what the police and the supermarket staff said, and because of the convenient lack of evidence – ultimately, deep down, I know she's telling the truth. I feel it.

Despite the alarm bells, I'm drawn to her in a way I can't fully explain. I know I'll be at Bateman's next Friday and I'll meet up with Mercy again. I can't give up on her, even if I want to.

I've rustled up a quick stir-fry with leftovers and, as Jamie walks in, I plate it up and put it on the table.

'Dinner's ready,' I say.

'Blimey.' He has barely shrugged off his coat, and looks at me with concern.

'I can be super-efficient when I want to be.' I offer a wide smile.

'So I see.' He saunters in and sits down at the table. 'I'm not complaining. Have you got ahead of yourself then?'

I frown. 'With my articles?'

'Yeah. You've seemed stressed, I guessed it was about hitting your work deadlines. I thought you had a backlog and would be working late every evening to catch up. But, you've managed it all?'

'Sort of,' I say, and cast around for a different topic to distract him. I can't very well admit that I haven't been working on my articles, that instead I've been getting myself entangled in someone else's business. 'Do you know the neighbour opposite us? The woman who's always sitting in the window?'

Jamie frowns, almost as if he's aware of what I'm doing.

'Erm . . . well, yes I've spoken to her on occasion. Why?' He shovels a forkful of noodles in his mouth.

'Just wondered. We've been living here for almost four years and I can't recall talking to her. Feel a bit bad about it. Not exactly neighbourly, is it?'

'I'm sure you must've spoken to her in four years, Erica.'

'I do wave,' I say, putting my hand up now to demonstrate.

'Well maybe you should go over then. But don't be upset if she doesn't invite you in.'

'Why would I be upset?'

Jamie shrugs but doesn't answer as he polishes off the remnants of the stir-fry then gets up and puts his plate in the dishwasher. As he bends, I stand and walk up behind him, pushing myself up against his back and reaching my hands around his middle.

'And what did I do to deserve this attention?' he says, swivelling around in my arms to face me.

'Nothing.' I feel the tell-tale prickling in my eyes and blink rapidly. I bury my head in his chest so he can't see me, or the cut in my hairline. I wince sightly as the pressure against it causes pain. 'Just wanted a hug.'

Mercy's words crowd my mind – 'I heard you rehearsing your little leaving speech to Jamie.' As much as I've planned my leaving speech, I've never even come close to telling Jamie. Something holds me back. Fear? I don't want to be on my own and I need him if I'm to realise my desire to have a baby. But I don't want to live this life either.

I'm in limbo.

'Have you seen Bea lately? It must've been a while since you guys had a catch-up.'

'Too busy. We can go months sometimes without seeing each other.'

Jamie takes my upper arms and gently forces us apart. 'Perhaps it would do you good to get together . . . You're spending a lot of time on your own.'

'Nature of the job. I can't just put everything down – I have a schedule too; just because I work from home doesn't mean I'm free as and when. You don't see your mates during work hours, do you? In fact, while we're on the subject, when last did *you* socialise?'

'But I do speak with people at work, Erica. There are people there I can have a laugh with, share my life with.'

'Huh, I bet,' I mumble, turning my back on him and starting towards the lounge. I hear Jamie following.

'What do you mean by that?' His tone is edged with condescension. I should quit. Back down now before I make this into an argument. But I don't.

'I imagine your female colleagues are very obliging when it comes to lending an ear, Jamie,' I say, immediately regretting it.

'Don't be so ridiculous.'

And in that moment, everything goes out the window. Him telling me not to be ridiculous is like a red rag to a bull and the mention of her is on the tip of my tongue.

'Your ex, *Gemma*, included in these people you can share your life with?' It's hard not to dredge this up during an argument; I can't seem to help myself. I could never let go of the weird coincidence that she followed Jamie from Bath to Devon, getting a job at the same establishment. I know they were both headed in a similar direction career-wise, and that's what Jamie always likes to point out, but there are plenty of other prisons in the UK.

'I don't see her. You know she works in probation – mostly in admin these days. I rarely bump into her.'

'But you do run into her sometimes. What do you talk about with her when you see her?'

'Erica, please. This wasn't meant to turn into an argument.' He sighs. Reluctantly adding, 'We exchange brief niceties, that's it.'

'You never talk about the baby?'

'What?' His jaw tenses. 'Why would we? It's in the past.'

'How old would she be? Four?'

'I don't know, Erica, I never think about it.'

'Really? I find that hard to believe.' *I* think about it. His apparent 'mistake' having taken place so close to us getting married.

'I did. Obviously, before. But not now. Unless you remind me. You tend to bring it up when you're avoiding talking about something I've instigated that you don't feel comfortable talking about.'

'Don't do that psychobabble shit on me, Jamie. You leave that at the prison, thanks.'

'You started this. And it's not psychobabble, it's a fact.'

I turn tail and walk back into the kitchen. I reach into the fridge, guiltily pulling the wine bottle from the door.

'You avoid any conversation that involves being honest with yourself,' Jamie spits, following me. 'Or with me. Somehow you always manage to turn things around on me when you're feeling trapped.'

'Well, don't trap me then. It's not nice to play games.'

'I'm not the one playing games. You know my thoughts on all of this.'

'All of what?'

'Don't play dumb. We're too far down the line for that.'

'If this is about the marriage guidance again . . .' It's a topic that's come up in previous fights. And to be fair, it

126

might be helpful. Yet, I can't allow someone else into our private lives. Share intimate details with a stranger. I shudder at the thought.

Jamie blinks rapidly. 'Sometimes I'm not sure if you're winding me up.'

I look at him now, straight in the eye. If there was ever a right time to say what's on my mind, now is it.

'I . . . I'm not . . .' My mouth dries, my tongue sticking. Jamie's eyebrows knit together, his lips forming a tight line. *Go on, say it. Tell him.* 'I don't think I want . . .'

'You don't want what, Erica?'

Finally faced with this opportunity, the words won't come; my mouth opens and closes but they remain unspoken. Under his intent gaze, pressure builds in my head. I rub my temples with my fingertips. Jamie's expression softens, like he's taken pity on me.

'The first step will be the hardest, but it's a step that has to be taken,' he says, softly.

I don't even know if we're talking about the same thing, but I'm drained – my entire body feels limp, and I just want to end this conversation. 'I'm not sure I can get through it, Jamie.'

It's the closest I've come to saying I want to leave him. And for now, it's all I can manage. I fill my glass and take it upstairs. As I draw the curtains, I see the cat lady looking up at me. We stare at each other for a moment, before I give an awkward wave. She gives a slow nod, her hands busy with the knitting needles. Doesn't she ever sleep?

Chapter 22

Erica

Over the days, thoughts of Mercy and her lost girl filled my mind almost constantly and culminated last night with my body refusing to relax. By five a.m. my muscles were rigid with tension, and I'd given up all hope. I crept out of bed, careful not to disturb Jamie, and fired up the computer in my office.

For all the good it's done me. Almost two hours have gone by, and still nothing. I'd blamed concussion for my lack of success on Friday night – that it was my inability to focus, rather than there being nothing, but seemingly not. A high-profile missing child case years ago – a supposed abduction from a beach while the family holidayed in Greece – is the only thing that keeps coming to the top of each of my searches. Some really far-out theories have been bandied about over the years. Conspiracy theories – like those Mercy spoke of, only in this case, they're against the parents of the missing child. The strangest one I've come across is referred to as the enigma theory – that the missing child never existed. My interest is piqued, because it's something that crossed my mind too when I realised there was only one single photo of Tia.

And isn't it what a lot of other people believe too? The supermarket staff, the police. I'm sure Jamie would say the same if I were to tell him everything that's happened so far. After all, which is easier to believe? A woman who has such little evidence of her daughter's existence but convincingly comes across as a grieving mother, or authorities that are adamant the child in the photo, whoever she might be, isn't Mercy's. That she never had a daughter in the first place. I've seen documentaries with distraught mothers who've lost babies who go on to buy lifelike dolls and pretend they're alive. It's sad but I guess I understand it, to a point.

If meeting Mercy is some sort of sign, if I'm meant to help her, I need to get to the bottom of this and decide which story I want to believe. I can't help her if I keep changing my mind. Because my internet searches haven't yielded much, the only thing I can think to do is pay a visit to Newton police station. Maybe the direct approach is the best one. I'll skip the usual gym session today, wait for Jamie to leave for work, then get ready. I must look the part; dress to impress. And that way, they might be more inclined to offer up information. I shut my mind to the voice in my head telling me that's a really dumb thing to even consider – as if wearing smart clothes will somehow trick the police into giving some random woman details of a missing girl. Still, it can't hurt to look good.

Jamie is sitting up, propped against the plush silver headboard as I walk back into the bedroom, his glasses balanced on the tip of his nose as he reads from the open book on his lap. I frown at him.

'Aren't you going to be late?'

'Erm,' he says, raising his eyes to mine and smiling. 'I'm not going in today. You know that.'

'No, I didn't, because you never mentioned having today off.' I stand in the doorway to the en suite, contemplating my next move as I slip my satin nightshirt off. 'Shame I didn't realise.'

'Oh?' Jamie's eyes glide down my body to the material now around my ankles.

'Well, if I hadn't cancelled my gym session and arranged to meet with a source instead, we could've had lunch out or something.'

'Ah,' he says, not hiding the disappointment in his voice. I suppress a smile.

'Sorry,' I say. 'Did you think other things were on the agenda?'

'I thought it must be "the right time".' He poses his fingers in air quotes. 'Anyway, lunch is a nice thought, but I'll still be working – just from home today. Have to try and get my head around this.' He indicates the open book and the file beside it. 'It's that challenging client I told you about.' He runs his fingers over his stubble – the scratchy sound grates through me, it's like someone running their nails down a chalkboard.

'Sounds like fun,' I say, scrunching my face up. 'Do you want me to bring you back a bagel and coffee?'

'Yeah, thanks. That'd be good. What time are you heading out?'

I reach across the bed and check the time on my phone. 'Nine-ish.'

'How long do you think your meeting will be for?' He isn't looking at me now, his attention half in the book, but goosebumps spring up on my skin. He doesn't usually question me like this. Although, I suppose I did just say I was going to bring him home a bagel and coffee, so he's probably just wanting to know a rough time he can expect them. Of course, currently I have no clue how long I'll be – it all depends how successful I am at the police station.

'I'll be a couple of hours. Don't skip brekkie just in case. Don't want you starving while you wait,' I say, moving towards him. I bend and kiss him on the top of his head, my breasts touching his chest. He reaches both hands up, brushing his fingertips over them, his thumbs rubbing over my erect nipples. His breath catches and for a moment I stay there, enjoying the contact. But then I pull away from him.

I'm not ovulating; there's no point.

Jamie, too, seems to snap out of his brief state of desire, his attention quickly returning to his work. I turn and walk into the shower cubicle, allowing the hot jets of water to caress my skin as I attempt to push unwanted thoughts from my mind. My IVF journey, the one I share on Instagram, isn't entirely the truth. The reality is it had already failed and I no longer 'fit' the criteria. But I can't very well tell my followers that. Because then, I'd have nothing left to give them. My only hope is natural conception, and thereby lies the problem. I want two different things, but one affects the other. My womb aches and I grip my belly with both hands. What a mess.

Chapter 23

Erica

Jamie watches me as I leave, my laptop bag slung over my shoulder to ensure my cover of meeting a source is credible. I pop it on the passenger side seat and wave as I reverse off the driveway. As I pass by the knitting cat lady, I have a sudden urge to stop. There's something about the curious expression on her face drawing me in. I carry on around the corner, but then Jamie's comment about me never socialising pops into my mind and I pull over and park again. When I'd mentioned being neighbourly, he'd suggested I should go over and see the cat lady. I've got all the time I need to visit the police station, it's not as though I'm under curfew. I can fit in a quick stop at the neighbour's, then go to the station and still be home in a few hours. No doubt Jamie won't even realise how long I've been gone and, as long as I return with the promised bagel and coffee, he'll be sweet. Mind made up, I get out the car and cautiously walk back around to our road. His head'll be buried in his books by now, so it's highly unlikely he'll see me.

I place my palm up towards the woman in the window as I stride up her path, long blades of grass whipping against my calves. Her face lights up and she springs from her chair, more spritely than I expected, and disappears from sight.

'I wondered when you'd be over,' she says, practically pulling me inside. The air is warm, stifling, like the windows haven't been opened for weeks, and the smell of cats mixed with floating fur clags the back of my throat. I cough to clear it before speaking.

'I'm so sorry, you know – I can't believe we've lived here so long without properly introducing ourselves, you must think us so rude.' I pause, stretching out my hand. 'I'm Erica Fielding, my husband and I live opposite.'

The woman takes my hand, her grip firm as she shakes it. 'Oh,' she frowns, still pumping my arm up and down. 'Yes, you both always wave up when you pass. Erica, you say?'

'Yes, that's right.' I smile as she releases me and I'm free to gaze around. 'You have a lovely cosy home, erm . . . Mrs . . .'

'Oh, my. Excuse my manners, Erica. I'm Jean. Jean Meneely.' Her eyes are fixed on mine, like she's waiting for something. God, did she introduce herself when we first moved in? 'You look very nice today, dear. Going anywhere special?'

I look down at myself, like I've forgotten what clothes I'm wearing. 'Thank you. And no, sadly nowhere special.' I don't want to mention my plan to visit the police station but she's still looking at me, as though I've not given her enough qualifying detail. 'A meeting. I'm off to meet someone about an article I'm writing,' I add.

'Ooh, that does sound exciting,' Jean says. She turns her back to me and heads to another room. The kitchen, I presume, if the houses have a similar layout. 'I'll make us a nice Earl Grey,' she calls. I screw up my nose. I loathe Earl Grey tea, but don't say so. I'm sure I'll be able to swallow the perfumed liquid without visibly gagging. 'Make yourself comfy.'

I cast my eyes around and am drawn to the high-backed leather tan chair beside the fireplace. It's cat-free. Hopefully fur-free too, or I'll be leaving here with a thick layer on my black trousers. I really didn't think this through. I hear crockery rattling as Jean walks steadily in with the tray of two fine-bone-china cups and saucers and a plate of Rich Tea biscuits. She sets it down on the coffee table.

'Ah, I see you've chosen that chair,' she says with a nod of approval. 'That was Frank's. God bless his soul.' A shadow seems to pass over her face as she signs the cross over her chest before passing me a drink. Then she takes her window seat, swivels it around and sits to face me. I wonder if my choice of chair has somehow told Jean something about me. I feel like lately everything is some sort of test. I sip the tea, pressing my lips tightly together as I swallow, hoping I've not unconsciously grimaced.

'Thank you,' I say, motioning to the tea. She gives a thin smile in return. I don't think I've fooled her. 'I'm sorry about your husband. How did . . .?' I let my sentence trail, but Jean answers.

'His heart, dear. So pure, yet that's what failed him.'

'Oh, that's very sad. I'm not sure I remember ever seeing him.'

'No? Oh, I guess he kept to himself a fair bit. We both did, really. This was our first house together.'

'That's so lovely. What wonderful memories you must have.'

'Oh, yes. That I do. I've one of the best memories, you know. Not so much for faces, but can always recall special occasions, or events. I can remember things from fifty years ago right up until now.' She gives a proud smile.

'That's very impressive, Jean. I wish I could say the same.' I laugh, then take a large swig from my cup. I want this tea gone so I can have a biscuit and rid my tastebuds of the cloying sensation.

'I see everything from here,' she continues. 'People aren't always aware of what's staring them in the face.' There's something about Jean's tone that causes a shiver to track down my spine.

'I bet you do. I'm sorry we're such boring neighbours, though. Not much goes on in this street, eh?'

'You'd be surprised, Erica. I'm practically invisible in that window, day after day. It's like people forget I'm here.'

My face flushes. Here I am, paying the first visit to my neighbour in four years, having treated her just the same as she's describing now. I do wave, though. I hope that counts for something. I must do better.

'Now I've finally dropped by – and again, my apologies for being such a bad neighbour – you will let me know if I can do anything for you, won't you? Like any errands, or,' I gaze around again, 'maybe any bits of DIY? Jamie will happily help out. Not that he's great at that stuff, I must add!'

'He seems pretty nifty with his hands to me,' she says, giving an exaggerated wink. I laugh, but I'm not quite sure what she means. I get up and wander to the window, looking up to our bedroom. Can she see us having sex from here? No, she can't possibly see in. Unless, of course, she does move from this window, and instead stares out from the one upstairs dead opposite our bedroom. I'm about to turn to face Jean, see if I can read her expression, when movement on the pavement outside catches my attention.

'No way,' I whisper.

'Are you all right, dear?' Jean joins me at the window. 'You've lost your colour. Who is it?' She looks up and down the street, then back at me. 'Did you see something?'

'Er . . . no.' I shake my head. 'I was mistaken. Just thought I saw . . .' I thought I saw Mercy. But this is a bit far out from Bateman's. It's also Wednesday. She said she only ventured into town on a Friday.

'Who did you think you saw?' Jean presses.

'Someone I met at the supermarket a few weeks ago. But it couldn't have been. She was there one second and . . . gone.' I turn now to face Jean. 'Did you see her a second ago? In a grey coat?'

Jean narrows her eyes. 'Maybe she went into a house.'

Maybe she went into *my* house. I look back outside, and stare at my door, then at each window in turn. I can't see any movement.

'Yeah, maybe.' It would be way too much of a coincidence if Mercy knew someone else in my street.

'Was your new friend trying to find you, do you think? Perhaps you should pop back into yours and see if she's there?'

'No,' I say a little too sharply. 'She doesn't know where I live. She can't have been going into mine. Even if she were, Jamie would've said I'm not there and sent her on her way by now. No one has come back out.'

'That's true.' Jean tucks her white hair behind an ear. 'Oh well, just one of those odd mysteries. Another biscuit?'

'Thank you, but I ought to get going.' I check my phone; I've already been half an hour. It didn't feel that long here with Jean. I'm glad I came over. My misconceptions, the strange feelings I had about her, have been quashed. Mostly.

'Do visit again, won't you? It's been nice to get to know you a little, Erica.'

'Absolutely, Jean. And don't forget to let me know if there's anything I can do for you.'

'Oh, I'll be sure to let you know. Thank you.'

I head out and back up the path, turning to wave as I reach the gate. 'Bye, Jean. See you later no doubt.'

'Yes, see you later. And Erica?'

'Yes?'

'Do be careful, won't you dear.'

I frown, unsure of what she thinks I'm about to do, or what she's worried will befall me. But I smile and nod before leaving her standing on her step.

Chapter 24

Erica

I fight the pull; forcing my legs to walk around the corner, not across the road. The only way of knowing if Mercy is indeed inside my house, which I know is ludicrous, is to march back across there and go inside. But, if I do that, Jamie will assume I'm finished with my meeting, and wonder why I'm bagel-free and coffee-less to boot. I can't convincingly leave again without raising his suspicion, then my plan will be lost for the day. I suppose I could pretend I've forgotten something I need for the meeting and am popping back to get it.

This idea almost causes me to cross the road but my internal voice screams at me not to be side-tracked. What if I get waylaid at home and then can't fit in a visit to the station? While I do have tomorrow, if something comes up and I lose that opportunity I'll kick myself. If I find out something interesting at the police station now, I'll be armed with that information when I meet Mercy again on Friday. I don't want to allow my paranoid mind to get in the way. And of *course* Mercy isn't in my house right at this moment. I give a cautious glance back over my shoulder. I must've been wrong about seeing her. It wouldn't be the first time, I remind myself. The second week, at Bateman's when I was seeking her out, I mistook another woman for her then. When you're desperate, it's easy to conjure up the thing you're looking for. It's a trick of the mind.

Now I've convinced myself of that, I get in the car, turn the radio up loud and drive towards Newton police station, singing with wild abandon to *One Step Closer* by Linkin Park. I smile as I imagine my brother headbanging to this in the Noughties – his long blond hair tangled and flying everywhere. Drove my mum nuts. Which is predominantly why he did it, of course. Anything to wind our poor mother up. If we'd known then our parents would die prematurely, I wonder if we'd have been different. Every now and then I find myself craving contact with the remainder of my family. It's just me, my brother Darren and Uncle Vern left. But Darren has been living at Her Majesty's pleasure for the past eight years and I've no interest in visiting – I'm not even sure when his release date is – and I haven't spoken with my uncle since he moved to Dubai.

It's like the *Mary Celeste* when I push through the glass door into the reception area of Newton Abbot police station. I tentatively step forward – is it even open? I'm not sure what I expected from a local town station, but it was more than this. A large wooden counter runs along the far side so, with shoulders back, head held high, I stride towards it, slamming my palm down on the old-fashioned brass bell on the top.

'Good morning,' a deep-but-cheerful voice takes me by surprise. I turn, but can't locate its owner.

'Hi,' I say, looking all around. 'I've an enquiry, please?' Is it an automated voice? Or is someone watching me from a different location?

'Don't look so worried, I won't cuff you just for asking a question.' A uniformed officer finally becomes visible from somewhere off to the left, behind the counter. I give an awkward laugh. He's bald, ruddy-faced as though he's fallen asleep in the midday sun. His smile is genuine, and I relax. He's right, I am only asking some questions, the worst that can happen is he'll tell me he's not at liberty to discuss the case, or something to that effect. Although I really hope that isn't the outcome. I want to leave here with some solid information.

'I wondered if you might be able to help with something,' I begin. How to word this so I don't get shut down straight away? Supposing I had some information *I* wanted to share? Would that help me to gain the information that they have? I'm suddenly aware he's staring at me. 'Sorry, right. Well, this might be a strange request.'

'Won't be as strange as the fella's before you, I'd bet on that.' He grins.

'Hopefully,' I say. 'I met a woman a few weeks back, I think she's known to the police.' I wait for this to sink in before continuing. 'And, the thing is, I've kind of got roped into helping her. She's lost her daughter, you see—'

'Hold it,' he says, his hands raised. He leans forwards, scrutinising me. 'Wait there.' And then he disappears. My pulse pounds in my throat. That was odd. Why do I have the feeling he immediately knew who I was referring to? Christ, do they get weekly complaints from people about Mercy bothering them at Bateman's? Before I can contemplate it further, a smartly dressed woman, early thirties, with her hair scraped so tightly into a bun it looks painted onto her scalp, lifts the countertop and comes through to my side of the reception. She stands with her feet apart, in what I can only describe as an army pose, with her hands clasped in front of her, rigid. My muscles tense up too.

'I'm Detective Sergeant Offord.' Her abruptness gives me a chill, goosebumps jut up from the skin on my arms and I shiver. 'My officer here says you want to talk about the missing child.'

Confusion clouds my mind at this overly dramatic approach. Couldn't he have waited to find out what my question even was before calling in the heavy squad? And I note she says 'the' missing child. Suggesting a) that there is only one, and b) that there IS a missing child! I'm buoyed by my deduction and quickly, and as succinctly as possible, relay Mercy's story to her.

The look of utter bewilderment on DS Offord's face when I finish speaking is like a punch in mine. Is this how Mercy feels every single time she asks for help finding Tia?

'So?' I prompt. 'Are you able to give me some background information? You might not be in a position to investigate; I understand with budgets and time issues and that – I'm sure you put everything into the initial search when Tia went missing.' I stop speaking as a hand obliterates my view of her face. I huff, indignant at the rude gesture. 'I was only asking—'

'Please,' DS Offord says. 'Stop. You've gabbled on so quickly I've lost the thread.'

'I've *gabbled*?' I open my eyes wide. 'I've done no such thing.' Perhaps I was a little overzealous.

'Sorry, what did you say your name was?' she asks, her

thick eyebrows joining in the centre of her forehead with the force of her frown.

I sigh. 'It's Erica Fielding. I live at 34, Westaway Road. Do you want to see my driver's licence too?' I muster all the sarcasm I can, but it falls on deaf ears.

'Yes, thank you.'

I jolt my head back. 'Really? I was actually joking.'

'You're asking a lot of questions, Ms Fielding. It would be remiss of me not to check out your identity, now, wouldn't it?'

She has a point. 'It's in the car. Hang on.' I turn to go out, but her shrill call halts me.

'God, no need. Don't worry for the minute. Look, I can't pretend I know what's going on, but I've got five minutes.' She takes a step back and ushers me behind the counter and into a small room off a corridor.

'Thank you. I appreciate it. I'm concerned about Mercy, you see. No one believes her and I just can't figure out why. I want to help her.'

DS Offord raises her eyebrows again. 'I just need to make a quick call, then we'll see if between the two of us we can put a few pieces together, shall we?'

The door closes with a soft thud.

Chapter 25

Dr Connie Summers

Police interview notes

Bateman's manager, Mr Simon Tyne, was interviewed at the scene as were several store colleagues and the retail security guard, Mr Wesley Little. Internal CCTV footage was obtained (detailed in a separate document) and external CCTV has been requested. No evidence of an abduction was found in the internal footage, nor was there clear visual evidence of the three-year-old wandering off alone. No witnesses came forward suggesting they'd seen a lone child, or one who was distressed or being forcibly taken from the store or surrounding area. Police dogs and specialist officers were drafted in to facilitate a full search of the location. Due to the mother's increasingly distressed state within the supermarket, emergency services were called and mental health input was gained from the CRISIS Team. Following an assessment, it was believed the woman who alerted staff to her missing child was in fact suffering with a delusional disorder. No further action taken at this time.

*

'I wanted to ask you about the day at the supermarket,' Connie says, getting comfortable in the chair and crossing her legs.

'I've gone over this so, so many times.' The woman's voice is exasperated, strained.

'This time, we're going to do some role play, though, so a little different from the other times.'

'Oh, my God. Are we back at school in drama class? I hate role play.'

'It can feel a bit uncomfortable to begin with, but it's a valuable tool and I've used it to great effect with other clients.'

The woman rolls her eyes like a grumpy teenager. 'How the hell does pretending to be someone else help me find my daughter?'

Connie chews on the end of her pen, choosing not to answer. Then she sits forward, her face serious. 'I want to take you back to the day in question, and this time you are inside the store, and you are a staff member. You're watching customers come through the entrance, and you're greeting them.'

'This is stupid.'

'We'll do it for a few minutes. Then we'll swap characters.'

'Seriously, Connie. I don't see the point in this.'

'Not right now, but I think you will.'

The woman sighs, her shoulders round as she slumps. 'Go on then. Get this over with.'

'You're standing by the doors as you see a woman walk in pushing a shopping trolley. She's not the only one – there's a crowd of teenagers. Can you see them?'

'Should I be closing my eyes?' She sighs.

'If that helps. Try to picture them as they pile in. They're noisy – a bunch of school kids. It's that time of day, you have to keep a close eye on groups of children, shoplifting is an issue.'

'My attention is on them, then. Not the woman and her child.'

'I didn't say there was a child. All you saw were the teenagers and a woman with a shopping trolley. But yes, your attention is initially on the group. You follow them up the aisle a bit, listen to their immature banter. Maybe you're focusing on what they're saying, listening out for any talk of stealing.'

'Little scrotes. One of them has just pocketed an apple.'

Connie allows herself a slight smile. Then she continues the role play exercise.

Connie watches her client as she leaves, a knot of anxiety wedged in her stomach. The session had progressed fairly well today, but she knows she isn't gaining the full picture from the weekly consultations; she needs more time with her. Connie also wants to know what goes on in the days between the sessions, because she's sure she's not being told the whole truth. But inserting herself into her client's life too deeply would be a mistake. Wouldn't it? A step too far. But then, she's already gone far beyond the boundaries with this case. What's one more step?

Connie turns back to her desk and snatches up the phone.

'Hi. It's Connie.' She doesn't wait for a response before carrying straight on. 'I'm taking the plan a little further. But I'm going to need your help again.'

MEETING 5

Chapter 26

Erica

'I thought I saw you on Wednesday,' I say when Mercy's stopped shuffling and clicked her seatbelt in place. She gives me a sideways glance and shrugs.

'I'd say "Where?" but given that up until today I didn't leave the cabin . . .'

'No. I guessed I must've been mistaken.' I keep my focus on her, but she doesn't look at me. Because she doesn't want me to see in her eyes that she's lying? 'Have you made any progress this week?'

'Shit, you sound like a shrink.' Mercy huffs. 'No. I haven't. But then, as I said – I've not been out.' She continues to stare out of the passenger side window.

Mercy's once-weekly trips to Bateman's to ask shoppers if they've seen Tia aren't enough. I find it strange that she's only trying to find her daughter one day of the week, and seemingly doing nothing in between.

'I went to the police station, spoke to a DS Offord,' I say lightly, like it's no big deal.

'You what?' She turns sharply to face me. At least I have

her full attention now. 'Why did you do that?' Her face crumples, her thin lips forming a pout as if she's about to cry.

'I thought it was the best way to gather information. Find out what they had, if there'd been any sightings or anything. You didn't seem to be getting anything from them, so I thought I'd try.'

Mercy looks thoughtful. 'And?' Her demoralised tone suggests she's not expecting a fruitful outcome.

'It was much like you told me, I'm afraid. No record of a Tia Hamilton, in fact, they were unable to find anything about you, either. Have you changed your name?'

'Hamilton is the name I took,' she says as she turns to look out the window again. 'He gave me my name and he gave me Tia. Parting with either isn't an option.'

If it was her married name, then surely there would be a record, though. I open my mouth to verbalise this, but Mercy cuts in.

'Whatever name I gave, they'd say the same bloody thing. They don't want to help me, Erica. You've witnessed that first-hand. They want me locked away, out of sight, away from others. They don't want me to prove what incompetent idiots they are. Best to get me sectioned.' Tears streak down her face, dropping onto her grey raincoat. I stare at the blurry-edged splotches and, in a sudden moment of sheer exasperation, I grab my handbag and jump out of the car.

'Stay there. I'll be five minutes,' I tell her.

Ten minutes later I hand the carrier to Mercy as I climb back in. 'Please take this as a gift.' Mercy narrows her eyes as she cautiously peers inside the bag.

'Why have you bought me this?' She pulls the coat fully out, holding it up high to look at it.

'I'm sure your raincoat has sentimental value, or something, but if I'm honest, I can't bear to look at its pathetic patchiness any longer.'

Mercy laughs. So loud that I reel back. When she stops, she smiles. 'Thank you. This is beautiful. I'll look like one of your Instagram friends in this!' She gets out, shrugs the grey blob of a coat off and puts the new, smart khaki, quilted jacket on. I see her twirl, then twist so she can catch a glimpse of herself in the wing mirror. Her smile lights up her face and a warm sensation tingles inside me. It's a small thing, of course, and in the grand scheme of things doesn't help her plight. But little acts of kindness go a long way.

Mercy pops her head back in the car. 'I love it, thanks.' She rummages in the pocket of her grey coat, retrieving Tia's photo, then bundles the material up in a big ball and shoves it roughly into the carrier. 'About time I let go of some things,' she says, her eyes clouding. Then she takes the bag and dumps it in the bin, displacing cardboard fast-food boxes as she does. I get out and help push everything back inside the bin. The two of us laugh as we push and shove, squashing it all in while seagulls watch in anticipation.

'Having fun, Erica?'

I inhale sharply as I see Sita – she's one of the psychologists who works with Jamie at the prison. I shoot Mercy a desperate glance, trying to convey my need for her to disappear for a minute. She seems to take the hint and backs away, mingling with some shoppers who are making their way to their cars.

'Just trying to outmanoeuvre the seagulls,' I say, smiling. 'Doing my bit for the community. I do hate litter.'

Sita's smile doesn't reach her eyes. For a psychologist, she hasn't got a very good poker face. I don't care if she judges me – she can think I'm barking mad if she wants. What I don't want is for her to relay her seeing me in the supermarket car park to Jamie. I've already gone against his instruction by coming to Bateman's on a Friday – although that in itself is something I could get around. But if Sita mentions she saw me laughing with some random woman while we rammed the bin with rubbish, that will raise questions. If you didn't know the backstory, it would seem a bit odd. *He* would certainly think it odd.

'You and Jamie absolutely must come over for dinner soon. It's been aaages.' Her exaggeration grates on me, but I force a smile and give the necessary response to get rid of her. As she reaches the end of the covered walkway, she glances over her shoulder, as if to check where I am. I wave and she looks away.

'How come you didn't want to be seen with me?' Mercy's back beside my car.

'She's a friend of my husband's. A work colleague. She'll tell him she's seen me, no doubt.'

'So?'

'So, I promised Jamie I wouldn't come back here on a Friday.'

'Because of *me*?' There's an edge to her voice and I catch a hurt look on her face.

'Come on,' I say, indicating for her to get back in. 'Let's get a drink.'

Chapter 27

Wes

Guilt comes and goes in waves – today's wave is nearing a tsunami in magnitude and Wes can't outswim it. He gives in to the imagined threat, his breaths shallow as he allows the water to drag him further into the depths of its black abyss. Sometimes when this happens, a panicky feeling overwhelms him – a sense that he's been found out to be a bad person making him flail, kick with all his might to push his head up and above the water. At other times, it's a calmness that washes over him. An acceptance, almost. Something he doesn't feel compelled to fight against. Those times don't happen as often. And in the moments between wakefulness and sleep, when he's at his most vulnerable and most honest, he reflects that if he were to properly let go, stop fighting it, he would actually drown.

He also believes that it's probably what he deserves.

But, he's not in a nightmare now. It's still daytime and he's in his room. His computer screen is blank, the game he'd been playing ended, and as he stares at the nothingness, the pitiful look on the woman's face as he marched her from the store for the umpteenth time shoots into his mind's eye. Something deep inside him twinges – like he's lifted too heavy a weight stack in the gym and pulled a muscle.

He's talked himself out of blame on many an occasion, but it's there, hovering, like the devil on his shoulder. It was too close to home; he really should've thought it through. His desires and needs had won out in the end. Now he's paying for it.

But he's not alone in that. He's not the one bearing the brunt of the cost.

Wes blinks, clearing his mind of the woman, and of all the news articles and online comments that he's obsessed over surrounding the girl's disappearance. But the image is seared into his brain. Her little face with the cute freckles, the innocent eyes boring into his, will forever remain, however far he buries it in his unconsciousness. He gets up to check his door is locked before clicking onto another screen and signing into his account. The homepage pops up but the usual thrill is absent. He scrolls through the images on the first page, but his heart isn't in it – none of them spark a reaction, either physical or emotional.

A dull, heavy thud draws his attention. It's from his mother's room. He jumps up, unlocking the door, and crashes along the landing. He bursts into her bedroom – the blackout curtains are permanently closed and so he has to whack the light on.

'Mum. You okay?'

'Get that, will you, Wesley.' She points her stick at the ground near her bed. 'Stupid thing. It's too big.'

He relaxes when he sees it's only her library book that's

fallen to the floor. He half expected her to be face down on the carpet, a broken hip or worse to contend with.

'I'll buy you a Kindle, Mum. It's lightweight. And you can make the words bigger, too. Much easier to read.'

'I don't want any newfangled thing. Just get me a paperback next time.'

'Yes, Mum.' Wes stoops to pick up the book and lays it on her lap again.

'Lost my place now.' She huffs and starts flicking through the pages. 'It was the part where Adeline was about to kiss her beau.' She stops her search and snaps her head up to look at Wes. 'When are you going to get yourself a nice girlfriend? You're not getting any younger and I'm not going to be here much longer to look after you.'

Wes gives a short laugh. 'Thanks. But I don't need any looking after.'

She tuts, disapprovingly. 'That's where you're wrong. Don't think I can't hear all the comings and goings, my lad.' She waggles her finger at him. 'I'm not deaf. I don't know what you're up to, but I can assure you, a good woman will set you straight.'

'I've no idea what you're talking about, Mother.' Wes turns to leave; a telling-off from his mum is the last thing he can face right now. And he certainly doesn't wish to get embroiled in a conversation about what he's getting up to. While he hopes his mum won't last for years and years, he doesn't want to give her a heart attack now by confirming her darkest fears about her only living child. The thought makes him shiver. If his brother hadn't gone into the army, hadn't suffered so badly that he eventually succumbed to his demons, Wes would have someone to share the load with.

'Ring your bell if you need anything, Mum,' he says, gently closing the door. He rests his head against it for a moment. If he didn't have his mum to look after, he would've left – run away from his life here; from his mistakes. But he didn't. Maybe his mum wasn't the only reason he stayed. To move forward, to stop the guilt, he must do something to make amends, and he can only do that if he's close by.

He slopes back across the landing, locks his bedroom door again and puts on his headphones. He clocks a familiar name on one of his screens and taps the icon alongside it.

Chapter 28

Erica

Against my better judgement, I've driven to Mercy's cabin again. It feels different this time, though. My insides aren't shaking – which isn't due to the roads being any less bumpy – and I'm not running through an endless stream of paranoid thoughts like I was before. There's an element of trust between us, and as Mercy pours me a coffee and hands it to me, I experience a lightness I've not felt in a long time. There's something to be said for this living off-grid. No one to impress, no one to answer to.

'You're thinking about it, aren't you?' Mercy gives me a knowing look.

'About what?'

'What it would be like to live alone. Or, at least, live without Jamie.'

I cast my gaze downwards, gripping my mug tightly with embarrassment.

'I didn't realise I was so transparent,' I say.

'You're not. Not to the casual observer,' Mercy says, coming to sit on the sofa beside me. 'Since losing Tia, my senses are heightened. Emotionally speaking – it's like I can read your thoughts.'

I shift my weight, edging a little further away from Mercy.

'Oh, you daft woman. Not like proper reading your mind. I just, sort of . . . link . . . to people who are also suffering. I think. It's the only way I can explain it, anyway. It's probably why I was drawn to you.'

I look at her now. She's right about some kind of connection – I felt it from the first time I saw her. It's why I've not been able to let this go. Why I'm still trying to find answers, help her find Tia, despite the overwhelming evidence suggesting she doesn't exist. I nod, gently.

'I feel it too,' I say. Mercy slips her arm around my shoulders and squeezes my shoulder.

'You need a friend – someone who you can really talk to. About everything. Talking in your head is fine, but if those words never make it to the right ears, you'll be going around in circles all your life.'

'It's hard. Once you start lying to yourself and it helps ease the pain for a moment, you're compelled to carry it on. It becomes easier. Then, suddenly, you're deep in your own pit of despair, living a life you don't want. Lying to yourself and everyone around you. I can't dig myself out of the hole now, Mercy. I'm stuck there.'

'I'm going to help dig you out,' Mercy says confidently. 'You need someone to give a big push. It's like you've got all the tools you need to escape the pit, you just don't know which to use first. Or how to use them.'

'I also don't think I have the strength. So much has happened . . .'

'I can be the one to give you the strength. We've got each other, Erica. Neither of us is alone now.'

'But I haven't done anything – not a single thing – to help you find Tia. It's been weeks.'

'How can you say you've done nothing? You told me about your internet searches, you went to the police to get information straight from them, you've been to the supermarket every week to meet me. You're here. Trust me, that's helping plenty. You have no clue how good it is to be able to talk about Tia, show you her room, openly grieve for her.' Her eyes widen and she stiffens. 'Grieve for her not being here beside me, where she belongs, I mean. I'm not grieving her because I think she's . . .' Mercy swallows hard, unable to say the word.

'I know what you mean.' I place my hand over Mercy's. 'And I'm so pleased I'm offering some kind of comfort. But I want to do more. There must be things you haven't tried. What about speaking with a journalist? Get them to run your story, put the word out there that Tia is still missing? I've got local connections at the paper I used to work for and they'll have wider ones.'

'That could help, I suppose. It didn't, back when it happened, though. Got loads of well-meaning people reporting sightings, but most were ridiculous – not even close to Tia's description – and others were a plain waste of time. It's disgusting how some people think it's fun to make up sightings, just to get a bit of attention.'

'Oh, no. That's awful, I'm so sorry.' I sit back, scratching around my mind for a different approach. 'I'm trying to think of ways to keep Tia in people's minds. Although there'll be false sightings, we only need one to be the right one.'

Mercy nods. 'Very true. So you think I should speak with someone you know from the newspaper?'

'You don't have to jump straight in with that if you don't feel comfortable.' I realise my enthusiasm could mean she feels pressured into doing something she doesn't really want to do. Then, it's suddenly obvious and I mentally kick myself for not having suggested it already. With my social media experience, I could actually be of help to Mercy – she doesn't seem to be particularly tech-savvy. An online campaign could bring Mercy's plight to the fore. Shame the police and authorities into doing something to find Tia. 'Why don't I begin by posting some stories on my Instagram? My followers will also then share my story with their followers. It's a good way of spreading the word to the accounts I already know to be engaged with me. It's worth a try.'

'Okay.' Mercy stands up and starts pacing the cabin. 'Yes. I mean, I hopped onto the social media sites when Tia was taken, it was a shit-show, but that was one of those "Spotted" pages where the comments are so stupid, or rude, or tagging in their immature friends, that it was upsetting. Making light of a child going missing – who *does* that?'

'I know. These things bring out the best and worst in people, don't they? Makes me so proud to be human.' I scoff.

'When will you do it?'

'As soon as I get home, back to—'

'Civilisation?'

'Hah! Well that, and the internet, yes. Do you have a phone?' With no landline, how would Mercy get help in an emergency?

'Not at the moment, no. I dropped and broke mine at Bateman's, during a bit of a kerfuffle with Wes!'

'Really? He should've made sure he replaced it if it happened because of his heavy-handedness.'

'I didn't realise straight away. Not that I'd have made a fuss even if I had. It was only a cheap pay-as-you-go thing and I have no call for it.'

'Bloody Wes,' I say. I'm not sure why I hadn't considered it before, or if it even makes the slightest difference, but the thought comes to me now. 'Was he there when Tia went missing?'

'Yep. He was there. As helpful as a chocolate fireguard.' Mercy's lips form a tight line.

'If he'd been doing his job properly, wouldn't he have seen her? Or someone taking her from the store?'

'You'd think. And trust me, I've brought it up many times.' Her eyes glaze over and she goes quiet; still. I give her a gentle nudge. 'Sorry,' she says, blinking rapidly. 'Look. I could blame him, Erica – make it all his fault. But I wasn't keeping an eye on my own daughter . . . if I'd kept hold of her hand . . .'

I realise I've pulled her into a bad place again, and decide getting back to the phone topic might be more helpful going forward.

'So you have no form of contacting anyone?'

'I'm not bothered,' she says, shrugging. 'Why?'

'I was thinking it would be good for us to keep in contact during the week, that's all. Keep you updated on whether I glean any leads from the Instagram story. I could grab you a phone – they sell them pretty much everywhere.'

'Oh, I don't like to be a bother. You've already bought me a lovely gift.' She beams as she looks over at the khaki coat hanging on the back of the door.

'It's no problem. Maybe I'll pick one up before I go

163

home. And we can meet before next Friday? Need to keep up the momentum.'

Mercy hesitates, biting on her lower lip. I'm alarmed to see spots of blood appear.

'What's the matter?'

'I don't know, Erica – I'm not that comfortable going out.' She casts her eyes around the cabin. 'I'm safer here. Once a week is plenty.'

'Oh, okay. Whatever you want.' If just mentioning additional outings causes concern, I don't want to push her. There's an awkward silence while Mercy looks everywhere but at me. Has she got a form of agoraphobia? I wouldn't blame her. Maybe she uses all her mental energy on her once-weekly trip to Bateman's.

'Well, that's me sorted,' Mercy says, snapping out of her trance-like state and sitting back down. 'Let's see if I can help *you*. Where shall we start?'

'Christ,' I say, sucking in air. 'It's such a huge, hot mess.'

'Oh, come on. I'm sure it's not that bad. I mean, look at you,' she says, dramatically eyeing me up and down. 'You're beautiful.'

'As you know – looks can be very deceptive.'

'Of course. I'm sorry, that was wrong of me. I should know better.'

I shrug. 'It's fine. I know on the surface, to everyone looking at me, it might appear that I've got everything. But, just like my Instagram selfies, it's heavily filtered. My real life is a mess . . .'

'How about you start at the beginning, then?' Mercy says, brightly. She grabs a cushion and plumps it, popping it behind my back. I half expect her to tell me to lie down on the sofa. I give a nervous laugh. 'Don't worry,' she says.

'Whatever you tell me won't go any further. Your secrets are safe with me.'

Her promise seems so convincing that my worries melt away and I'm suddenly desperate to talk about everything. With a warmness spreading inside me, I find myself telling Mercy all about my failed IVF, how I pretend I'm still going through cycles of it for my followers because I'm so afraid of losing them all, how I haven't told Jamie that I'm only staying with him in the vain hope of falling pregnant naturally. And then, in a moment of reckless abandon, I open up about my fear that Jamie's been conducting an affair for the past year.

'I think that maybe . . . maybe he wants a baby with her, not me,' I say, wiping tears from my face with the back of my hand.

'Oh, Erica. Surely not. I'm not trying to play down your concerns, and I'm certainly not trying to say it's all in your head – but are you *sure*? Sounds like you've had quite the time, emotionally, it's easy to . . . well, blow things up out of proportion, you know?' Mercy makes a face. 'I know, that's rich coming from me.'

'No, I understand what you mean. And I've tried to remain unemotional, think everything through logically. There are just too many little things that all add up to one whacking big affair.'

'Have you asked him? Outright?'

'Of course not.'

'Wouldn't that get it all out in the open? You can't fight what you can't see, Erica.'

'Asking him might involve him giving me the answer I don't want to hear.'

Confusion crosses Mercy's face. I know what's coming.

'But, this whole time you've been gearing up to give him the big leaving speech, no? This could give you the excuse you need to make the break.'

'Yep. That's the way a normal person would be thinking. But all I can see is a man I used to love – still do – slipping away from me. I am aware I've been planning to leave him. But it's all tied up in a big, fat emotional knot. The reason I was wanting to leave was because of my fears, do you understand? Like, I'll leave him before he can leave me, sort of thing. Stems from what happened in my family growing up, I think. My parents left – not that they could help that, they died – didn't purposely leave me, but it felt that way for a really long time. Then my brother got himself in trouble, always in and out of secure centres, then finally he was sent to prison. And I *was* purposely abandoned by my uncle – he upped and left without discussing his new living arrangements abroad. So, you see, if I can control the losses, I can also control the pain better.'

'Ah,' Mercy says, nodding. 'I get you.'

'Mad, isn't it? Why is love so complicated?'

'Because anything worth having is difficult to gain, and even harder to keep.'

We both stare off into the cabin, silently contemplating Mercy's words.

Chapter 29

Erica

'Film night?' Jamie slides up behind me as I'm slicing the beef, his hands on my hips. 'I've got wine and chocolate.'

'You know how to woo a lady,' I say. I hear the flatness of my tone at the realisation my chances of conceiving are slim – I may as well have a drink. Jamie's hands slip from me.

'What's up?' he says.

'Nothing.' I force a smile. 'What film are we watching?'

'A comedy, I thought. We could both do with a laugh to take us into the weekend.'

'Sure.' I wipe the cutting board down, spread the plates over the worktop. 'Do you want to pour the wine, then?'

'Apparently you bumped into Sita today outside Bateman's.' His face is obscured by the fridge door as he grabs the chilled wine, but the slight edge to his voice is clear enough. He's trying to be nonchalant, stealthily dropping this into conversation so as not to alert my spidey senses to his game. I knew that cow would say something. But when? She obviously wasn't on the same shift at the prison as Jamie today. I wonder if I could get away with saying she must've been mistaken as I haven't been to the store today. Seeing as we actually spoke, though, that seems risky. There's no point skirting around this.

'Yes, I saw her briefly. When did you see her?' I raise my eyebrows at him as his face reappears from the fridge. He takes his time to pop the cork and pour the wine into the two flutes.

'Passed her in the lane, driving home. Wound down her window to tell me the cows were out.'

Apt.

'She looked well,' I say, waiting for the inevitable question.

Jamie nods, his lips pressed down. 'Cut her hours. She's less stressed.'

'Maybe you should think of doing the same.' I know my change of topic won't act as the distractor I want it to, but it's worth a shot.

'And fail to keep you in the lap of luxury you've come to expect?' He gives a dry laugh. 'I'll be working until I'm seventy.' There's an undercurrent of discontent that riles me. Why does he do this? He starts off all perfectly amicable, setting up a lovely evening and weekend ahead, then turns, as quick as a flash, into a cruel, sarcastic idiot. He wasn't always this way. The soft parts of him have hardened – and I know it's his way of coping. I honestly don't think he intends to hurt me. Or, that's what I tell myself.

'I'll have to find another job, then. The freelance work was only meant to be temporary anyway, to fit around a family. But, as that's not working out . . .' I lower my face, start dishing food onto the plates to avoid looking at Jamie.

'We've gone off topic,' he says, moving beside me to take the plates to the dining table. 'I was surprised when Sita said she'd spoken with you at the supermarket.'

Here we go.

We sit opposite each other at the too-long-for-two-people glass table, the distance between us both literal and figurative. Jamie plants both elbows on the table and stares at me. He's waiting for an explanation. I'm not going to make it easy for him. I don't see why I should feel like a naughty child, going against his wishes – I'm a grown bloody woman.

'Did you see that woman again? The one that tried to latch on to you?' He's skirting around the fact he's mad that I ignored his professional opinion and went ahead and shopped the same day I knew Mercy would be there. He's likely saving that scolding for later.

'No,' I say without an ounce of guilt. 'But if I had, it wouldn't have been a problem. It's not as though I'd bring her home with me, Jamie.'

I wait for the inevitable 'So who were you with when Sita saw you, then?' but it doesn't come. The scraping of knives and forks on plates is the only sound for what feels like ten minutes. Finally, Jamie breaks the silence.

'I'm glad. I just don't want you taken advantage of, that's all. You're a kind person, Erica – you'll be easily sucked in because you want to help people.'

'As do you,' I say, pointedly.

'Yes. That's my job. But I leave it at the prison gate.'

'Do you?'

Jamie pushes his chair back and takes his plate to the dishwasher. 'There's loads of leftovers. Could plate up a meal for the neighbour. I'm sure she'd appreciate it,' he says.

For all these years, he's never once suggested such a

thing and I can't help feeling a tinge of suspicion – like he has an ulterior motive somehow.

'Suddenly have a neighbourhood conscience?' I ask, lightly.

'Something like that. Can't hurt to be kind, eh?'

'You do know we've lived opposite the knitting cat lady for four years, don't you?'

'Jean? Yes, of course.'

I swivel in my chair. 'Jean? You've never mentioned her name before. Have you known it all this time?'

'Really, Erica? Are you being serious right now?' Jamie stands with his hands splayed, a mask of confusion on his face.

'What do you mean?' I stand now, too, a mix of annoyance and anxiety propelling me up.

'She introduced herself the day we moved in, don't you remember?'

'Well, that was ages ago. And if it was one time . . .' So, I did know her name. No wonder she was put out when I suggested she'd never told me.

'Anyway, as I say, maybe you should take it around. Be good to have someone else to chat to.'

'Fine, but not now. You've planned a film night, *remember*?' I say, mockingly.

'I've got to jump in the shower, so now would be the better time actually. She probably goes to bed earlier than us, so may as well do it right away. I'm sure she won't keep you talking for long. We'll have plenty of time to fit in the film and stuff our faces with wine and chocolate.' He covers the plate of food with clingfilm, then pushes it into my hands. He smiles. 'See you in a bit, then.' He walks out, and I hear him taking the stairs two at a time.

170

I stare down at the plate, warm in my hands. What just happened?

It's like Jamie's trying to get me out of the house. So he can have a phone call with his lover? I huff. Part of me wants to make it awkward for him. Dig my heels in and stay put so he can't make his stupid call. Or, at least make him sweat a bit.

The other half can't be bothered.

I open the front door, letting in the cool evening breeze. Jean Meneely is in her usual position at the window, knitting, with a clowder of cats jumping all over her. As I cross the road, I look behind me, at our bedroom. The curtains are drawn, but I see Jamie's silhouette as he walks back and forth, his hand to his ear and my mind wanders to who the woman on the other end of the phone might be.

Chapter 30

Erica

'Oh! How very kind of you . . .' Jean gives me a brief look up and down, then her eyes lock onto mine. 'Erica,' she says, pleased with herself. I feel a bit better that she'd forgotten my name, too, even if momentarily. Unless, of course, she did that on purpose. She seems the type to want others to be at ease.

'Sorry to disturb your evening,' I say. 'Jamie was adamant I should bring this over right away.'

'Please give him my thanks.' Jean takes the plate and disappears into the kitchen. When she comes back, it's with two glasses in her hands. 'I like a little tipple of an evening. Sets me up for the night. Sleep like a log after one of these,' she says, setting the glasses down. A cat jumps up, knocking the glass, but Jean quickly rights it and shoos 'Barney' away.

'Great reactions,' I say.

'Have to with these troublemakers.' She gives me a wink as she pours two fingers of whisky. I'm about to object, but sod it. 'This'll warm your cockles, lovely,' Jean says. We clink glasses, then take the same seats as we had the other day.

'I can't stay long,' I say, then take a slug of whisky.

'That's okay, dear. A moment of your company is a pleasure.'

My cheeks glow. It couldn't be an effect of the drink this quickly, I think it's more likely from Jean's kindness. Tears sting my eyes and I pat the corners of them with the fingertips of one hand. The lump in my throat stops me from speaking.

'How's the rest of your week been?' She eyes me cautiously over the tumbler. 'Any interesting developments?'

I cast my mind back to our previous conversation, attempting to pinpoint what she means. I can't remember telling her anything much.

'It's been the usual, really,' I say. 'Not exactly filled with excitement, at any rate. Yours?' I take another sip of my drink.

'Well, now you ask,' Jean says, her face lighting up. 'A fair bit of coming and going as it happens. Some police visited number ten, two uniformed officers, but they didn't stay long. I hoped it wasn't bad news and I think, had it been, they'd have gone inside, not stay on the step. Do you?'

'I suspect you're right,' I tell Jean. 'But still, a bit of action, eh?'

'Of course, you had a few visitors too – but not quite as exciting.'

I make a face. 'Oh? No one comes to ours. Ah, well, apart from damn cold callers, I expect,' I say.

'No, I don't think so. I assumed it was a friend of yours. You thought you saw someone when you were here, didn't you? A woman?'

I sit up straighter. 'Yes, but I was mistaken. What did

this woman look like?' I attempt to keep my tone level, but my adrenaline is soaring. 'And when was this, again? Because Jamie's been at work . . . and as you know, I work from home.'

'It was the day you came here, the first time.'

The first time I came here, does she mean? Or the first time she saw this woman? Jean could well be confusing the days, I get that, but there's obviously something in what she's saying. My chest feels tight, like an elastic band is constricting my lungs.

'First time?' I squeeze the words through my larynx.

'I saw her again, I think. I've seen someone a few times, actually, but can't be *absolutely* sure it's the same person each visit.'

'Sorry, can you describe her, or them?' How many women are we talking about here?

'You know my eyesight isn't the best. But I usually recognise people's shapes, their walks, that sort of thing. The woman took short, quick strides, like she was in a hurry.'

I bet she was. Probably trying to get in and out before I came back and rumbled them. I curl my hand into a fist, digging my nails into my palm until the skin stings.

'Did you happen to notice how long she was there for?'

'No, dear. I'm sorry. The cats, you see, they wanted my attention and then I must've missed her coming back out again.'

'But you think you've seen her before?'

'As I say, I can't categorically tell you yes, but the walk is similar.'

'But I'm almost always in the house. And Jamie is rarely there when I'm not.'

'I'm fairly certain I've seen them when you're out. Your

175

Friday shopping trips or when I see you leave with your gym bag. I envy your fitness.'

'I go to yoga classes. But when Jamie's at work, though. You see him leave, don't you? Every morning? And come back each evening?'

Jean looks thoughtful. And, I think, a little wary.

'Well, yes,' she says, her voice uncertain. She puts her fingers to her head, straightening a non-existent wayward strand of white hair. Does she know more than she's telling me? I decide to get back on firmer ground.

'So, the woman – apart from the walk, is there anything else that stands out about her?'

'Oh yes,' she says with a nod of her head. I widen my eyes in anticipation. 'The coat.'

My heart sinks and I'm scared to ask. 'What about it?'

'It struck me as a bit frumpy for a young woman. Even I wouldn't wear something so shapeless and bland.' Jean chuckles, then must see my expression and turns serious. 'An old-fashioned wishy-washy grey raincoat it was. And I've definitely seen that before.'

Jesus. What is going on? I stand to leave. 'I must get back, Jean. It's film night,' I say, heading for the door.

'You will come again, won't you?'

I plaster on a smile. 'Of course.' I pause at the threshold, looking back at Jean. I feel bad asking a favour like this of her, especially as I've only just started visiting. But someone like her would be really useful. I walk back to the lounge. 'Would you do something for me, Jean?' She looks up, smiles and nods. 'Would you keep an eye on our house, see if that woman, or any other, comes knocking?'

Jean studies me for a moment, then moves towards the window.

'Oh, I don't mean like right now. I don't want you in the window all night. But maybe if you see me leave . . .'

'I always sit for a half-hour in the evening, until the streetlights go on. I'll be sure to keep my eyes peeled in future.'

Pressure builds in my head as I cross back over to our house. The lounge lamp glows softly through the window, projecting a square of yellow on the lawn. I breathe deeply a few times while pressing my fingers to my temples. Before I was approached by Mercy in Bateman's I was in a bubble of my own creation. It wasn't a happy bubble, but I'd been muddling along. Ignoring the issues, glossing over the cracks. Since Mercy, things have escalated out of my control and I feel as though I'm being swept along on a wave. One that's about to break over the rocks.

I look back at Jean's house. True to her word, she's sitting in the window waiting for the streetlamps to be lit. If what she says is right, and I can't see her being wrong, then a woman, who fits Mercy's description, came here last week. I thought I saw her while I was at Jean's, before going to the police station, but Jean didn't see her then. So when? Jean's assertion that the same woman has been to my house before, supposedly when I'm out – possibly at the gym – makes my stomach churn. But Jamie would be at work. Last Wednesday seemed like a one-off working from home, he's never mentioned doing that on a regular basis. And besides, Jean saw him leave the house at the same time as usual and not return until the end of the day.

Unless he used the back entrance.

It's a faff, and we never use it because we have a perfectly good drive and the slope to the rear is so steep it's not worth the hassle. The huge gate is always padlocked. But doesn't it make it perfect, then? He could leave, making sure Jean sees him, then drive around and park in the road behind the house and enter through the back door. From the front of the house no one would know he was in. For a moment, this theory holds water. But then, if he went in the back so as not to be seen by Jean, why would *she* blatantly come to the front, in full view of my neighbours?

The only explanation I can think of is that she wanted to be seen.

Chapter 31

Dr Connie Summers

Local News

Police have confirmed that a child reported missing from the Newton area has been located. Further details are unknown at this time.

Raj Antony

What does that even mean? Located? As in alive? Dead? Or wasn't missing in the first place as we suspected? Such shoddy reporting.

Kaycee Smith

All a fuss over nothing then.

Sammi Peters

What's the betting we'll never find out what the hell happened?

Carmen Allan

Does it matter? God, you lot – can't you just be thankful the child was found?

Max Gardner

Not if the kid's dead, dumbass. What's the point of

reporting this? Tells us nothing. Could be a child killer on the loose or anything!

Kaycee Smith

Bit dramatic.

Pete Landon

If it was something bad, we'd know about it. Can't keep murder quiet in a place like this.

Lou Thomas

Yeah, good point.

Kaycee Smith

Back to it being a fake then.

Emily Hellyer

Well, whatever, let's hope the person concerned gets the help they need. There but for the grace of God go I.

Shaun Pollard

Bible freak.

Libby Drake

Actually, I know the mother. Your cruel, pathetic and ignorant attempts at psychology are laughable. If you don't know the details, I suggest you all shut up.

Andy Wethers

Oh yeah? Of course you know the mother. Stop talking shit to get attention.

Unless you are the mother, of course.

Shaun Pollard

I bet she is. Hey . . . spill. What really happened then? Did you lie to get attention? Are you sick?

Libby Drake

Leave it out . . . Get a life.

*

'It got ugly really quickly. So many accusations flying about.' The woman cries softly into a tissue as Connie takes the printout back.

'And that's why you came off social media?'

'One of the reasons, yes. I mean, who wants to read that about themselves?'

'Tell me about this time. What was the catalyst for this particular media outburst?'

'I don't remember.'

'You said it got ugly quickly – that suggests you recall some of it. Tell me the bits you do recall.'

'I don't want to.' The woman gets up from the sofa and takes a few paces towards the window. Her back is rigid, shoulders pulled back. 'I can't,' she adds.

'I'm here to help you.'

'Are you?' She turns sharply. 'Seems to me you're very keen to put words in my mouth, Connie.'

Connie steeples her fingers, leaning her chin on them as her focus remains on the woman. 'I'm asking you to relay the events in your own words. Take your time.' Connie's patience is used to being stretched; it hasn't snapped yet. But there's always a first time and if anyone is going to be the first, it's this client.

'What do you want me to say?' A flash of anger crosses the woman's face. 'You're trying to trap me, aren't you? That's what's happening here. I told you. Over and over. My daughter is missing. Why doesn't anyone believe me? You are meant to be on my side—'

'I am. I'm working with you. We're coming to the point when you need to work with me, too. If we're going to reach a place where you're fully accepting past events, you have to start being honest. With me and yourself.'

'If I can't?'

Connie sits back in her chair, takes several deep breaths in and out through her nose.

'Then I can't be of further help to you.' Connie holds her breath, hoping she hasn't blown this opportunity. When the silence becomes too much to bear, she breaks it. 'It's up to you. Your future is in your hands.'

'The question is, do I want a future?'

'Only you know that. I think it's worth a try, though. No one knows what's just around the corner.'

'I guess.' The woman pushes the palms of her hands down the front of her trousers, flattening the material. Then, she takes a big breath. 'I don't have a missing daughter, do I?'

Connie rips a tissue from the square box beside her and reaches forwards. 'No,' she says, handing the tissue to the woman.

Chapter 32

Erica

Jamie asked me if I was going to the gym when he left for work this morning. My skin is alive with tiny electrical impulses as I pace the bedroom floorboards, my bare heels slamming hard against the wood, making them sting. I'm dressed as if I'm going to do a yoga session, but it's only for show. How dare he think he can get away with this. I can't believe I've been so blind.

I'll drive out, as I usually would, heading towards town for a few minutes. I'll go right around the roundabout before returning, parking in a side street close enough to walk back. My initial plan was to go to the back entrance of our house, see if I can spot Jamie's car. But if he is using that way, he might well see me and that'll be that.

Dragging my old winter coat from the wardrobe, I stuff it in a holdall. I'll wear it on my walk to Jean's; I haven't worn it in ages, Jamie won't recognise it as mine. If he does happen to look out the window at the exact moment I go into the neighbour's house, hopefully it'll act as a disguise. It's the best plan I have. From Jean's I have the perfect view. Maybe I'll ask to go upstairs as she did mention Jamie being 'nifty with his hands', which I'd taken to mean she'd seen us together in the bedroom.

Now I'm wondering if she's seen him with someone else.

Shit. Had she been trying to tell me in her own way? Did she know about him having an affair but wasn't quite sure how to broach the subject? The times she's been staring at me, even beckoning me to hers that time – I bet she was trying to warn me. I slam the wardrobe door closed, screwing up my eyes as I hear the glass door crack.

'Dammit!' I run my fingertip over the lightning-bolt-shaped line. Now I'm going to have to explain that. I laugh. As if *that's* the worst of my worries.

After Jean described the woman at my house – specifically 'the coat' – my mind hasn't stopped conjuring theories as to who this woman is. If it really is Mercy, the biggest question is *why*? Meeting her at Bateman's was an encounter I'd assumed was random. Or partly. I mean, I shop there weekly, have done for years, and she admitted she'd seen me there on other occasions. But Karen, the checkout woman, said she was there every week, bothering loads of customers, not just me. It's not as though I was purposely targeted; I was simply there at the right place, and the right time. And, with no disrespect to Mercy, what would Jamie see in her anyway? She's literally the opposite of me – dowdy and plain.

She might not have always looked that way, of course. It might only be since her daughter went missing that she'd 'let herself go'. Her cabin is spotless, well looked after – she herself probably was too before all of her trauma. I close my eyes, bringing the photo of Tia into my mind's eye. Is there a familiarity about her? Something had struck me – I believed it was an emotional punch, the sheer devastation I felt coming off Mercy in waves. Now, as I try to grasp hold of a memory, I have the feeling I've seen that photo before.

Just before Jamie and I met up again the second time, following uni, he'd been in a long-term relationship with Gemma, his mate's sister. She'd fallen pregnant, but they'd separated and she'd later miscarried. Or, that's how the story went. The one Jamie told me when we became serious. She happened to work at the prison – again, Jamie told me that his ex was there, he was 'upfront' because he didn't want any secrets between us. No skeletons that might leap out at a later date to cause issues in our relationship. I've never met her, and he's denied having any old photos. I tried searching for her on social media, but failed. I hadn't found it odd because a lot of prison staff stay off social media.

I've only Jamie's word that she miscarried their child. Telling me he had a daughter might've thrown a spanner in the works during our first years, so he could've chosen the simple lie that while Gemma *had* been pregnant, the pregnancy hadn't continued. Later on, during the 'trauma years' as I've come to think of them, if Jamie had come clean, admitted he had a child, it most certainly would've spelled the end of our marriage. So, is it feasible this child exists, and that 'Mercy' is the ex? Her reasons for not meeting with me except on Fridays could be because she works the rest of the week.

In a fit of impulsivity, I grab my mobile and dial the prison. As it rings, I realise I don't know Jamie's ex's full name. I do know she works in admin, according to something Jamie said.

'Hello, can I be put through to Gemma, in admin please?' My heart beats out my chest while I wait for the 'What's her surname', but with a snap of relief, the words I hear aren't that.

'Gemma Flavel, in probation admin?'

'Yes,' I say quickly, as that rings a bell. 'Please.'

'I'm afraid she isn't in this morning.'

My jaw slackens. No way. It can't be this simple, surely? 'Oh? I was told to call her today.'

'I'm so sorry, you've been given the wrong information. Can I take a message?'

'Oh, erm . . . it's fine. I'll call back. When's the best time please?'

'What's it regarding, Mrs . . .?'

'Mrs Fielding.' I wince slightly at my mistake. Too late now – and it's not as if this person is going to tell Jamie that his wife called for his ex-girlfriend, there are loads of Fieldings. 'I'm freelance, working on an article that Gemma is helping with.'

By the time this lie surfaces, it won't matter. I'll have what I need.

'Well, you should catch her Monday to Thursday . . .' My mind wanders.

'Not on a Friday?' I venture.

'No, she doesn't work Fridays.' Having a Friday off isn't exactly conclusive, many people do. Am I jumping to the conclusion Mercy is really Gemma purely because it happens to fit with my wild theory? It still begs the question: why?

'Okay, thank you for your help.' I'm about to hang up when I realise something. For my theory to be correct, Jamie would need the same times off. 'Could you put me through to the psychology department please?'

My heart booms as I hear the different tone while I'm being transferred and I become so light-headed I have to sit down on the bed and take some deep breaths.

'Psychology,' a female voice says. 'How can I help?'

All power leaves my voice. 'Can I speak with Jamie Fielding please?' I needn't worry about attempting to disguise my voice, the squeak that escapes my lips sounds nothing like me.

'He's not in this morning,' she says.

How many coincidences can there conceivably be before it's considered a design?

Friday is shopping at Bateman's day – the only day Mercy can manage to visit the store. And it was a Wednesday morning that I thought I saw her here, right outside my house. Jamie always discourages phone calls to the prison, unless I have a dire emergency. And of course, he's not allowed his mobile inside, so I have no contact with him during the day. How perfect for him.

'Oh, okay. Thanks. Sorry to trouble you.'

I catch the tail end of her asking if I want to leave him a message as I hang up. There are some things I'd like him to know, but it would be unwise to leave them in a message. If he's not at work, then where is he? I check the time. Five minutes before I usually leave the house to head to the gym. What does he do, wait around the corner watching for me to leave before coming back in? Isn't that risky? I might change my mind, or have a shorter session and return before he's expecting me. Perhaps it's that danger that's exciting. Like when you're a teenager and having sex downstairs knowing full well your parents are in bed and could catch you at any point.

The bastard. How could he do this? I grasp my stomach,

the hollowed-out feeling bringing hot tears to my eyes. They've made a mug of me. I tilt my head back and let out a cry to release the pain.

As I make a big show of leaving the house, I think about how I'm going to react when I see Mercy strut up my path and waltz into my house. Is she trying to take my entire life? Because she's lost her daughter, does she now want a replacement with *my* husband?

Why drag me into this warped game? I'm not needed. They could carry on their sordid affair without involving me in some elaborate hoax. Jamie himself warned me against seeking Mercy out. He said it was a bad idea. He couldn't have wanted me to do the opposite. Unless he doesn't know what she's doing. I clench and unclench my hands, digging my nails into my palms. Should I have realised that Mercy and Gemma are one and the same before now? I hear this thought so loud in my mind it's as if I've spoken it, and I know instinctively that Jamie's response to this accusation would be that it's ludicrous – that I'm allowing paranoia to take over. Only he'd confuse me with all the psychological jargon. But his basic argument would be that I didn't make the link because there isn't one.

I'm overreacting.

I shake my head as I walk towards my car, as if the swirling questions will somehow exit via my ears.

I could twist myself up in knots trying to figure this out. Climbing in the car, I buckle up and turn the music full blast. In half an hour or so, I'll have at least one answer to this riddle. What I do about it then is a whole other matter.

Chapter 33

Erica

'You look terribly peaky, dear. Come and have a seat.' Jean bustles around me, guiding me to what I've now come to think of as 'my chair'.

'Oh, I'm fine. Just been rushing about, is all.' I remove my 'disguise' coat, flinging it over the back.

'Have you eaten breakfast?' Jean gives me the once-over and tuts. 'No fat on those bones,' she says. 'I'll rustle up a round of sandwiches.' Once she disappears into the kitchen, I go and hover by the window, careful to stand to the side so I can't be seen from the street. My pulse trips along at an unhealthy rate as I anticipate seeing Mercy walk up the pavement and into my house.

'Here we go.' Jean's voice startles me; it's as though I'd forgotten I was in someone else's house for a second. I turn to see her place a bone-china side plate on a small, round occasional table beside the chair. 'Not very breakfasty, but eat up. Can't have you passing out. And if you wait too long, Marmaduke here will swipe it clean off your plate.'

The ginger cat sits beside the table, eyeing the plate, its tail swishing from side to side. I feel like saying, *go on, have it*, because I've such a hard lump in my throat I might vomit if I try to swallow solid food. I thank Jean anyway, but don't move from my position behind the curtain.

'A watched pot never boils.' Jean's voice is soft, but I sense she's trying to be firm. I want to point out that she's always watching, but bite my tongue. Jean's been wonderful to me, being rude isn't the way to repay her for her kindness.

'I can't tear my eyes away,' I say in a whisper. 'I might miss something.'

'Oh, my dear. You could be putting yourself through this for nothing, you know?' From the corner of my eye, I can see Jean's head shaking.

'It's my gym day, though. If she's going to turn up, I'm placing my bets on it being now.'

'And you're sure Jamie isn't at work?'

'He isn't home. Or he wasn't when I left. But he's not at work, either.'

'Oh,' Jean says, sucking in air through her teeth. 'I see. As far as you were aware, that's where he went when he left this morning?'

'Yep. Whatever is going on, Jean – he's lying.' I hear a deep sigh, like Jean has been forced to admit what I already suspect.

'What will you do?' she says.

'If I see another woman go in my home?' I clench my teeth so hard I expect to hear the crack of enamel. I can't answer her question because I haven't thought that far ahead.

'Look, it's none of my business . . .' Jean guides me away

from the window. 'But it might be a good idea to talk this through, eh? Before getting yourself in a muddle.'

'What do you mean, in a muddle?'

'Seems to me you are in a . . . situation . . . with Jamie at the moment and things aren't going as smoothly as they might.'

'Huh! Yes, that would be correct,' I say.

'When emotions are running high, thoughts can become erratic. Jump about all over the place. And things which appear one way, might well have very simple explanations. We've all been there. We've all had moments of irrational behaviour – particularly where love is concerned.'

'So, what are you saying?' I crane my head so I can still look out the window despite Jean's attempts to move me away. I don't want to miss anything.

'Take a step back, look at the situation objectively. Start at the beginning. Don't try and jam pieces in so they fit your puzzle. Find the correct pieces.'

I turn to face Jean, squinting at her while I contemplate her words. 'That's very sensible advice, Jean.'

So, why do I get the feeling she's trying to side-track me – like a good illusionist, she's getting me to look this way, while the trick is happening that way. I shouldn't let her distract me. I pull my attention away from her, back to the window.

'Erica?' she says, her voice soft. 'Look at me, dear.'

She's being kind – motherly – and I find myself turning slowly towards her. She smiles.

'I've had many more years of practice,' she says.

'Does Jamie visit you?' It's a sudden thought that I can't stop bursting from my lips. I swear I see Jean stiffen, her spine suddenly more upright. She pushes the edges of her mouth down.

'Not really, no. I mean, he's popped by on the odd occasion over the years.'

'Right, of course.' I begin pacing around the lounge; cats scatter just like my thoughts. I shouldn't read anything into her attempt to talk me around. She's probably genuinely concerned and doesn't want me to make a fool of myself, flinging wild accusations before gathering enough information. I get that. And Jamie was surprised when I said I hadn't visited our neighbour, implying he had at least made contact during our time living in the street. It's me who's the bad person here. God, I must appear to Jean as though I've totally lost the plot. Maybe I have.

But a niggle remains. If Jamie is aware Jean watches from her window and could have seen him carrying on with another woman, might he have pre-empted it and come across to have a word with Jean? Would he go as far as to threaten her to keep quiet about his affair?

I screw my eyes up. God. This thinking is *exactly* what Jean's referring to. Jamie isn't like that. It doesn't make sense either, because if that were the case, why would he have encouraged me to visit Jean? All he wanted was for me to socialise a bit – get out of the house, outside of my own head for a while.

'You're right, Jean.' My upper body slumps; tiredness swooping in. 'I'm sorry. I don't know which way is up at the moment.'

'Shall I make us a nice cup of tea?'

'Okay, thanks.' I watch Jean retreat to the kitchen. 'Actually, do you have coffee, Jean?' I call. The thought of that floral Earl Grey stuff makes my stomach churn.

'I got some Gold Blend, especially for you, Erica.'

It hits me that I'm more transparent than I realise. I didn't tell her I disliked her last offering, yet she clearly noted it. Jean is instinctive and observant. I really should trust her judgement over the Jamie thing.

The chinking of china brings me back to the moment and Jean sets a tray down on the table and hands me my coffee. My eyes fixate on her as she pours herself a drink from the teapot. I wonder if I've overestimated her age. Her bobbed hair is pure white, but her face has a more youthful appearance. Her hands are wrinkled, but there's no sign of arthritis, no trembling fingers as she's pouring. My nan always used a teapot too. There's something comforting in it. And very British: everything can be solved with a nice cuppa.

'Tell me about Jamie, Erica,' Jean says as she sits, her cup and saucer rattling slightly in her hands. 'Why is it that you think he'd lie to you?'

For an uncomfortable moment, the thought that Jamie's asked Jean to delve further, find out what I know or suspect, consumes my mind. Surely this unassuming, kind woman wouldn't do such a thing? No. Of course not. I'm being stupid, again.

'Maybe it's what all husbands do, eventually, Jean. Lie to their wives. Cheat. Because what they have right under their noses no longer holds their attention.'

'Oh, no, no. Not all of them are like that, dear. Some of them are pure gold.' Jean is thinking about Frank – her gaze drifting away from mine towards the sideboard and a silver framed photo of their wedding day. 'My Frank gave me the world. Or at least that's what he wanted. He used to say, "I'll give you the best life, Jean, or die trying." God rest his soul.' Her smile is sad – she obviously misses him hugely.

'I'm so pleased you found the nugget of gold, Jean. I thought I'd found mine, too, but . . .'

'But what?' Her eyes narrow and, for a moment, I sense I've offended her. Perhaps she feels angry that she's lost the love of her life and I'm not treating mine with respect. Or is that my own conscience pricking?

'Things change, Jean. Life is so different than it used to be for you and Frank – packed with extra stresses, more pressure; it's not a simple life. We've gone through tough situations, and both come through them differently.' A tightness grips my chest. I don't want to talk about my struggle to get pregnant, my longing for a child. It's personal. I feel Jean's eyes on me, like she's gazing into my mind and seeing things I don't want to share.

'I won't pry, dear,' she says suddenly. 'I can see you're hurting.'

Jean's kindness brings tears to my eyes and I bite my lip to stop myself crying.

'Another time,' I say. 'I'm not ready yet.'

Jean nods just as a cat leaps onto the back of my chair.

'Shit!' I jolt forward, spilling the dregs of my coffee.

'Barney! I'm sorry, Erica.' Jean gets up and shoos him away. 'I'll get a cloth.'

I sit, the brown liquid seeping through my trousers as a familiar, sinister suspicion hits me again. Because I haven't been able to conceive, Jamie might be looking to another woman not merely for comfort, but to give him a child.

Chapter 34

Erica

After a futile wait at Jean's yesterday, I've concluded I must be imagining things. There are times I'd like to talk to someone – really talk, not just share a status or type a carefully constructed caption. There are others when I'd prefer to bury my head in the sand, pretend nothing is wrong. At Jean's I was so close to talking, opening up and letting it all out. I was intending to go there to watch – lie in wait – for Jamie's love interest and then confront him. But Jean did such a great job of distracting me, gently advising me it was a bad idea and to wait before acting on my suspicions. The niggling feeling that Jamie is somehow manipulating the situation, and that Jean is working on his behalf, made me hold back and I avoided any mention of it all after Jamie eventually got home. The evening was mostly taken up with him doing paperwork and me absently flicking through Netflix, so we didn't really speak anyway – though my thoughts were eating away at me.

Watching him now, his attention on the TV, the urge to

broach the subject of why he wasn't at the prison yesterday is too great to suppress. I'm still taking Jean's suggestion of not rushing in with accusations on board. I'm merely gathering intel now. I must be smart. He was in a strange mood the second he stepped through the door earlier, brushing aside my attempts at finding out about his day – 'too tired to rake over it'. Now, though, he's unwound with a few glasses of wine and seems relaxed, so it's my best opportunity.

'I popped over to see Jean before I hit the gym yesterday,' I say in the breeziest tone I can muster. He sighs, and, sitting forwards, he lays his elbows on his knees, cupping his chin in his hands. My breathing accelerates. One sentence uttered and his mood darkens. What is wrong with him? I want to scream in his face, ask why everything I say is met with such contempt.

'You went to Jean's, then the gym yesterday, did you?' His lips press together, forming a harsh line.

'Yes. As I said.' Irritation bubbles beneath the surface. 'And anyway, while I was having a cuppa, I thought I saw someone go into our house!' I'm aware I too am now lying. But it's only a white lie.

Jamie's face remains neutral. There's no hint of concern, no flash of panic that he's been found out. 'Like, just walk in?'

'I don't know. I couldn't really see. But obviously I rushed over to check. I was worried there was an intruder.'

'And you're telling me this now. Why the hell didn't you mention it yesterday?'

'You seemed too preoccupied; I didn't want to stress you out any further.'

He gives me an incredulous look, but doesn't try to argue the point. 'Did you call the police?'

'No. I called you,' I say, studying his face closely. 'At the prison.' Now I note a slight flicker; a twitch in the corner of one eye. I pause to wait for his response. I'm not giving him any more – I need to hear what he comes up with. What reason he gives to wriggle free of this. He reaches to pick up his wine glass and takes a slow sip before locking his gaze with mine.

'And, as I wasn't there, what did you do?' he says, his voice quiet and level.

Damn. He's not giving up additional info either.

'Well, I was forced to check around myself. I knew you wouldn't be able to do anything anyway. I suppose I just wanted to hear your voice on the other end of the line. You're always so calm in such situations.'

'Sorry,' he says with a shrug.

That's it? Nothing else? 'How come you weren't at work?'

'Had an appointment outside of the prison. I often do on a Wednesday. Didn't you remember?'

And, just like that, I'm on the back foot again. He's so clever – twisting it so it's my faulty memory that's the problem. Although, now I think about it, there is something about a Wednesday that rings a bell. Court day, or probation meeting or similar. It does explain everything nicely. I didn't even see anyone at the house on Wednesday. I should probably face facts – I was wrong. I've conjured up this entire, convoluted story and for what purpose?

In which case, Mercy really is who she says she is. Not Gemma. And she would say I'm trying to find fault in Jamie so I can make it easier for myself to leave him.

Creating drama where there isn't any. I'm beginning to wonder whether Mercy and myself have that in common.

Jamie gets up, taking his glass with him. I hear him refill it and listen as his footsteps ascend the stairs. It's barely ten o'clock. Surely, he's not going to bed now – without so much as a 'Goodnight, Erica'? I swing my legs up onto the sofa and gaze blankly at the TV. After flicking through all of the available channels and finding nothing I want to watch, I grab my mobile and click onto Instagram. I've neglected my grid, it's been several days since my last post.

My heart plummets and I sit up so quickly my head spins as I remember the conversation Mercy and I had at the cabin the other day. I'd said I'd do an Instagram story to help spread the message that Tia still hasn't been found. Shit. How had I forgotten to do that? The most important task I had this week. I've allowed my anxiety and muddled thinking to overwhelm me. As I begin adding info to my story, I make out Jamie's muffled voice through the floor. He's in our bedroom, above the lounge. He's talking to someone. I quickly publish my story and creep out, edge my way up the stairs and hover outside the bedroom door, my breath held.

'That's what she said, I swear.' His tone is one of incredulity.

My blood runs cold. He's talking about me. I step even closer, tilting my ear to the door.

'No, I didn't tell her. How could I? It needs to be the right time.'

There's another gap as whoever the person on the other end is talks. My pulse is banging like a bass drum; my fists are hard at my side, every muscle tense. I'm coiled ready to spring. Tell me what?

Ping.

A glow of light illuminates the landing. For a moment, confusion strikes and I don't know which way to turn. Then, I realise it's my phone – I stupidly left it on the banister when I crept up the stairs. I rush to grab it, fumbling as I attempt to hit the mute button. I manage it, but not before another ping rings out. The bedroom door flies open.

'Hey,' I say. 'Assumed you'd come to bed, thought I'd follow suit.' My voice is strangely normal, no hint of the anger coursing through my veins. Jamie shoots me a quizzical glance. Luckily, I had at least got to the landing and turned to make it look as though I was just reaching the top stair when he opened the door. I don't think it's obvious I heard his conversation. My eyes fall to his hand, to the phone still in it. His gaze follows, and he holds it up.

'Quick work call. I'll finish it now.' And he does. He taps the button to end the call without a single word of explanation to the other person. If it really was a work call, he'd have at least been polite and wrapped up the conversation first.

No. That was another woman for sure. And for some reason, I'm doubting my suspicion that it *is* Mercy. I can't quite fathom why – she could have lied about not having a phone, after all – but I need to keep an open mind. My evidence, which is scant at best – not to mention circumstantial – led me to focus entirely on her. That she must be Gemma. It's all about the misdirection, isn't it? I won't exclude her as a possibility though, but I will keep my cards close to my chest.

While I might not have pinned down the who, it does

seem an inevitability my husband is having an affair. Should I be happy, really? It means that at least some of my irrational thoughts were not, in fact, irrational at all. *I'm* not wholly irrational. That's a good thing. And ultimately, I'm likely to get what I want: a separation. A new chance at life. Perfect. Isn't it?

I brush past him to go into the bedroom and our eyes meet. My unasked questions seem to float between us and it's all I can do to stop myself giving voice to them all right now. Jamie's eyes are wide and I catch fear in them. He's waiting for the explosion he knows is coming. But not yet. I can hold it together a while longer. The crushing silence continues, like we're both afraid to confront the elephant in the room, until we utter a brief goodnight and turn off the bedside lamps.

As I lie next to Jamie, his body radiating warmth, his soft breath whispering against my cheek, I know that as well as not being honest with him, I've not been honest with myself either. I've always struggled with it, even as a child I told fibs. Or, as my mother used to refer to them, the untruths: tall tales. 'She's got a creative mind, our Erica.' And 'She'll be a fabulous author when she grows up.' I never lied to hurt anyone, though. I lied to protect myself. Over the years, I came to understand that it was mostly myself I was damaging. The lies became less dramatic, told more out of necessity than to gain attention.

Until more recently, anyway. The IVF stories I've been telling *are* for attention. I have a desire to be needed. Another ping on my Instagram confirms this is what I'm probably doing now, too. Am I using Mercy's trauma to gain more followers, more popularity? I shield my screen so the brightness doesn't wake Jamie and I look again at one of the reels I made. This fake online Erica is happy – her complexion is bright, she's smiling widely as she speaks with passion about her journey. She has hundreds of fans who think she's something special.

But I know I'm not that Erica.

And Jamie knows it too.

MEETING 6

Chapter 35

Erica

Friday has rolled around quickly. I lie on my side, listening to Jamie going about his usual routine like nothing is different. The jets of water hit against his skin, then glug down the plughole as he hums some tune or other. The water shuts off, and I quickly turn to face the window, pulling the duvet up towards my head so I don't have to speak to him. He flits about the bedroom, opening and closing the cupboards, then I hear his gentle grunts as he dresses. Finally, I hear his footsteps descend the stairs and I get up.

Downstairs he's sitting in the kitchen, his nose in a file the same as any other day, one hand spooning cornflakes from the bowl, the other keeping his place, and his light and breezy attitude causes a numbness to invade my body. I'll skip breakfast because the thought of sitting opposite him at the table is too much; I can't face him. Not after what I heard last night. He said to the woman on the other end of the phone that he had to wait for the right time. There'll never be a right time. Is he as much of a coward as I am? Scared to be without me, as I am him?

Perhaps we're both playing the same game, but with differing rules.

I snatch my jacket from the hook and, without explaining where I'm going, I sneak out the front door. His attention was on his work, he probably didn't even realise I'd left. After filling up with petrol, I buy a breakfast sandwich, crisps and drink from the garage shop. Getting it here means at least I won't have to venture inside Bateman's. The thought of that gives me weird butterflies – not the nice nervous kind, more the impending dread kind.

With my preoccupation on Jamie having an affair, I failed to act on the plan Mercy and I made until last night. Sitting in Bateman's car park waiting for Mercy to show up now, my mind is awash with guilt. Instead of helping her, as I'd promised, I suspected her of conspiring to steal my life. Conspiracy theory at its worst. Oh, the irony. I cross my arms tightly over my chest. I'm not liking who I'm becoming.

I can pull this back, though. Mercy doesn't need to know I only just put the story up last night. I've had a tonne of responses, as I suspected, so there's lots I can tell Mercy. I unwrap the plastic of my meal deal sandwich and almost drop it when I see him.

Wes, the security guard, walks by the bonnet of my car heading in the direction of Bateman's entrance.

In a moment of rashness, I fling my sandwich on the passenger seat and leap out the car.

'Hey, wait,' I shout. 'Wes!'

He turns, stops. I note a brief hesitation before he carries on walking. Is he blatantly ignoring me?

'I said, wait up, Wes.' I run to try and catch up with

him. He comes to a halt, but keeps his back turned to me. With his shoulders round, head low, he just stands there waiting for me to reach him.

'Do you mind if I ask you a question?' I'm slightly out of breath from having chased him down.

'If you must,' he says.

My mouth opens and closes a few times, taken aback at his rudeness. The urge to respond with an equal lack of respect almost wins over, but if I want information, I'll have to overlook it.

'My friend . . .' That was a mistake, I'm sure. I should've pretended to be a journalist; someone like Wes seems like the type to enjoy being the one with interesting information to 'sell'. Might not be too late, actually. 'My contact at the *Mid-Devon* put me onto you.'

Wes looks at me, an expression of incredulity on his face. *Too much.*

'Pull the other one,' he says and starts walking off.

'Okay, sorry, that's a lie.' I take two steps to every one of his, tripping along beside him towards the store. 'I'm trying to help my friend.'

'Look, love. Give it a rest. I'm late.'

'Please. I only want to know about the CCTV footage. From the day Mercy's daughter went missing.'

'Bloody delusional,' he mutters, taking larger strides now.

'Seriously, stop!' I yank hold of Wes's forearm. 'What harm does it do you? Come on. You're the one with the power here. You're the only one who can help. It's a quick look at the—'

'Look, even if I wanted to help – I can't get you in there.' Wes throws an arm towards the entrance of Bateman's.

He's right. It's not like he can waltz in with me and let me into the room where CCTV is located.

'But you can get access to the footage?' I say, my voice sickeningly sweet.

'Yes. I can. But you're talking about footage from a year ago. It won't be stored here anymore.'

'Not even if it was part of a police investigation?'

He tilts his head. 'Hmm. Maybe, I guess.'

'I'll make it worth your while,' I say, rubbing my thumb and forefinger together so he's clear I mean money, not sex. 'The date I'm after is—'

'I know the date.' He contemplates my request for a few seconds, his eyes wide. 'You're wasting your time, though, aren't you?' He looks at me, a mix of sadness and pity in his eyes. 'Not like you'll find anything the cops didn't.'

'She doesn't really trust them,' I say. 'Wouldn't you want to see for yourself, if you were in that situation?'

Wes closes his eyes, takes a deep breath. The moment stretches – it's like he's in a meditative state. Finally, he snaps his eyes open and nods. 'Sure. Why not?'

'Oh, that's great. Thank you.' I feel the muscles in my face relax.

'I'm not making any promises,' he says, glumly.

I ignore his statement. 'If you find it, record it on your phone and forward it to me.' I reach for his top pocket and snatch the pen from it. Then I take his hand and scribble my mobile number on it. He shakes his head in defeat.

'If I do this, will that be it? You won't harass me again?' His words aren't as harshly spoken as their meaning suggests.

I flash him a smile. 'I'm not making any promises.' A

slightly giddy feeling reminds me of my more flirtatious days – and maybe I've still got it. I did just talk him around, after all.

I get back inside the car just as Mercy raps on the window and opens the passenger door. I swipe the sandwich from the seat and she plonks herself down, her old grey coat flapping open. *Unbelievable.* Where's the nice one I bought her?

'I've had the worst morning,' she says, heaving a huge sigh.

'Oh, no. What's happened?'

'As I was walking to the bus stop, some boy-racer came hurtling through the lane, narrowly missing a squirrel at the roadside, then sped through a huge puddle, spraying me completely with muddy water. I had to go back to the cabin to change. Tosser.'

'Could've been worse, I guess,' I say, but my attention has drifted. The horrible grey coat looks just the same, yet she bundled it up in the bag and rammed it into the bin in this very car park. I helped her do it. She must've sneaked it back out again when I was talking to Sita. What a strange thing to do. I'm about to ask why but stop myself as the most likely reason hits me. Maybe she felt weirdly attached to it because it was from the time in her life when she had her daughter. She wasn't ready to let go of it, but my actions forced it on her. I really need to be more mindful, empathic. Grief is a complex process. She has to go through the stages in her own time.

'Are you listening?' Mercy says, lines streaking across her forehead like lightning.

'Yeah, sorry,' I say. 'Glad he didn't hit you – those lanes are lethal.'

'No, it's idiot drivers that are lethal, not the lanes.' Mercy shakes her head. 'Then, of course, I missed the bus. Had to get a taxi. I swear they've put their prices up since the last time.'

'Probably, Mercy. There's a fuel crisis – the cost has rocketed.' As she gives me a mystified look, I realise that she's unlikely to be keeping up with the state of the economy. 'Anyway, hopefully I'll be able to make your awful morning better,' I say. Her face lights up, and, too late, I know I've made it sound as though I have better news than I actually do.

'Go on,' she says. She's already reached into her pocket to retrieve the photo of Tia. She sits with it gripped between her fingers, hope glinting in her eyes.

'I've had a great deal of engagement from my Instagram story. Loads of shares. Like, thousands. That's a positive start, don't you think?' I'm not sure I'm selling it well. 'And I've convinced Wes—'

'Security Wes?' Mercy's eyes widen at his name, my Instagram news seemingly less important.

'Yes. He's going to find the CCTV footage from the day Tia went missing and record it, then send it to my phone so we can see it for ourselves.'

'Oh, my God. That's fantastic. Thank you,' she gushes. 'I've been trying to set eyes on that since day one. I'm sure they're hiding something from me. How long did he say he'd take?'

'Oh, well. I don't think it'll be a quick thing. I imagine he'll have to make excuses to access where it's held, find the right day, then make sure he's on his own when he records it. I don't suppose it'll be easy.'

'It's a step further than I've ever managed.' Mercy gives

me the once-over. 'Looking *that* way can't hurt of course.' I'm unsure what to say, so I turn the topic back to the Instagram story again.

'I'm hopeful some of my followers will recognise the photo of Tia. I know you show it here every week but a wider reach will target a different set of people. A memory might be triggered.'

'I'm grateful for you trying. It's a long shot, but worth a punt. The photo itself is one thing, but teaming it with the description and key information in the way you have could really make people take notice, so thank you.'

'You've seen it? How?' My words are abrupt, literally out of my mouth as I think them. Mercy seems to freeze, but quickly recovers.

'I went into the library, used their internet.'

When? She couldn't possibly have had time to do that prior to meeting me here. She herself said she'd had a terrible morning. Oh. Unless that was a cover story for what she'd really been doing before seeing me. Something niggles me – a feeling I know I shouldn't ignore. If she's not being straight with me, then why not? What is she trying to hide from me?

The knot in my stomach intensifies as I consider whether to give her the benefit of the doubt, or dig deeper. Question her. I scratch my head roughly, irritation making me itch. If I make a big deal about this, I'll alienate her. But then, my suspicions about her *are* mounting and I've already overlooked so many other things, worried that I'll upset her – cause her precarious state of mind to topple. I take a deep breath and, deciding to wait for a better time to confront my worries, I ask her what she felt about the story, the music I paired with it.

She seems happy – although now she'll be aware I only did it last night. But stories only last for twenty-four hours, so I could say it wasn't my first story.

'What's your account on Instagram?' I ask, casually. 'I'll tag you in on my next one.'

She looks at me blankly. 'I'm not active. Being off-grid, there's no point.'

My previous sense of unease creeps back. I swear she said she didn't have an account, now she's just said she's not active. Those are two different things. Is it her story that's muddled, or my memory of our past conversations? She carries on talking and these thoughts about the inconsistencies are displaced by her rush of words. It's almost like she knows I'm trying to intervene with questions she won't be able to answer.

'And besides, I loathe social media. Hence you're doing this part,' Mercy says with a tight laugh before changing the subject and asking me about Jamie. 'How's your week been? Did you get any closer to telling him how you feel?'

Just thinking about Jamie, about everything that's happened the past week, sets my nerves on edge. I twirl a long piece of my hair round my fingers, curling it faster and faster while I consider if I want to share anything with Mercy given I can't fully reject my suspicions of her. Sometimes, I think we've built an element of trust – other times I find myself questioning that. I decide to err on the side of caution for now.

'I didn't, no,' I say. But as I speak the words I see my reflection in the visor mirror and my breath catches. It's like my true thoughts are etched on my face – plain to everyone. I'm talking about trust, about suspicion, and yet it's very possible Mercy is rightfully questioning *me*. My motivation for helping her. Perhaps she's struggling to fully trust me, too.

'You can do it without him, you know. Life. You will manage. It doesn't seem like it now, but you'll find the strength, regain some independence. You'll surprise yourself.'

'You think?'

'Absolutely. Look at you! You're beautiful inside and out, you're intelligent – you don't need a man, Erica.'

'But I do need a baby,' I whisper. I cover my face, embarrassed for allowing my emotions to spill out. I feel the warmth of Mercy's hand on my shoulder.

'I understand that need. Obviously. But you have plenty of time. Maybe the reason you haven't conceived with Jamie is because it's not meant to be. He's not destined to be the father of your child.'

'You believe in that? In destiny?'

Mercy turns to look out the window. 'Yes. I suppose I do. We were destined to meet, for example. I knew it was you I had to get to help me.'

'Had to?'

Mercy slowly turns to face me. 'It always had to be you, Erica.'

I touch my hand to my stomach, to try and still the flutters.

Chapter 36

Wes

Wes had made it sound harder than it was to access the CCTV. He knows it was partly to put her off, but admittedly, it was also so he can emerge as some kind of hero when he delivers what she wants. His own thoughts and feelings – the things he finds himself focusing on, obsessing over – are so jumbled he doesn't really know what he's doing, or why, anymore.

Why has everything become so confusing and complicated? He feels he's being pulled one way, then the other. Boundaries have blurred, the law has been bent, and he's pretty sure that ethically he's breaking all the rules having anything to do with the missing girl case. Being at this place, seeing the aftermath, it's not good for him. If he'd picked the target from somewhere else, he wouldn't have to be reliving it all week after week. He might have been able to put The Incident to the back of his mind if he didn't have to face it again.

Stupid, stupid idiot.

Now, every fibre of his being is shouting at him not to

get involved again. He should leave it well alone, let them get on with it. The other pretty woman is clearly helping her, and in turn, she's approached him for his help. If he says no repeatedly, he's going to look a complete dick. Not only that, he'll appear suspicious for refusing. But on the flip side, he's not doing himself any favours putting himself in the firing line. The pressure in his skull mounts as he walks through the store to the back. If it continues to build it'll blow, like a watermelon exploding after being dropped from a height onto concrete.

Keep your head down. That's been his mantra since that day, so why is he ignoring it now? Wes shudders, pushing away the dark thoughts, the fractured images.

It's all about self-preservation.

But then why when he looks at her, sees the pain in her eyes, does he long to step in and help despite the fact he always does the opposite?

It's my job, he tells himself. He has no choice.

You always have a choice, Wes.

The nagging voices in his head, the devil on his shoulder arguing with the angel – his conscience – all need silencing because the thunderous booming of voices threatens to overtake him completely.

It's too late to change what happened, and he hasn't acted in her best interests before, but he can do what's right now. To a degree, anyway. His stomach bubbles – his digestive system is all out of whack lately. Is what he's experiencing just guilt? For as long as he can remember he's always looked out for number one. Apart from his mum. He has to be there for her, he owes her. But he doesn't care about anyone else, usually.

He does what he does to feel good. To fulfil his desires

and make his life worth living. No matter the cost to others. So why now is his conscience trying to rectify his mistakes?

Slipping inside the security room, Wes casts his eye over the wall of monitors, then begins to search the archived CCTV footage. If he does this one thing, maybe this hideous feeling in his gut will go.

Chapter 37

Erica

Later, as I'm in my office checking responses to the story before it disappears, I realise I've set it so only followers can see the story. I tut loudly. Last night, I was keen to run upstairs to see who Jamie was speaking to – so must've hit the wrong button. I need to do another anyway. I make a similar story, this time adding new music, then I make certain to choose the correct public share button and also highlight the story so it can still be accessed after the twenty-four hours is up.

Then it hits me, like a punch to the stomach. Mercy said she'd seen the story when she accessed Instagram in the library. But without an account, and also not being friends with me, she wouldn't have been *able* to see it. My ears fill with the thrum of my pulse. Why would she say she had? I can't see that it would be to please me. Although, as she says I'm her only friend, perhaps that would be something she'd do. The only other option is that she does have an account.

And that she does follow me.

'It always had to be you, Erica.' Her words repeat in my head and make me go cold. I knew her story didn't ring true earlier, but then she'd side-tracked me, just as she always does.

'You okay?' Jamie pops his head around the door of my office. 'You've been holed up in here all night?'

I'm not okay. In every sense, I'm not okay. 'Yep,' I say, leaning back in the leather chair to look at him.

'You're pale. You sure you're not unwell?'

Why the sudden concern, I wonder. 'Tired. Long day.'

'Come to bed, then.' His hazel-green eyes seem even more intense this evening. If he thinks I look poorly, I'm assuming his desire to get me to go to bed isn't to have sex with me, or to tell me whatever it is that he's waiting for the right time for.

'I'll be there in five,' I say, leaning forwards again to denote I'm carrying on. He hasn't passed comment about why I'm on Instagram. He knows I'm heavily into my grid, but he doesn't know *what* it is, or the pictures I post, the IVF journey I share. He's no interest in it himself, he just thinks it's mostly people posting pictures of cats or their meals. I wait for him to leave, then click back onto my page. There are another load of new messages.

They could wait until tomorrow.

But, like a drug addict being drawn to their next fix, the number 8 encased in a red circle over the white arrow calls to me. My fingertips twitch. I can't go to bed not having checked them.

The first few I read are a waste of time: people sharing their shock at the length of time Tia's been missing, offering their best wishes, good luck and prayers and the like. All very thoughtful and lovely, but not offering anything helpful.

Then my stomach lurches.

LoobyLou Hi Erica, I remember this.

The three words start my heart thumping violently.

I lived locally at the time, I've since moved to Manchester. It's that dear little face, the smattering of freckles over her nose – always reminded me of my little sister, so it stuck in my mind. But I'm confused.

Here we go. This is where my hopes are dashed, I can sense it. I almost shut the computer down rather than experience the deflation that's inevitably coming. But I force myself to read on.

I'm convinced this little girl is no longer missing. I'm afraid her name has escaped me, but it wasn't Tia. Something similar, maybe? I don't know where your source is from, I don't want you to be sharing something that is incorrect, I know you pride yourself in your accuracy – so I wanted to reach out. Louise x

With my pulse racing, I tap out a response.

Erica_IVF_Journal Hi Louise, thanks so much for your message, I really appreciate you reaching out like this. I have shared Tia's picture at the request of her mother. The little girl is still missing. The mother's name is Mercy Hamilton – does that sound familiar?

I can't go to bed now; my adrenaline is rushing through my veins at a rate of knots. I wait, my fingernails drumming on the melamine desktop as my mind fills with questions. My pulse leaps as a reply comes through.

LoobyLou No, I'm sorry, it doesn't. But I'm very sure it's the same photo that was used at the time of her disappearance. And the same one I remember seeing in the papers after they found her.

What? She was found? All the energy drains from my body. I don't understand. If she was found, why is Mercy doing this? There's no evidence of a child living at the cabin. There's the bedroom of course, but there's definitely no child. But more to the point, the supermarket staff, and from what Mercy said even the police – wouldn't be suggesting the child never existed if there's a record of her being found. A shooting pain above my eye makes me wince. Too much time staring at the screen, I expect. Plus, a tonne of confusion swimming about in my head.

I start to type out: I don't understand. If they found her, why is her mother still adamant she's missing? But before I press enter, a new message appears.

LoobyLou It was so desperately sad. Such a waste of a life not yet lived.

Bile burns the back of my throat. What? No, no, no.

Erica_IVF_Journal Sorry, I think I've misunderstood. Waste of a life? You mean, she was found dead?

LoobyLou Yes. There's no mistake in my mind. My mum told me. The little girl was found in woods just outside of town, by a dog walker.

Chapter 38

Then

Flames burst from the vehicle.

The sound of cracking glass punctuated the quiet of the woods as the fire engulfed it. The heat became so intense it could be felt from over twenty metres away.

But not by the little girl lying on the leaf-covered ground, her Peppa Pig top grubby.

She could no longer feel temperature. She would no longer feel pain.

She wouldn't feel anything ever again.

Chapter 39

Dr Connie Summers

Devon Live – body of child found in woods
The market town of Newton has been left in shock after the discovery of a child's body in nearby woodland. Police are treating the death as 'unexplained' while an investigation has been launched. A heavy police presence remains in the wooded area on the outskirts of the town while forensic teams continue their investigation into the incident. No further details have been released but a senior police source has told Devon Live a press release will follow later on today.

Connie rereads the previous session notes. She feels more confident this time will work. She's taken it at a slower pace than the previous attempts, involved other professionals and the woman's support network. Anticipation makes her skin tingle. She envisages the finish line. Of course professionally this would mean the world to her – but it's become so much more than that. It's personal now. The woman's success is Connie's success.

And she's so very close.

But, there's a slight bump in the road ahead that needs flattening.

Connie takes the newspaper clipping and pops it inside the cardboard file with the others. There's a collection – all the information gathered over the months has been categorised, catalogued. It wasn't easy but, with her colleague's help, the last piece has enabled her to gain the full picture. Connie closes her eyes, soaking up the silence. Today, she needs to delve into the woman's belief system a little deeper – and she needs to ask her about her 'friend'. The one she's convinced is going to help solve everything.

The doorbell rings.

Connie pulls back the edge of the curtain and sees a dishevelled-looking woman standing on the doorstep, her grey raincoat hanging from her tiny frame. Connie takes a deep breath, goes to the door. She hesitates slightly before opening it.

'Mercy.' Connie forces a smile.

'I need to speak to you,' she says.

'Sure.' Connie steps back as Mercy pushes past her, heading straight for the therapy room.

Chapter 40

Erica

I swill cold water over my face, the shock of the temperature on my skin bringing some clarity of thought. Over the weekend the most horrific images permeated my mind and even cleaning didn't stop them crowding in. I need to talk to someone about Friday night's finding and it can't be Jamie.

Jean? She's the only one I can even think to go to. I've cut myself off from almost everyone in my life, choosing my social media followers over real friends when things became overwhelming. It's so much simpler talking with those who know exactly what you're going through – not having to listen to the fake sympathy, see the awkwardness in their eyes. And yes, it's also easier when people don't know you, know what you're really like. Fabricating details of my life became addictive, and of course, friends IRL tend to know lies when they hear them. Yes, Jean likes to listen to me. She knows what it's like to feel alone. Not thinking for another moment, I walk across the road to the familiar house and tap on the door.

'I've got myself tangled up in something, Jean. I don't know how to proceed.' I give her a desperate look.

'That sounds like something that calls for a coffee and a pot of tea, dear.'

'It's a long story, but basically there's this woman called Mercy . . .' My mouth moves faster than my brain as the words start pouring out.

'Mercy?' Jean glares at me over her cup of tea. 'The woman you thought you saw going into your house?'

I don't remember mentioning Mercy's name in relation to that, but I guess I must've.

'Yes, her,' I say. 'Anyway, she accosted me at Bateman's, shoved a photo of a little girl under my nose, and asked if I'd seen her.'

'So . . . the girl is missing?'

'Well, that was my assumption, yes. But the supermarket staff said she's there every week, showing anyone and everyone the photo and begging them to help her find her daughter.'

'Oh, that's so very sad. The poor woman.'

'It is. But it's even worse than that. I've just found out that a girl was found dead around here at the time Mercy says her daughter went missing and I think it's the same girl. It's Mercy's daughter who was found dead. Do you remember the case, Jean?' I take a breath, I feel light-headed from having talked so quickly.

Jean sits back, a look of sadness crossing her face. 'Oh, dear.' She shakes her head. 'Yes, I remember it. Terrible business.'

'Why don't I remember it, then?' My frown is so deep it hurts my head.

'Probably had a lot going on yourself, lovely. There was limited exposure – not the usual television appeals by the parents and it didn't stay in the media long. That bomb went off in the Exeter shopping centre just after and the fickle nature of journalism meant it was buried in the aftermath of that. Poor little mite.'

That might explain my inability to recall it, but I would've thought, with my links to the *Mid-Devon*, that I'd have been all over it. Is Jean right, that the media simply found something more newsworthy to replace a dead girl being found? The fact this was once my profession makes my chest tight – anger surging through me.

'Honestly, that's appalling,' I say. 'Makes me ashamed to have been involved in journalism.' I lower my head, disgraced. But this is my first real opportunity to gain some information from someone who's actually aware of the case. Someone who's willing to admit they know about the missing – the dead – girl. I just have to tease it out of her and hopefully fill in some missing pieces. 'Do you remember the girl's name? The parents'?'

'Ah,' Jean says, her lips pursing. 'Names aren't such an easy thing to recall, I'm afraid. As I told you.' She gives an awkward smile. I gaze into her eyes, suddenly wary. If it was something so terrible, I'd have thought at least the girl's name would be imprinted in her mind.

'Why are the police making it seem like Mercy is suffering from a mental health issue – that she's lying about having had a child, then? They must know what happened to her daughter.' I'm verbalising my thoughts as they come to me – there are so many questions now this piece of information has come to light.

'I really don't know. Perhaps if she's adamant she's

missing, not . . . dead, they maybe don't realise?' Jean squints, and it's obvious to me that she, too, thinks there's still something amiss.

'No. That's not it. Mercy told me that as far as they're concerned, she didn't even have a daughter. She's convinced it's some kind of conspiracy.'

Jean scratches her head, then picks up one of the cats that's rubbing her calves.

'You say someone messaged you about recognising the girl in the photo?' Jean asks.

'Yes, someone from my Instagram. But she couldn't remember the girl's name. Although, when I mentioned the name Tia, she said that wasn't it – but perhaps something similar, though, she thought.'

'Then maybe Mercy didn't give the right name,' Jean says confidently, like she's solved the mystery. 'There'd be no record to show if that were the case.'

I bite the edge of my fingernail. 'But why give a false name when you're asking people to find your daughter? It doesn't make sense.'

'You're assuming all this time that Mercy *wants* you to find her daughter.'

I blink a few times, then frown.

'Well, yes, Jean. That's the point. She's literally desperate for someone to help find her!' I stretch my shoulders; knots have formed in my neck and back, the tension too much to bear. I'm trying not to get annoyed with Jean – she's only trying to help. But agitation works its way through my muscles anyway.

'I'm playing devil's advocate here,' Jean says. 'But what if that's not what Mercy wants?'

I shake my head. 'What other possible reason could she have, Jean?'

Jean takes a huge gulp of air and blows it out. 'What if Mercy just wants someone to listen to her? She might need help in a different way. If everyone knows her daughter is dead, there's no reason for people to offer to help her. If she's lonely—'

'Christ! There are far better ways to seek companionship, Jean. It's a hell of a lie.'

'Or, she's simply in denial. If you tell lies often enough, you can start to believe them yourself.'

'So you think she's traumatised by the death of her daughter, doesn't want to let go of her, so is keeping her alive by pretending she's missing, not dead?' I say, summing it up. Jean gives a thoughtful look.

'I'm no psychologist, but the brain is a complex organ, Erica. People are compelled to do far more strange things to cope with terrible situations. It's a theory, is all, dear. Wouldn't you like to think it's that, rather than her reasons for lying and befriending you being sinister? I mean, you don't *really* believe that her motive is in any way malicious, do you?'

I shiver as a cold sensation like icy water trickles down my back. I'm not sure what I believe anymore.

Chapter 41

Erica

As I'm drifting off to sleep, my phone pings and my eyes fly open. Jamie is still, his back towards me. His breaths are rhythmic. We'd chatted for a bit before settling down; the conversation was chilled for a change. Mainly because it avoided anything emotionally challenging. Talking about other people's lives is a safer bet these days.

Slowly, I rotate my body to face the bedside cabinet, wait a few seconds to ensure I haven't disturbed him, then reach for my phone. Under the covers, careful the backlight doesn't glare, I unlock the screen. It's a text from a contact I don't have saved. I almost delete it, but then see there's a link in the text message with the word 'video' in it.

My heart jolts me fully awake. Well, well, well, Wes came through. With a rush of anticipation, I sneak out the bed and downstairs to the kitchen. Sitting at the breakfast bar, my shoulders hunched, I open the message and click the link. It's not exactly clear on my mobile screen, but it's watchable. I stop it, though, and email it to myself so I can watch it properly on the large monitor later. Then I restart it, my breath held. With my face inches from my mobile's screen, I watch the footage.

Two and a half minutes later, it goes blank.

I start it over. All in all I watch it fifteen times – each viewing focusing on a different aspect. At the end of it I sit back on the bar stool, rubbing my eyes. This is the footage which apparently doesn't show evidence of a little girl being with the mother. The mother – a woman dressed in what appears to be a blue coat – could well be Mercy, it's difficult to say one way or the other. I could show it to Jean because she might recognise the walk. She's seen Mercy – or so I believe – and she said she always recognises specific gaits. As for the little girl, I can see why no one is able to say without doubt that she's there. But I swear I can see her a few times, just tucked behind the woman, or other customers. No one clearly, or obviously, takes her, though. I wonder if CCTV outside might yield more.

From this, it's looking likely that Mercy is mixing some elements of the truth with some fiction. I don't think there's something underhand, or sinister about her actions, just as Jean suggested, but there are things that are bothering me. If the Instagram messenger is right, the little girl could've gone missing from the store, but was later found dead. Mercy, however, hasn't come to terms with her loss and is still keeping Tia alive in her mind, ever hopeful someone will help find her daughter and bring her back safe and well.

A deep sadness makes me double over. I cross my arms over my stomach.

Having a sliver of hope is better than the alternative.

I let out a puff of breath. If that's how Mercy copes, who am I to tell her otherwise? How would I even start to

234

suggest to her that she's wrong? Should I attempt gently implying that Tia could be dead? I've no way of telling what damage that would do to Mercy's state of mind. This isn't something I should be involving myself with. Jamie is right, she needs professional help. When I see her on Friday, I'm going to have to pull back. I'm not doing her any good by feeding her delusions, adding to them even, by telling her I can help her find Tia. If I could find out her daughter's real name, then I could find the information about her death.

The thought it wasn't a natural death, that someone killed Tia, swoops into my mind and my stomach knots. If she was abducted from the store and then murdered, that would be a huge trauma to deal with. I know if that were to happen to me, I'd blame myself. And as Mercy was the only one with her daughter that day, it's safe to say she'd blame herself for losing Tia. How do you ever get over that?

I felt bad enough when the little girl in the pink coat lost her mum at Bateman's the day I met Mercy. My immediate concern was either that someone would think I was trying to abduct her, or that if I didn't step in, someone else might coax her out of the store. If I were responsible for a child and that child was not just taken, but killed, then that would be the end of my life.

When I make my way back up to bed, my limbs feel like lead. Tiredness, I tell myself. But I know I'm lying – it's more than that. The last few weeks have been stressful. Sleep doesn't come quickly, but when it does it's permeated with dark shadows and shapes moving ominously through thick woodland, the bark of the trees glowing orange. A child's screams . . . and then my own.

Chapter 42

Erica

The days between my meetings with Mercy seem to blur into one and I have to check my mobile each morning to remind myself where I am in the week. I'm reliably informed it's Thursday. A flurry of thoughts whirl around in my head as the toothbrush vibrates against my teeth and I stare outside rather than at my reflection – at the heavy undereye bags and dull complexion. The sun is yet to make an appearance, the autumn sky still a gloomy grey. The en suite window overlooks our back garden – it's not frosted like most people's bathroom windows because the room was originally meant to be a dressing area. Jamie talked me out of it, saying the en suite would add value to the property – more so than a 'poncy walk-in wardrobe'. I gave up arguing my case the day the plumber and his team rocked up.

My entire head buzzes; the toothbrush bristles feel as though they're burrowing into my brain but I press them hard against each tooth like a punishment. A seagull swoops past the window and I jump back, my teeth clamping down on the toothbrush. Living here can be a curse, the squawks beginning in the early hours and lasting all day. It's why we disappear onto the moors some weekends – Dartmoor ponies, Highland cows and sheep are preferable and offer a more calming experience.

I turn away, leaning down to the sink to spit white residue into it, then as I bob back up, I do look at myself. My face is in dire need of some pampering. And I really should take a decent selfie and whack it up on Insta – it's been too long since my last post. As I apply the layers of make-up, I think about Mercy, imagining her dark eyes filling with tears as I broach the topic of grief and loss. My own eyes blur and black mascara smudges at my lash line. Pulling off a square of toilet paper, I dab gently at the blotches.

Energy oozes from every pore, like something is sucking it out of me, leaving me like an empty shell, tired and lifeless. Even my Instagram doesn't give me the thrill it once did. The past six weeks have slowly drained me of enthusiasm. With a burst of anger, I turn the tap on full, lowering my face and splashing it with the cold water. I rub at my skin until it's sore, until all traces of make-up are gone. I don't want to wear a mask anymore. I think I hear Jamie shouting up the stairs, but I don't respond. He's probably leaving to go to work. With light pats of the cream towel, I dry my face and exit the bathroom.

It seems it was easy enough for Wes to access the CCTV, so now I have his number, I could call and ask him to get me the outside footage. Jamie once told me how some prisoners use coercion and manipulation: if you do one thing for them, like smuggle in contraband or take a bribe, they have you – you're vulnerable to further manipulation.

A twinge of guilt pulls at my gut as I think about how I can get Wes to cooperate. Am I that kind of person now? But needs must.

I check that Jamie has definitely left the house then, sitting on the bed, I dial Wes.

'Hey, Wes. It's Erica.'

'Who?' The voice is groggy.

It's only seven a.m. I've likely woken him up. 'Sorry, I didn't realise it was so early. I wanted to thank you for sending the CCTV.'

'Ah. It's you.' I hear a yawn, then a rustling. 'You said you wouldn't bother me again if I did that. Yet here we are.' His voice is thick with sleep. And I suspect, exasperation.

'I know, I'm sorry. I'm really grateful for your help. But I could do with seeing the CCTV for *outside* Bateman's?'

'Oh, for God's sake.' Wes lets out a long, irritated groan and my hand grips my mobile a little tighter.

'Please, Wes. I think something bad happened to Mercy's daughter. A girl was found dead in the woods around the time of Tia's disappearance. I think it was her.'

Silence.

'Wes? You still there?'

'Er . . . Yeah,' he sighs. 'I'm here.' I can hear him breathing – shallow, almost hyperventilating if I'm not mistaken.

'Is something wrong?' I ask, my voice lilting. Mentioning my suspicion that Mercy's daughter is in fact dead seems to have knocked him. Is it that he really didn't believe her and feels guilty now? A more alarming thought is that he already knew, and has been treating her like this regardless. The man comes across a bit full of his own self-importance, arrogant, even, but he *did* offer to help, eventually. With a bit of arm-twisting. Surely, he can't be all bad. His continued silence is doing nothing to quash my anxiety, though. 'Wes?'

'Look, meet me at Bateman's at one forty-five.'

Relief swoops through me. 'Thank you,' I say.

'Don't get ahead of yourself, I didn't say I was going to do it, I just said to meet me.'

'Sure.' I smile to myself, knowing I have him in the palm of my hand.

'But hey,' Wes says. 'Maybe bring your friend, too, eh?'

'Oh.' I suck air through my teeth. 'It's not a Friday.'

'Riiiight. So?'

'She only goes out on a Friday.' As I speak the words, I realise how dumb they sound. 'She works the rest of the week,' I add quickly.

'Wait until tomorrow then?' I envisage Wes giving a shrug.

'No.' My tone is sharp. 'Sorry, no. I can't wait. It needs to be today. I'll see you at one forty-five.'

I hang up before he can protest. He could, of course, text to tell me to forget it. But now I know he's on shift at the supermarket today, I feel sure he won't. He knows I'll just find him inside. And that would be far more awkward for him.

Chapter 43

Erica

Jean isn't in the window when I leave the house. I fling my handbag onto the passenger seat as I climb into my car and start it. A flutter in my stomach raises a red flag, like my gut is trying to warn me of impending trouble. A warning regarding what I'm about to do? Or about Jean? I look in my rear-view mirror, squinting at Jean's house. It looks as it usually does, bar the cat woman herself. It's a bit odd, although I mostly see her later in the day, sitting behind her window to the world, her cats leaping all over the place or sleeping on the windowsill. She's allowed a change of routine, I remind myself. But still, a tightness in my stomach persists as I drive past.

I hope she's okay. Maybe I'll check in on her when I get back.

It's a slow drive into town, tension is tight across my shoulders as I hunch behind the wheel. I've been following this huge tractor from the moment I pulled out onto the main road and it doesn't look as though it's going to pull in to let me and the other three cars past anytime soon.

241

Ignorant shit. Jamie would be quick to quote the Highway Code – 'He doesn't need to do anything until there are six vehicles behind him.' But there have been two opportunities to let me pass and he's ignored both. For some reason, despite me living in the countryside for years, today this has irked me.

I beep my horn, throwing my hands up in disgust as he drives on by another pull-in space. I know the gesture is futile, but it temporarily makes me feel better. After crawling along for another mile, the bloody thing finally begins to turn off. I jam my fist on the horn again as I drive past, just for good measure.

Sweat trickles down my back as I near Bateman's. I'm not sure how pleased Wes will be to see me, given I've practically blackmailed the guy into helping again. I draw into the far end of the car park instead of my usual spot, unclip my seatbelt and lower the window. I'm dead on time. I prefer to be early to everything, but with the tractor impeding my journey, that ship has sailed. I hope I'm not too late and that Wes hasn't already gone into the store.

Fidgeting with my wedding band, I consider what I'll do if I can't get Wes to agree to this second misdemeanour. On the phone he appeared keen I should bring Mercy; without her maybe he'll fob me off.

He's five minutes late now.

I shuffle in the seat then begin biting my nails. If he thinks he can avoid me, he's wrong. I will go inside and I will approach him. I've come this far in my drive to help Mercy, I need to see it through. A shadow crosses behind me and I turn sharply. The figure looms beside my window.

'Where's the other woman?' Wes says, ducking low. I catch a strong waft of aftershave and stifle a cough.

'She couldn't make it,' I say, quickly adding: 'Christ, did you empty an entire bottle of Burberry on yourself this morning?' I put my hand to my face and allow my cough to escape.

'Wow, you're ruder than usual today.' He straightens, and begins to walk off.

I jump out of the car. 'Sorry!' I run after him. 'I'm nervous, I say stupid shit when I'm nervous.'

Wes stops and turns. 'Why are *you* nervous? Are *you* about to break the law by accessing security footage you're not permitted to?' His blue eyes flash but it's not anger I see in them; I think he's really worried about the consequences of doing this.

I tuck my hair behind my ears then jam my hands into my pockets. 'Well, no. But I'm aware that I'm asking you to.'

'Oh, well that's all fine and dandy, then.' He lets out a long sigh. We both stand, casting our gazes around. 'What exactly are you hoping to find anyway?'

'I thought that was obvious.'

He shrugs. 'It's all been checked before, I mean. So, what are you expecting to see that no one else did?'

It's a fair question and one I don't actually know the answer to, so that's what I say.

'Are you sure you're looking at the right date?' His voice is curious, not sarcastic, and gives me pause.

'It's the one Mercy gave me.' I shrug.

Wes shoots me a strange look. 'Okaaay.' He scratches his stubble. 'What if it's all got a little mixed up? Trauma can do that. Twist things. You can remember things in the wrong order. Or . . .' He squints a little at me. 'Not remember them at all. Happened to my brother after Iraq.'

'I hadn't even thought of that.' The realisation hits me like a brick. Is that why no one believes Mercy? All this time she's been going on about losing Tia on a specific day and time – but if it's the incorrect date, that could explain some of the confusion. 'It's a theory. But if that were the case, they'd still have found a record of her child's *existence*.' I lean back against a pillar under the walkway to the supermarket. 'Ah, shit.'

'What?'

'Something my neighbour said. She couldn't remember the child's name from the news – the one found dead in the woods near here – but wondered if perhaps Mercy gave a false name.'

'And you think it could be why you can't be sure if you see a kid being taken inside there?' Wes nods towards the store. 'I'm assuming Friday is a relevant day, though. As in, it must be significant, just the dates aren't right.' He fidgets, tapping his hands on his thighs, then over his jacket.

'Or she doesn't want me to find out what really happened,' I say more to myself than him.

'You are as confusing as hell, you know that?' Wes shakes his head, then reaches inside his pocket and takes a cigarette packet out. 'Want one?'

I contemplate it. I haven't smoked since I was fourteen, when my dad caught me dragging on a fag hanging half out the bathroom window, but right now, it's looking an attractive option.

'I'd probably cough my guts up.'

'Like when you smelled my expensive aftershave?' He narrows his eyes.

'Oh, worse. Much worse.' I laugh and it catches me off-guard, the sound almost foreign to my ears. When did I last laugh? I take a few seconds to look at Wes's face. I'd thought it hard, unkind even, when I came across him all those weeks ago. I must've seen him on previous occasions of course, but I'd obviously never had reason to study his features. Caught up in my own world, I expect. Now though, I decide he's gentle, maybe even compassionate. Quite good-looking too. He's giving me the time of day, anyway, and seems genuinely concerned about Mercy's daughter. 'So? Are you willing to do a bit of detective work, Wes?'

Wes leans back against the pillar beside me, blows a smoke ring, then turns his head to look at me. 'This is all a bit . . . well, *odd*. I'm not really sure how, or even if, I can help. It's not like I can go back through days and days of footage. And as I told you before, if it's after a certain length of time it'll have been wiped.'

I reach across and take the cigarette from Wes's fingers. 'Stuff it,' I say, putting it to my lips and drawing on it. My throat burns and I immediately begin coughing. Wes laughs. 'Don't,' I say, my voice croaky. 'Look, you're right. This is a waste of time, isn't it?'

'That's not what I said.'

'It's what you meant.' I hand back the cigarette stub.

'You said it yourself the other day – the only reason the CCTV from the day you gave me was still available is because it was part of a police investigation. Which means it's likely the date *was* right?'

'So, we're back to the beginning,' I say.

'Strike all the above,' Wes says, his tone firm, like he's made his mind up about something. 'Theories are all well and good, but most will be totally off the wall. You ought to listen to some of the ones online – those groups of people who do nothing else other than pick apart criminal cases and throw a dozen madcap theories around. That'll make you realise this case is actually pretty straightforward.'

I sigh. 'Would you take a look at the outside CCTV then? Just in case.'

Wes nods slowly, while keeping eye contact. My pulse skips – the way he's looking at me, there's something behind his eyes. I'd say it was sadness. That, or pity.

'It's not for me, you know,' I add. 'I said I'd help Mercy and I really want to keep my word. I've been pretty selfish lately, had my head up my own arse, you know? It would be good to do something for someone else.'

Wes scratches his nose, then checks the time on his phone. 'Whatever. I'll do it.' He pushes off the pillar and walks off. 'I'll be seeing you, no doubt.'

Chapter 44

Erica

The conversation with Wes plays over in my mind as I drive home. I need to go back to the start, do another search of online news articles relating to the child's body found in the woods, but with a more open mind. Finding out her name is crucial because what if the body in the woods really *isn't* Mercy's daughter? I'd be doing her a disservice if I'm barking up the wrong tree. It's a shame Jean can't recall more, because that would save a lot of time.

Jean. My heart stutters – I'd almost forgotten.

I peer at her window as I slow down to swing the car into the drive and relief cascades over me. There she is, sitting in her favourite spot, knitting. Good. One less worry. My strange feeling of impending doom first thing was clearly because of meeting Wes, then. Not a weird sixth sense that Jean had come to harm. Unless of course it was a premonition. A little dramatic, but I've a vague memory of something similar happening before. I guess everyone has those odd déjà-vu moments though, and with my swinging up and down emotions it's no surprise I'm feeling a bit jittery.

Just before walking into the house, I turn and wave to Jean. She looks up from her knitting, but doesn't return the gesture. Odd. Her face is upturned now, looking towards mine, so I wave again; perhaps she didn't see the first time. She flicks her hand up in response, but she looks quickly away. Something's off. Did I offend her before? Maybe I said something I shouldn't have. We only talked about Mercy. But she did seem keen to shut down the negative thoughts I shared with her about Mercy. Although, thinking about it, it was actually Jean who put it into my mind that Mercy's motivations might be sinister – I don't think I said that. What was it she said . . . 'You don't *really* believe that her motive is in any way malicious, do you?'

I'm overthinking. She was likely just upset by talking about the girl who was found dead in the woods. I mentally chastise myself. I dragged up something that was possibly difficult for Jean to talk about without giving any thought to her feelings. I'll have to pop across in a bit, make sure she's okay. That we're okay.

After making a coffee and taking a selfie with it sitting cross-legged on the sofa, I go upstairs. Notebooks are piled to the right of my keyboard, a reminder to myself that I must get my freelance articles written at some point. Mercy and Tia have taken up so much of my time, I've put everything else on the backburner. I've even ignored the majority of my Instagram followers. Sitting in my office chair, I open the app now and post the selfie I've just taken with a caption reading: *A little me time*. A stab of guilt makes me catch my breath when I spot the number of comments I've not replied to, and the sixteen messages I've not opened. I'm scared to check how many followers I've lost. Despite this, I mute my notifications – something I'd never have done before.

Swiping my guilt aside, I type the usual key words into the search engine, hoping for different results. Nothing relating to Mercy's missing daughter, Tia, or a name for the girl found in the woods comes up. I pull at my hair and let out a frustrated yell. If it was such a huge local story – how come I can't find mentions of the girl's name? There are a few mentions of a missing girl, then a single Devon Live story with vague details, no names. It's bizarre. It's almost as if search engines have been wiped clear of the finding. 'Conspiracy theory' springs into my thoughts again and I rub my temples. Nothing about this case makes any sense to me. What am I missing?

Can articles be redacted or altered even after they've been published? Or details of particular cases be explicitly forbidden to be reported? I guess there could be rules in place if the deceased child had siblings, in order to protect them? The police weren't forthcoming when I went to see them, but I got the impression they know something, just didn't want to share it with me. If the people involved are in protective custody, or have been given new identities, that might also explain their reluctance. I'm reminded of the high-profile murder of a child that I heard so much about when I was growing up – how the young boys responsible were provided with new identities when they were released. They could live among us and we wouldn't know.

My mind storms to a conclusion I know is outrageous: it's one of those boys, now an adult, who took and murdered Tia. That's why everyone is so cagey and the police refuse to give credence to Mercy's claims. Why they're adamant she has mental health issues and tell everyone she never had a child in the first place. Jesus. If this is even close to the truth it's scary as hell.

Is it possible someone could be married to the perpetrator and not have any inkling of their past identity?

The front door slams and my eyes snap to the clock. Damn – Jamie's home – where has the time gone? I haven't even taken the pie out of the freezer that I planned to cook for dinner.

'Fancy a takeaway?' I say as I bounce down the stairs towards Jamie. He umms and ahhs for all of two seconds, then says yes.

'Shall we go collect, it'll be quicker and I'm ravenous.' He's in a good mood, and it lifts my own. I force the question of *why* back down; I don't want to ruin the evening.

'Good idea,' I say, reaching for the coat hooks. Mine's not there. 'I'll just grab my coat.' I run back up the stairs, into our bedroom, and pull the wardrobe door open. I stand there, momentarily confused as it's not hanging there, either. I flick the coat hangers quickly, in case it's slipped off. My eye catches a patch of dark green on the wardrobe floor. I duck down, pulling at its edge.

I lift out a khaki, quilted jacket.

I stop breathing.

What the hell is this doing here? *How?*

'Erica? Hurry up!' Jamie shouts up the stairwell, but it barely registers; the pounding of my heart overpowers it. The only way this coat could've got inside my wardrobe is by Mercy putting it there. Which means she *has* been in my home.

In a flash, I rewind a week and I'm back to thinking that Mercy isn't who she says she is. She has to be Jamie's ex. It's why things are familiar. The photo. There'd been a fleeting familiarity – I thought I'd seen it before, but not from any news or social media, it was closer to home. But where? In Jamie's wallet? Tucked inside a drawer? I screw up my eyes, trying to remember. If I'd found a photo I didn't recognise I'd have asked him about it, though, so it can't have been among his things, surely?

His parents' house.

My breathing escapes my lungs in short, shallow bursts. That's it. It was in a frame on their dresser in the hall last time we visited. It had been off the cuff. My idea to drop in unannounced as we'd been to a wedding nearby. Jesus. I bet Gemma had the baby, just like I suspected, and she gave Jamie a recent photo of their daughter, and, as he couldn't keep it, he'd passed it on it to his parents. Of course they wouldn't ever tell me – they'd keep their precious Jamie's secret. I suspect they usually hide the photo when they know I'm coming, but Jamie didn't have enough time to warn them of our arrival on that occasion.

It was Jamie's daughter who'd been found dead in the nearby woods. The child he'd had with Gemma – the woman I've finally convinced myself *is* Mercy. As I grip the jacket even tighter, my knuckles blanching, I realise timing-wise it must've coincided with Jamie's bout of depression. I know we were going through a difficult time but not sharing any of that with me cuts deep. How could he go through something so horrific without me realising? Maybe the question I should be asking is *why*? Really, there'd have been no need to keep his child secret anymore once she died. He could've simply told me he wasn't aware of his daughter until recently, that's why he'd never said anything.

He did spend a lot of time out of the house, though. Working late at the prison, evening meetings with colleagues to discuss offenders' cases. Looking back, he could quite easily have been spending time with Gemma, them both grieving the loss of their child together.

He wouldn't have needed me.

My nose tingles with threatening tears and I blink rapidly to prevent them.

'Erica? How bloody long does it take to grab a jacket?' Jamie shouts. With no further hesitation, I feed my arms through Mercy's coat and, with my pulse banging, walk down the stairs towards my husband.

His pupils dilate as he looks at me; his Adam's apple bobs. He parts his lips but no words are uttered.

'What's the matter?' I say, my words dripping in sarcasm.

He appears lost for words. 'Oh. Nothing, Erica,' he manages, his eyes still on me. 'Erm . . .'

'You've seen this coat before, haven't you?' Does he know I'm testing him? His eyes fall away from mine, and he turns to open the door.

'No. No, I don't think so,' he says, as he steps outside, holding the door for me to go through. 'Is it new?'

He gives me a thin smile as I move past him. My insides burn with the need to have this out with him right now, but it's not enough yet – if I say it's not my coat and that I don't know how it got inside my wardrobe, Jamie will somehow wriggle out of it, give a perfectly plausible reason like he did when I confronted him about not working on Wednesdays. Either that, or he'll turn it around, back onto me, like he often does.

'Yes,' I say with a shrug, deciding to leave it there. Despite the anger and the mounting paranoia bubbling away, I manage to hold it all in as I walk to the drive, my legs like liquid. Once inside the car, he asks me about my day and I do the expected thing and ask about his. This mundane chit-chat has come to signify the state of our marriage.

We get Indian and the heat from the foil trays is burning my thighs by the time we reach home again. I pass the bag to Jamie to get out the car and automatically wave up to Jean as I head to the door, as does Jamie. When I see her hand immediately rise, I'm pleased. But the paranoid part of me wonders if she's responding to Jamie, not me.

'You've been seeing quite a bit of her lately,' Jamie says. He pushes the door open, stooping to pick a leaflet off the mat.

'That's what you wanted, wasn't it? For me to be more social.'

'Yes, absolutely. I'm pleased. Having someone to talk to is important.'

Not that lecture again. Or is this a precursor to him finally telling me his confidante at work is really his ex? Who is really Mercy. And all this time he's been seeing her, allowing her into *our* home. Do they have sex in our bed? My skin prickles, like my blood is bubbling hot beneath it. I take a long, slow breath in, releasing it even more slowly. I need to keep it together.

We eat at the dining room table. It's so quiet I can hear the click of his jaw when he chews each mouthful of food: *click, click, click.* The sound burrows into my brain like some kind of torture method and I snap.

'I have to ask, Jamie.' And suddenly, I really do need to. The burning question, the one I've avoided for so long for fear of being right, is one I must ask this second. His fork pauses midway to his mouth.

'Right.'

'Who were you talking with on the phone the other night? I heard you say you're waiting for the right time to tell me. So, who is she? Who's the woman you're having an affair with?' The words have been so long in the making, they rush from me as if a dam is busting. My chest is tight, my spine rigid. Tears aren't far away.

'Oh, God, Erica.' Jamie's head hangs, then he drops the cutlery to his plate with a clatter and rests his forehead on his interlaced hands. He looks like a destroyed man.

My breath judders from my lungs in weird hiccuppy sobs.

'Why are you crying?' He looks up, reaching for my hands.

'Why?' The strength has left my voice, my body; my spine suddenly feels as though it's become liquefied and can no longer offer the structural support required. I slump over the table, my head banging against my crossed forearms. Heat flushes my skin; I'm so hot that for a crazy moment I fear I'll spontaneously combust.

'I'm not having an affair, Erica.' He shakes my arm until I look back up at him. 'I have no idea why you'd think that.' His words seem empty, his eyes too. He's lying to me and this knowledge makes something inside me break.

'Oh really? You've no idea, you say?' The power in my voice returning. 'I'll enlighten you, shall I? There's the late-night calls, the woman who's been coming to the house – even Jean's seen her.' I'm shaking now, the tap is open and the pent-up anger begins to pour out. 'The missed work days, the fact you've wanted to get me out of the house, the months of acting strangely towards me. Then there's the coat.' My face burns, but Jamie continues to look at me with disbelief. I can't have got this all wrong, he's just good at lying.

'You need to calm down,' he says, slowly, deliberately.

Those infamous 'calming' words that always have the opposite effect. 'I am calm.' I accentuate each word.

'Why do you have to ruin the evening with this nonsense, eh?' He pushes his chair back, the scraping of wood on wood grating through me.

'Why do you have to ruin our marriage with an affair?'

'Jesus. I'm going out.'

He snatches up a coat, and as he opens the front door the loud hiss of rain bursts in, then is muted again as he slams it closed. I listen to the roar of his car engine until it disappears around the corner, then I run out into the rain, get into my car and head in the same direction. I'm vaguely aware of Jean's silhouette in the window as I pass, the rain streaming down the windscreen so heavily the wipers don't even clear it. I don't wave.

Chapter 45

Dr Connie Summers

MUMSNET TALK

Losing your kid in a store
MisfitMumma
How the hell did this happen? A child was taken in broad daylight, right under the noses of not only the mother, but the security and other customers too. The mum must feel like shit for ever letting go of her hand.

Karenlovescava
The woman got what she deserved. Who's going to feel sorry for her when she clearly wasn't paying attention to her own child?

YouDoYou
Can't believe in this day and age that a mother would let their 3-year-old go off in a supermarket – what did she expect?

OpinionatedNat
Did no one learn from the Bulger case FFS?

MrsPM

I'd NEVER let go of my DD's hand in a store. Too many weirdos around.

Runragged

Oh, come on – you've never ONCE let go of your kid? What do you do, shop with one hand? It's not practical. You shouldn't have to worry about someone taking your kid while shopping in a supermarket!

YouDoYou

But that's the way it is. You can't let them out of your sight. The mother knew that, it's why she did zero publicity. She failed to keep her DD safe and the girl paid the price.

Karenlovescava

Yeah, if I'm honest, I think she should be done for neglect. Stupid woman. I heard she was flirting with the bloody security bloke! He should've been sacked. If both he and the mother were doing their jobs, the poor little girl wouldn't have been taken and killed by a paedo.

Connie waits for the woman to stop crying, then takes the proffered ball of soggy tissues from her with one hand as she offers the box of new tissues with the other. The first minutes have covered some old ground, with little in the way of progression. The woman had stared at Connie as though her words were foreign to her; a language so confusing she failed to comprehend any of it.

Connie moves to her desk, pulling the cardboard file from beneath another folder. She places some paperwork from it on the table between them then sits again. The lump in her throat is proving difficult to dispel, even with several hard swallows.

This could go horribly wrong.

Connie holds in her breath as the woman leans forward, nudging the paper closer to her.

'I don't know why you want me to look at these – some weird online group all talking about the Bulger murder. Why are people so macabre?'

'It's not about that,' Connie says. 'Read it again.'

'I don't want to.'

'Why not?'

'You know why not.'

'Take your time,' Connie says, patiently. And she purposely sits back; looks around the room. The ripping sound makes Connie's head turn sharply back. The paper, now in pieces, is scattered on the floor. 'What's wrong?' she says.

'I'm not looking at that. You can't make me.'

'It's time. I think you're ready now.' Connie shifts in her seat, unsure of her own statement.

Chapter 46

Erica

For a split second, I think I've lost him; I waited too long before following. I squint in the darkness, frantically searching for a hint of his black car ahead. I'm on the road that takes you to town; if he came this way it's perfectly reasonable to assume he's simply driving around aimlessly, going anywhere just to calm down. He used to do that a lot when we were first together. Any argument would result in him jumping in his car and racing off and I'd wait impatiently at home until he felt he'd cooled off sufficiently to return. He said it was because he hated to argue. His parents' marriage had been difficult over the years, and it was one of the things Jamie was adamant he'd never put his children through.

Always better to walk away; take yourself out of the situation. Before things are said that are too difficult to take back. I don't share his need to eject myself from the situation, I'd rather tackle the argument head on. Admittedly, that hasn't been the case recently, but I don't run off. It infuriates me that he walks away from me. At the traffic lights by B&Q I catch sight of taillights. It's Jamie, I'm sure. He's going towards Kingsteignton. Which makes it less likely he's simply driving around, surely? He's going there because he knows just where he's headed.

But Mercy doesn't live in Kingsteignton. In which case, does this mean that, yet again, I'm wrong about her? Although, it might be that Jamie's just choosing not to drive straight to his mistress's house because he's predicting I'll follow him. Or, of course, I am wrong about Mercy being his mistress – and it's a different woman's house he's driving to. My head throbs. I don't know what's real or imagined anymore where Mercy is concerned – but in my gut I know that my husband is lying to me and he's having an affair with *someone*.

I turn the radio up loud to drown out my hammering heart. Adrenaline pumps violently through my blood. Anger, hurt, betrayal swirling and mixing together – how could he do this to me?

You were going to do it to him.

'Arrrggghhhh!' I slam my hands repeatedly against the steering wheel, hitting them on the leather until my palms sting, then numb. I should've had the strength to leave a long time ago. I've been too weak, too pathetic. Mercy was right. Whatever the truth turns out to be, we needed each other. I have been her strength as she's been mine. She's certainly gone to great lengths to show me that I don't really need Jamie – that I was hanging on to him for dear life for all the wrong reasons.

I have a sudden desperation to make him suffer. How dare he treat me like this?

Jamie's car slows just after the Rydon pub. He's approaching the speed humps that litter all the roads in this area. I back right off. I don't want him to catch a glimpse of my car in his rear-view mirror. I give it a few seconds, then follow. We're deep in the estate now, so it's clear he's heading for a specific house – there's nothing else now we've passed the pub and, as far as I remember, none of these roads take you out of the town, it's the opposite direction to the dual carriageway. Saliva floods my mouth and I swallow repeatedly as I squint to find his car. The problem with following so far behind is I could have easily missed his destination because there are so many roads off-shooting this one.

My foot slams on the brake. Ahead, I spot Jamie walking up a driveway. Shit, I hope he doesn't look my way, I've nowhere to hide. I duck down. Not that it'll help, he'll recognise the car. He's parked directly outside this house, not further up, like I'd expect of someone not wanting to be caught out having an affair. Arrogant. Even after I've just accused him and he denied it. In this moment, I hate him.

I give it a few minutes, then carry on driving up the hill. Both hands shake violently on the wheel, my thighs tremble, making it difficult to negotiate the pedals. I almost stall the car as I get level with Jamie's, but manage to keep going, kangarooing past. I hope no one is watching. No doubt *he'll* be too preoccupied.

I turn so I'm facing down the hill, but I stay a fair distance away. New rainfall splatters the windscreen, obscuring my view of the house he's in. The wipers swish across, clearing it, but the rain is so heavy it's immediately obliterated again. I can afford to get a bit closer, so I edge my car towards the redbrick semi-detached house until it's clearly visible on my right-hand side. I can watch the door,

263

see him come out. If he does. He might stay there all night. My muscles twitch and jump; I want to get out. Do something. I want to bang on the door, make sure he knows I know. Pressure builds and builds inside me until it's unbearable.

In a blind rage, I rummage in my glove box. Finding what I need, I slip it up my sleeve, then, checking the surrounding area to make sure no one's watching me, I get out the car. The sheets of rain assault me, and within seconds my hair is plastered against my scalp and my jumper is wet, heavy – but I don't care. There's no CCTV around here, or not that I'm aware of. But some people's homes may well have those video doorbells, so I should be as inconspicuous as possible. I reach back into the car, grab a cap and pull it low over my eyes, then cross the road, my head turning in each direction. When I'm confident I'm not being watched I crouch down beside the car. Taking the tool from my sleeve, I flick out the knife. With a satisfying force, I slash the knife into the nearside tyre of Jamie's BMW. Then the other. That'll teach him.

Outside the house I saw Jamie enter, I stand motionless, drenched to my skin and numb with cold. Is he entering her right now? There's movement inside, the soft glow of light letting me see just enough. I sneak closer. I want to know exactly who this woman is, yet at the same time I'm afraid to find out. I position myself behind a large shrub on the edge of the garden and I watch, heart beating out my chest. They aren't close – they're sitting apart, and the woman isn't Mercy.

Should I feel relieved? I could well have jumped to all the wrong conclusions – been too rash. All this time I've been holding everything together, not sharing my fears, my suspicions, because, deep down, I didn't want to face it. Then, in one fell swoop, I've let loose and given Jamie both barrels. I bet this woman is a colleague – one of those ones he shares his life stories with. And right now he's probably sharing how his wife has just lost it and accused him of having an affair. Will he be asking for her expert advice? I feel as though my insides are withering with humiliation. Why didn't I hold off? A numbness replaces my anger – there's a sudden and inexplicable emptiness in my stomach, my heart – my head.

There's nothing to think about anymore. I turn to leave.

But I can't. And, like I'm being pulled by an invisible magnet, I move closer to the window. One step, another . . . my feet acting as though disconnected from my brain.

They're going to see you, Erica.

Ignoring my internal warning, and oddly unafraid of being caught lurking outside, I draw close enough that I see my own reflection in the glass of the window. Jamie and the woman are too engrossed in talking to look my way. If I'm not going to bang on the window to alert them to my presence, I may as well go. My limbs are heavy as I slowly begin to turn away.

And that's when I see someone else in the room. Jamie stands to greet her. Where did she come from? She must've already been in the house as no one has walked past me. As she sits down next to Jamie, he leans in and kisses her. My heart skips a beat.

As Jamie sits back, the woman's face comes into view.

It's Mercy.

Chapter 47

Erica

What the fuck is going on? I stumble backwards as though an invisible force is pressing against my chest, pushing me. This is a trick, an illusion. Has to be. I right myself, before stepping back behind the shrub. I scrunch up my eyes, then relax them, suck in a deep breath and take another look. Jamie is in the house with two women – one of whom is definitely Mercy, there's no mistake. I pull my gaze away. My head is spinning, my brain not able to join the dots. Half an hour ago we were sitting at the table and it was only my accusation that sent Jamie hurrying out the house. Wasn't it? Supposing he'd been going out anyway, and just used the opportunity I gave him to go without having to explain himself? I inadvertently provided him the perfect reason to storm out of the house, but all along his plan had been to come here. To meet Mercy at this woman's house. But why?

As I look around, I spot a small plaque on the wall of the house to the left of the front door. It's raining too hard to decipher the wording, but it looks like a professional sign. Like those used by therapists who work from home. A jolt of adrenaline shoots through me. Are Jamie and Mercy having couple therapy? The thought is madness, but at the same time makes total sense if my earlier theory is correct. If they've lost a child, then maybe they're having sessions to cope with their grief. But if they're no longer together, why on earth would they be *here* together?

Because he's planning to leave you.

Perhaps he left me a long time ago. And it's me who hasn't come to terms with *my* loss. I can't bear to look any longer; can't bear to even think about what I've seen and what it means. I could hammer on the door, confront them and hear all their lies, or I could leave with a minuscule amount of pride intact and go about uncovering their lies in a more dignified way.

Despite the hot ball of anger heavy in my stomach, I choose the latter and slope back to my car and drive away. Tears distort my vision, the rain on the windscreen adding to my reduced visibility. With each speed bump I go back over, a little bit more of me fades. It's as if the life is being sucked from me and, in a few minutes, all I'll be is an empty sack of skin. I'm at the dual carriageway before I realise I've driven that far.

If I put my foot down flat, close my eyes, I could let fate decide what happens next.

A voice fills my head: *Are you really going to give up so easily? You deserve more. This isn't the end – it's your beginning.*

It's what I wanted, wasn't it? I have been practising my 'Dear Jamie' speech for ages, now I don't have to bother. A sob erupts from somewhere deep inside me. Who am I trying to kid? If I truly wanted to leave him, I'd have done it by now. I've been hesitating, putting it off for a reason. The reason, though, isn't clear – not really. Everything is cloudy, like I'm in a room filled with steam. It's all so complex, probably only a therapist would be able to unpick it. Maybe I should turn back, waltz into the house with Jamie and ask *his* therapist if she offers a discount for group bookings.

I laugh. At the absurdity of the situation or my own ridiculous thoughts, I don't know, but, once I start, I can't stop. Tears run down my face, my lungs hurt from the manic laughter. I'm reminded of the time I consumed a handful of magic mushrooms, when I thought I'd literally die laughing. But soon, it'd given way to crying. Hysterical sobbing.

And that's just what happens now.

I grip the steering wheel, hunch over it as the sobs rack my body. Where shall I go? I can't return home – and I'm not in the mood to talk to Jean, especially as she appeared a bit cold towards me earlier. I've half a mind to call Wes. He's the only other person who I've spoken to recently. My friend Bea has no clue what's been going on in my life; if I rock up at hers, it'll be awkward.

I lose track of time as I drive aimlessly, no destination in mind. My petrol light flashes; I've five miles left in the tank. Who cares if I run out in the middle of nowhere? No one will even know for hours. If Jamie chooses to stay out all night, he won't miss me until morning. Though I'm guessing if it's Mercy – or should I call her *Gemma* now – he's going to stay with, he'll go to her cabin.

The cabin. Of course.

If Mercy is busy with my husband and the therapist, I've time to go to the cabin and turn the place inside out. If the child found dead in the woods is hers and Jamie's, I might find evidence of it there – things she's kept hidden so I wouldn't see them when I was visiting. Quite what I'll do with any evidence if I find it, I'm not sure. But I need to know for my own sake. He can wriggle out of the affair, deny all wrongdoing, but if I have proof the child was his, at least that gives me grounding; a valid reason to blame him for everything that's gone wrong in our marriage.

I can't allow him to make me out to be paranoid, stupid for jumping to conclusions – or, worse, say I'm imagining it all. Jamie's always been good at talking himself out of situations – he has certainly had enough practice over the years while working in forensic psychology. I won't let him talk his way out of this.

Bolstered by my decision, I sit up straight, flick on the radio and pull off the dual carriageway. After doubling back, I head out of Newton and take the turning that'll bring me out on the road I need to follow to get to Mercy's. After a few minutes the glow of streetlights decrease, each pole getting further and further apart until they disappear completely. I force down the rising anxiety branching up from my stomach into my mouth. There's something innately scary about the dark. Rainclouds still obscure the moonlight, so I don't even have that as reassurance.

I pull into a passing space as I spot a car approaching, but the landscape becomes more remote the further I travel. There are no headlights in sight, no house lights even. It's as though I'm all alone in the world, like everyone else has simply disappeared. In the darkness, the dirt tracks appear even more narrow, they're bumpier, more eerie. It all looks so different at night. The roads are longer. It feels like an age before I reach the fork in the road and take the left one. The cabin comes into sight, but instead of my muscles finally relaxing, they tighten further – sharp pains stab at me like knives. Now I'm here, I'm suddenly unsure. Once I cross the line, break into Mercy's house, there's no going back.

So no one will be able to see my car from the front, I continue driving around to the back of the cabin, my tyres crunching and slipping on the uneven ground. I hope I don't get stuck in the mud here. Something even darker than the night catches in the beam of my headlights and I gasp, my foot involuntarily slamming on the brake. Is someone here? I lurch forwards, taking my eyes off it, and when I straighten it's gone. My heart flutters, my blood running cold. There's a structure there, looks like a well. Was that what I saw? I could've sworn it was a person, that they moved. My eyes flit around the car, but nothing is visible beyond the beam of the car headlights.

The most sensible thing would be to turn the car around and drive back home. I look at the fuel gauge. The needle is on empty. It's never precise, though, I'm sure. They're bound to manufacture cars with a little leeway, aren't they? Empty probably means I've a few miles left in the tank. I look around again, wondering if it was just my imagination – my heightened emotions playing tricks. There's no one else here. It's just me and the wildlife. That's probably what I saw. A fox or something. Yes, that'll be it.

It's almost eleven. If I attempt to go home now and run out of petrol, alone in my car in the complete darkness of the lanes, that's a far scarier prospect than remaining here, breaking into the cabin and staying inside until daybreak, then driving back. Running out of fuel in the broad daylight I can cope with.

271

Mind made up, I kill the engine. The headlights stay on for a few moments, then extinguish, leaving me in a pitch-black void. Quickly, I tap my torch app on my mobile. I jump at the sight of my own face reflected back at me in the windscreen.

'Fucking hell.' The words come out as a hoarse whisper and I shake my head to clear it of the cloud of fear. I'm not cut out for spooky adventures. I never watched the horror films everyone else raved about – the scariest thing I've seen is *The Little Vampire* and that's a kids' film. A shiver judders through my body and I look down at my sodden clothes. I need to get into dry ones. I slowly get out the car. The density of the trees seems to protect me from the rain – only a light drizzle reaches me. I hold up my phone so the torch app can light my way as I stealthily circumnavigate the cabin to find the best entry point.

It takes a while to come full circle. There are four windows in total, but they're all fairly high off the ground and it would be a struggle to climb in, especially if I break the glass. The front door is in clear view if a car were to come this way, so that's risky, despite the unlikeliness of a random person driving by. Still, the back door looks the best bet so I step onto the wooden veranda and tiptoe across it. I'm not sure why I'm creeping, it's not like I'm going to wake anyone. Mercy is with Jamie and no one else lives here. But I should hurry this along in case she comes back soon.

Moving the light around the ground, I find a stone I can use to break the glass. With some effort, I pull off my soggy jumper and wrap the stone inside it, then bash it with a short, sharp movement against the glass pane near the handle. There's a dull clink, then a cracking noise, but it doesn't shatter. I sigh. I need to do it harder.

I bring my arm back further, then slam it against the pane again. This time, shards of glass fall into the cabin with a tinkling sound as they hit against each other and fall onto the doormat. With my hand wrapped in my jumper, I push it through and unlock the door. The crunching of splintered glass as I walk over it sounds loud in the eerily silent room. Pressure builds in my skull, as if my brain is warning me not to continue. I stand still, waiting for it to pass. But the pain is all I can focus on. I drop my jumper and mobile as both hands cup my head. Thankfully, as quickly as it came on, it's gone. Now, in the darkness, my heart races as I try to remember where I am and why I'm here. It's like being in the throes of a nightmare, that experience of pure panic and disorientation before realising it's only a dream.

'You're in Mercy's cabin,' I say quietly. 'Pull yourself together, Erica.'

I bend to feel around for my phone, then after fumbling with it, I manage to aim the torch app around the room. It's not how I remember it.

The few times I'd been here, it was spotless. I'd been surprised at that, having assumed, due to Mercy's appearance, that her house would be messy. But that is just how it is now. An unnerving feeling makes my skin tingle. The place is in total disarray – like someone was looking for something in a hurry. I'm hoping it was Mercy herself who was the one searching.

Or it was the figure I thought I saw outside.

Had I disturbed the person responsible for doing this? Maybe they thought I was Mercy and scrambled as my car approached. The thought doesn't do much for my nerves and I shiver. Ignoring the mess, I head for the second door that goes off the main room in the cabin. I've not been in this room before, only Tia's. With a hesitant push, the door creaks open. I'm already cold from my wet clothes, but now an icy chill invades my body. I stand, rooted to the spot on the threshold of Mercy's bedroom. It's immaculate, as the rest of the cabin had been the last time I visited. And on a small wooden dresser sits a framed photograph of a couple. I'm too far away to see the detail, but it's obvious who they are. They're sitting encased in each other's arms. From the closely cropped dark hair and familiar face, I know the man is Jamie.

My lip curls: I want to snarl like a dog at the photo but as I run at it, swiping it from the dresser, all anger seeps away and instead an overwhelming sadness envelops me. I pick it up, place it back exactly how I found it. They belong together.

At least this is physical proof.

I sit on Mercy's bed, shivering and rubbing my hands together. I could lie down right here, maybe hypothermia will take me. But I don't want to die on a bed where my husband has likely fucked another woman. I spring up and start rummaging through Mercy's clothes for something dry to wear.

'This bloody thing!' I say out loud as I find her grey coat hanging in the small oak wardrobe. Although, at least she's gone out wearing something different this evening. Dressed up because she's meeting Jamie, no doubt. Has it all been an act? I grip the material of the coat, screwing it up as I clench it in my fist while my mind struggles to make sense of it all. I can't understand why Mercy would've gone to such great lengths to create this . . . this *hoax*. Why?

To steal my life.

I've been well and truly suckered.

I tear the coat from the hanger and storm out of Mercy's room with it, open Tia's bedroom door and throw it inside, tears stinging my eyes. I can't stand to see it, or Tia's room again. I slam the door and return to Mercy's wardrobe.

After I've dressed in a pair of Mercy's jeans and an oversize hoody and taken a bottle of water from Mercy's cool box, a huge wave of exhaustion overwhelms me and nausea churns my stomach. My eyelids are heavy, swollen from crying, and every breath I take is a huge effort. It's like I've been drugged. I need to lie down. I drag the large blanket off the back of the sofa and settle myself on the two-seater, pulling the blanket over me. Even though it's been a horrific night, I'm comforted by the soft, brushed cotton – there's a familiarity about it. I think it's the one Mercy placed over me when I tripped on the rug that first time I was here. My eyes close and I'm carried off on a cloud; I feel as light as helium as my brain shuts down.

Chapter 48

Wes

Wes looks down at her as she sleeps and sways a little. He's been off-kilter, he knows that – the usual things he finds exciting and derives pleasure from aren't doing it for him. His mother is right. She usually is.

A good woman would straighten him out.

But they're not the ones he goes for. For some reason that he's never been able to fathom, he prefers women who aren't exactly within his reach. Ones who are older, or married, or otherwise unattainable. Saves having to spend precious time getting to really know someone and it means he doesn't have to share himself, let them into his headspace, his house. Wes takes a shuddering breath and drapes the fallen blanket over her still body. If he's honest with himself, it's also to prevent having to bare any emotions, because once they're on the table, getting tangled up in proceedings, that's when the trouble really starts. The thought of an actual relationship makes his head spin. Much better to love them and leave them than to get involved in all that feeling stuff.

Or, that's how he felt until recently. Until the mess inside his head started to untangle, and he began to understand some things he'd been struggling with. She seems to trust him – *wants* his help; that's why he drove to the cabin, so that he could do the right thing.

But he knows he shouldn't really be here – it's not the right time. He creeps out the front door, careful not to disturb her.

In the darkness, he crouches and rewatches the CCTV footage, a dull ache squirming inside his gut. This is what she was after but hiding it a little longer might be more beneficial in the long run. The truth can wait.

Wes drops his phone and presses a hand to his face, his fingertips becoming wet. Then, he lowers his head to his knees and softly cries as he remembers that day.

MEETING 7

Chapter 49

Erica

I awake with a start.

Sunlight pours through the gingham curtains and I'm momentarily dazed, unsure where I am, why I'm not at home. Then, like I've been hit by a bulldozer, my memory of the past evening's events floods back, knocking the wind from me. I sit up, gasping. But even taking large gulps of air, none seems to reach my lungs. It's a panic attack, I'm sure, but as a pain crushes my chest it crosses my mind it might be a heart attack. I check around me for my mobile, but my trembling hands don't find it.

Oh God, oh God, oh God. This is it.

'You looking for this?'

I turn at the sound of the voice and my heart leaps.

Mercy is standing behind me, my mobile in her hand. I open and close my mouth, but no words form.

'Won't do you any good, you know that. No signal.' She slowly walks around the sofa until she's opposite me, but she keeps her distance.

I still can't catch my breath. I reach my hand out, but

then pull it back and put it on my chest, feeling the panicked beat of my heart against my palm.

'Pl . . . ease . . .'

'Erica. Calm down,' she says, lurching towards me. 'Slow breath in. Hold it . . . One, two, three, four, five. Gently blow it out.' She ducks down in front of me, guiding me, breathing with me to help me overcome the attack. I both love and hate her in the same second. After a few more minutes, my breathing is steady. Normal.

'You can always dial 999,' I say, my eyes narrowed. Of course, that's dependent on whether there are other networks available but I don't say this because Mercy is likely right – there's literally no reception from *any* network here. That realisation makes my palms sweat.

'The crisis was averted; it wasn't needed.' Mercy gives a tight smile. Is she intending to come across as nasty? It certainly feels that way, like she's taunting me. Not allowing me to get to my phone – to alert Jamie of my whereabouts. With a shiver, I realise that perhaps he already knows where I am. I hold my hand out.

'Can I have it, please?' I stand up, so I'm level with her. I don't want to be in a submissive position sitting on the sofa while she towers above me. I've had enough of power games. Mercy looks down at my phone in her hand. I note that her clothes are different today – more modern, clean-looking. Neat. It strikes me that I might not have been looking at her properly – seeing only what I wanted to see. She hasn't asked what I'm doing in her cabin, it must be clear I've broken the glass in the door to get inside.

Ah. Maybe that's why she seems wary, why she appears less than willing to give me my phone. I am the intruder, after all.

'Sorry about that,' I say, pointing to the splintered glass on the doormat. 'You weren't in and I didn't know what else to do.' I'm amazed at how calm I sound, when in my head a different scenario is playing out. One where I'm yelling that she's a liar, that she's Gemma, that I know about her affair with my husband. That Tia was their baby.

'No problem.' Mercy shrugs, giving the broken glass a quick glance before locking eyes with mine. 'I was expecting you.'

My mouth dries. 'What do you mean?' Is this it? Where she finally comes clean about what the hell has been going on?

'Well, I knew it wouldn't be too much longer before you figured it all out. I was aware my time was running out.' Mercy sighs, and my stomach flips with anticipation of what's to come. She flings my phone at me and I quickly pocket it as she walks to the kitchen area. 'I think we should have a little chat. Drink?' She opens a cupboard, pulls two champagne flutes out and places them on the table.

'Um, no. No thanks, I'm good.' I rub my hand over my forehead, wooziness swooping in.

'It might help,' Mercy says, pouring liquid from a carafe. Not champagne, clearly. 'Here. This'll take the edge off it.' She thrusts the glass into my hand. 'Sorry for the inappropriate glass, I don't have tumblers here; there's limited supplies.'

I sniff the brown liquid.

'Brandy,' she says. 'It's warming. You look like you could do with it.'

'It's been a long night,' I say, through gritted teeth. I'm not sure how to play this – it's like waiting to see who will sacrifice their chess piece first to achieve an advantage.

'Cheers. It's at least a little different seeing you here first on a Friday. We giving Bateman's a miss today?' I take a tentative sip, screw my nose up as the liquid burns the back of my throat.

'Yes. On both counts.' Mercy looks around, a look of annoyance on her face. 'You had quite the rummage, I see.'

I frown, then remember. 'Oh, this wasn't me. It was like this when I got here.' I take another swig. She was right, it is warming.

Mercy's nostrils flare as she expels a sharp puff of air. 'Sure. Did you find it? What you were looking for?'

'Really, it wasn't me. I think someone was here just before I got here, though. I'm sure I saw a figure lurking outside, near the well. But they disappeared when my headlights picked them up.'

'Oh, Erica.' She shakes her head. 'You really don't know?' She swirls her drink around in the glass. She hasn't drunk any and too late I think it could be because she's laced it with something. Poison?

'Know what?' I wish I hadn't fallen asleep. I wonder if she used that opportunity to remove the proof that she and Jamie had been together. That the 'missing' Tia was their child. I need to question Mercy right now – sit her down and get her to admit their child died. That she's not merely missing. I have to tell her that I know she and Jamie have been seeing a therapist, that I witnessed them all cosied up at her house last night. Tell her I know she's stealing my life.

But for some reason, all the words stick to my tongue and I can't form them or get them out of my mouth. I want to scream at her that I do know. I know everything.

But I can't speak.

My legs shake and my head becomes heavy. The glass slips from my hand as my grasp weakens. With no control over my body, I tumble backwards. Just like when I was here before, only this time, the sofa breaks my fall.

I'm vaguely aware of Mercy moving about the cabin as my eyes close.

Chapter 50

Erica

A door slams.

My eyelids lift, slowly, with huge effort; they feel like they have weights on them. Then they flutter closed again.

A sensation of being on a boat wakes me. As I open my eyes, more easily this time, I'm greeted by Jamie's face looming over me, his hands on my arms, gently shaking me.

'What . . . I don't . . . How did you get here?' I sit bolt upright, the blanket slipping from me.

'Slowly, slowly. It's all right, Erica. Did you take something?'

'Where is she? No, I didn't take anything. She put something in my drink! Did you save me?'

'Shhh-shhh, Erica, please.' Tears make the green of his eyes sharper. 'I'm sorry.'

'So you fucking should be.' The events of last night and from when I first awoke this morning, flood back and suddenly I'm standing, squaring up to my cheating husband. 'Is she in her room?' I stomp around, my head splitting with a crushing pain. A hangover, it feels like. 'The bitch *drugged* me,' I shout, pushing Mercy's bedroom door wide open. The metal handle bangs, like a gunshot, against the wooden wall. She's not in there. I run outside and call her name. Nothing. With each passing second of silence, my confusion doubles.

'What are you doing, Erica?' Jamie says.

'Where is she?' I demand to know, as I push past Jamie on the veranda and stomp back into the cabin.

'Where's who?'

'Bloody Mercy. Or Gemma, or whatever her name is.'

'Gemma?' The frown lines intensify. 'Sit down, Erica. Please. We should talk.'

'Damn right, you *liar*,' I spit. I launch myself at him, jabbing my finger into his chest. '*I'm not having an affair, Erica*,' I say, mocking his voice. 'God. You must think I'm a pushover. So easy to manipulate. You've learned well from your fucking inmates, haven't you. Well, turns out you can't have your cake and eat it, *Jamie*.'

'No.' He drops down on the leather footstool, his head in his hands.

'Not so cocky now you've been caught out, eh?'

'I've never been cocky. All I've been doing is trying to get through each day.' There's no power to his voice; it's weak. Broken. The words uttered as though he's said the same ones over and over. Has he? Have we been through this argument already? 'It's okay, Erica,' he says. 'I know you're confused right now. It'll be all right soon.'

'Yeah, it will. Because I'm leaving you, Jamie. Something I should've done a long time ago but never quite found the courage to. Until Mercy.' I huff. 'Jesus, it's ironic. She was so keen for me to gain the strength to leave you, and now I know why. Because she wants you. You and her want to be together, don't you? Just admit it.'

'No, love. I can't admit what isn't true.' His eyes plead with mine, but I can't let him off the hook. I won't stand for any more lies.

'Sure. You tell yourself that, you coward.' I storm into Mercy's room to grab the photo of Jamie and her. The dresser is clear – no framed photo. I check the floor. Obviously I didn't pick it back up like I thought. Nothing. Of course – Mercy will have taken it. I let out an animal-like groan. Now what?

I wonder if Tia's photo might still be in her coat pocket though. I can show him that at least – see how he reacts to being confronted with a picture of his daughter. My heart flutters as I remember where I threw it in my state last night. I have no choice but to go into Tia's bedroom. I hesitate with my hand on the door knob.

'Erica, wait. What are you doing?' Jamie's voice is close behind me now. I ignore him and go inside Tia's bedroom. The giraffes on the wall cause my breath to freeze in my lungs, like it's the first time I'm seeing them. Mercy *has* copied my room, I'm sure of it. She stole my future child's room design and she's stealing my husband to boot. I shake myself out of my thoughts and remember why I'm in here. I'm relieved to see the grey heap on the floor. Can I dare to hope that Mercy left the photo in it? She's always had it on her when we've met. With a deep breath and no expectation, I snatch up the coat and delve my hand into the pocket.

It's there. Did she leave in that much of a rush she forgot it? I pull out the little girl's photo and stride back towards Jamie.

'Have you seen her?' I thrust the photo into his hand. 'Do you recognise this little girl?'

His face pales. Yes. I've got him – he can't wriggle out of this now. 'Well?'

Tears fill his eyes and I feel a pain deep in my stomach. Am I being cruel doing this? I wanted him to suffer when I realised he'd been cheating, but all of a sudden this seems all wrong and I have the urge to hug him – hold him in my arms and cry with him, tell him I'm here for him no matter what.

'Yes, Erica. Yes. I recognise her, okay. Are you happy now?' He turns away from me, still holding the photograph, slumping down onto the sofa.

The fire inside me extinguishes, his words pouring cold water on them.

I sit down beside him. It's time to hear the truth.

Chapter 51

Dr Connie Summers

Bateman's external CCTV – transcript of requested CCTV footage

CAMERA 6 – TIMING: 00:01:38 Small child exits the store. Can't see clearly, but she appears to go out and to the left.

CAMERA 8 – TIMING 00:01:56 A white van is seen, partially obscured by trees surrounding park area. Side door appears to open.

CAMERA 8 – TIMING 00:02:45 Child is seen walking alongside the far fencing of park area.

CAMERA 8 – TIMING 00:2:59 Van leaves. Unable to gain visual of driver.

No further sighting of child.

*

Devon Live

A murder investigation is under way following the discovery of a child's body in Berry's Wood near Newton Abbot.

Police were called at 06:05hrs on Wednesday, 21 September after a dog walker reported the find.

Officers attended along with the South Western Ambulance Service and the child was pronounced dead at the scene. The death is being treated as suspicious, but no arrests have been made.

Detective Chief Inspector Lucinda Burnley, who is leading the investigation, said: 'This is a tragic incident and we are carrying out a number of enquiries to piece together the circumstances that led to a child losing their life.'

This comes following the report last week of a missing girl, thought to have been abducted from Bateman's supermarket. Police have yet to confirm the identity of the child, but said: 'A number of enquiries will be carried out in the area over the coming days, and it is likely that the local community will continue to see a high level of police activity. We thank them for their support and if anyone has any information please call 101, quoting reference number 0703.'

Connie angles her chair so it faces towards the window. She wants to spot them before they reach the front door. A few minutes spent preparing herself is better than none. Her erratic heart rate might have an extra bit of time to calm, settle into its usual rhythm. Although she doubts that. Everything has been building to this moment. It's not how she'd planned it, but these things are rarely predictable.

Her notes about Mercy lie open on the desk, together with details of past sessions over the last year. The nature of her client's problems means Connie isn't sure quite what she'll be faced with. They'll be here shortly. All of them, hopefully. She's prepared as best she can. The right people have been involved this time, she's researched well. What could possibly go wrong?

Connie hears the slam of a car door. Then another.

Pushing her shoulders back and taking a deep, diaphragmatic breath, she stands and walks to the front door.

Chapter 52

Then

The girl's gaze didn't waver. She kept her focus straight ahead of her as she walked through the play area adjacent to the supermarket. Few people used it and today, with the remnants of a storm the previous night, it was deserted.

The perfect conditions to commit the perfect crime.

Her mouth formed a tiny 'O' shape when she saw who was waiting for her beside a white van. She paused, a frown settling on her forehead. She turned to walk away, but the toy she'd been holding fell from her grip and so she stooped to pick it up. She had a sudden sensation of weightlessness as her legs came off the ground and, before she could yelp in surprise, something rough covered her mouth and the world went black.

Chapter 53

Erica

'You need to tell me everything, Jamie.'

'I'm not sure I can.'

'Shall we start with Tia?' I reach across Jamie and touch my fingertip to the fading photo, but don't look at the girl. He's gripping it tightly with both hands, his face contorted. 'When did you know she was yours?'

Ever so slowly Jamie turns his head to look at me and the pain in his eyes steals my breath. His chin wobbles, his barely contained emotion threatening to erupt. 'Always,' he says, and I pull back, the single word sending a shockwave through me.

'Why didn't you tell me? I don't—'

'Erica, stop. Just . . .' He stands, placing the photo on the table. 'Just stop. Please.' He begins pacing and I watch, my thoughts and feelings all jumbled.

'But I need to know! You owe me an explanation. How did you get here, anyway?' He couldn't have driven his car. Unless he got the tyres replaced quickly. I check my mobile for the time. It's late morning – I've been here hours; Lord knows what's been going on in the time since Mercy drugged me. 'Oh my God. Did you come here with Mercy and stand in the shadows while she plied me with drugs? Did you both plan to knock me out for the count, so you had time to figure out what to do with me?' The tendons in my neck tighten as heat flares, making my face hot.

'No, no, no. Look, you have it all so very wrong. Fuck!' His voice rises as he roughly runs his hands over his hair. 'I can't do this on my own,' he says.

'Ahh, so you need Mercy to wade in now? Are you leaving it up to her to spill the beans? Tell me how she's manipulated me, dragged me into her fucked-up game. How she wants to take what's mine.'

'Not exactly. Will you come with me?' He holds out a hand, but I bat it away. 'Please, Erica. I want to explain properly.'

I look around the cabin. 'Fine. I don't want to stay here anyway.' I also know I don't have enough petrol to get me out of this hellhole, so I kind of need him. He heaves a huge sigh of relief and heads to the door. I follow.

'Whose car is that?' I say, noting the bright blue Ford Escort parked a few metres from the door.

'Well, Erica, my car was *vandalised*, but you know that don't you? I was given this one on loan and we need to take it back now.' The fob in Jamie's outstretched hand unlocks the doors with a beep and he opens the passenger side and holds it open for me to climb in.

'Oh, I get it. We're going to the place you and Mercy go to for your grief counselling or whatever.'

Jamie gives a gentle shake of his head, but his eyes are filled with sorrow. Or guilt. He knows he's screwed up and now there's no getting away from it. 'Yes, I'm taking you there.'

My pulse pounds in my ears. 'Is Mercy going to be there?'

The silent pause stretches, then I hear a whispered 'Yes.' My heart slams against my ribcage almost as hard as Jamie slams the door closed.

Chapter 54

Erica

'I – I don't want to go,' I say as Jamie gets in and starts the engine. I go to pull the handle, but there's a loud click. He's activated the lock; I'm trapped in this car.

He says nothing as I rant at him, keeping his eyes dead ahead like he can't hear me. He's blocking me out. Like I'm nothing to him.

I grip the sides of the seat, each hump we go over jolting my brain against my skull.

'I'm going to be sick.'

'It'll be the meds you took, I expect.'

'That I took? You mean that your *mistress* gave to me!' I gag – a dry retch that scores my throat. 'Pull in,' I say, grappling with the electric window so I can get air.

Jamie does as I ask and unlocks the door in time for me to empty my guts at the side of the road. I feel better afterwards. He hands me a bottle of water and I thirstily gulp from it, almost choking on each mouthful but now so desperate for liquid, I don't care if I throw it all back up again.

'Better?'

'It helped. I don't think I'll ever feel better again, though, Jamie. You and Mercy have destroyed any hope of that.'

'I'm sorry for all of this.' He says it like his apology is good enough to make it all go away.

'For lying to me? Not telling me about the child you had with your ex, or that you've been having an affair with her? Or are you sorry I met Mercy? You did try and warn me,' I shrug. 'At least now I know why.'

Except, I don't, really – not the reasons for all of this. Why, why, why would they concoct such an elaborate plan that included me in such a way? I've a million questions swarming inside my head and they're threatening to explode through my skull.

We're at the B&Q roundabout now. I've the speed humps to look forward to in a minute. I'd best brace myself for those. I sit with my arms clamped against my stomach – as if that'll somehow ensure none of its contents are expelled. Jamie takes the bumps slowly. Much more slowly than when I followed him last night. Then he was more desperate to get to the house. I'm guessing now he'd rather put it off for a few moments longer. Avoid the massive fallout he must know will come.

The liquid sloshes about in my tummy, but I manage to retain it. Jamie swings the car into the drive of the house I was standing outside last night.

'Oh, so it's your therapist's car you've borrowed. How nice of her. You shagging her too?' Jamie doesn't respond, just gets out of the car. I watch him as he walks around to my side and opens the door for me. 'I'm capable, thanks.'

An onerous dread sits inside me; I literally feel heavier as I attempt to walk to the therapist's front door. Now, in the day, and with no rain, I can see the plaque.

I frown. Not quite what I expected. I imagined the words: 'Couple Therapist' or similar, and minus the doctor title.

'That's quite hardcore,' I mutter. 'Know her from prison?'

'I do, yes,' Jamie says. He knocks on the door. 'She was a colleague.'

'And you chose *her* to counsel you and Mercy?'

He doesn't have a chance to respond because the door opens.

'Hi, Jamie,' the woman says, then looks to me. 'Come on in, Erica.'

'Clearly you've talked about me then. Does she know you're having an affair?' Neither the woman nor Jamie look directly at me as I enter the hallway. I'm not keen to hear whatever I'm about to be told, but I *am* eager to face Mercy. If I get to her first, I can cause *some* damage before Jamie and Connie step in. I walk into the room but there's no sign of Mercy yet.

Maybe they predicted what I might do, given what I did to Jamie's tyres.

'Take a seat, Erica,' Connie says, coming into the room and closing the door.

'Where's Jamie?' I stare at the door. 'Gone to get *her*, I suppose.'

'I wanted to speak with you alone, just for the moment. If that's all right with you, Erica?' The way she's saying my name is grating on my last nerve.

'I don't know why. It's him who needs to do the explaining.' My nerves skitter, causing one eye to twitch

303

– I press my fingers to it to stop it. 'That's why he brought me here, he said. So he could properly explain.'

'And he will,' Connie says, her voice soft. She smiles and something clicks.

'I've seen you before,' I say, my mind whirring. 'I mean, before last night. Jamie said you were a colleague – have we met?'

I have a vague memory of talking to Connie. Jamie went to a work do a few years back – some team-building activity with a meal in Exeter afterwards. I picked him up, but was early so ended up joining them in the restaurant for one drink. Did I chat with Connie then?

'Yes, we have.' Connie seems to freeze in mid-movement, like she's been paused by a TV remote. Then, she carries on reaching forwards, a folder in her hands. She holds it out for me to take.

'What's this?'

'A file,' Connie says. 'But before you open it, I'd like to talk about Mercy.'

'At fucking last! Thank you. That's apparently what I'm here for. To find out what the hell is going on with her and my husband. Why have you been counselling them both together? Is it because of Tia? Are they planning on being together?'

'Let's deal with one question at a time. So things don't get too confusing.'

'It's a bit late for that,' I say, slumping. 'Since I met Mercy literally *everything* has been confusing.'

'When did you meet her?' Connie crosses her legs, settling in her chair as though readying herself for a long story.

'I met her about six weeks ago? At Bateman's. She came

up to me when I was at the checkout and asked me if I'd seen her daughter. But she'd apparently seen me before; she'd already been watching me. Which, now I think about it, is very odd.'

Obviously, Connie doesn't share my take as she doesn't even blink. 'Can you recall what happened in the lead-up to her approaching you?'

'And the point of this is?' I pull at my fingers, click my knuckles. I don't understand how this is explaining anything.

'To obtain the full picture,' she says.

'Whatever. Well, I was shopping, obviously. Like I do every Friday. And the checkouts were rammed, so I cheated a bit – took my chocka basket to the ten items or less till, which annoyed Karen.'

'Karen?'

'The checkout woman. She was the one who acted all weird when Mercy came up asking if I'd seen her and thrusting a photo of Tia in my face.'

'Ah, I see. That was at the end of your shopping trip. Anything happen prior to the checkout?'

I'm genuinely baffled now. 'What's the relevance of that? Look, where's Jamie? He's the one you should be asking all the questions.'

'He'll be here in a moment. What happened when you started your shopping?'

The girl in the pink coat.

'Oh, of course. Right, well there was a little girl crying because she was lost and I took her to the customer service desk. That's it. But I did get confused when Mercy asked if I'd seen the girl in the photo, because initially I assumed it was her she was looking for. Of course, it turns out that

a) Mercy's child went missing a year ago, and b), sadly, Mercy's child was found dead in the woods outside of town. I only learned of this recently. And after some research that's when I realised that Mercy was really Jamie's ex and that they'd had the child together but Jamie never told me. You're seeing them to help them over their grief. What I need to know is why Mercy lied about who she was and held back the vital info that Tia was dead, and whether Jamie is leaving me for her.'

'That's certainly a traumatic tale. Would you like a glass of water?' Connie offers me a glass with iced water.

My mouth is dry from my rambling monologue, so I gladly take it and gulp it down.

'Yes. It is traumatic. And I felt so very bad for her to begin with. Couldn't get her, or the photo of the girl, out of my head. All I wanted to do was to help her. What an idiot I am.'

'Not at all,' Connie says. 'Can you open that file now please?'

I'd forgotten about it. It sits flat on my lap. I lift the cover. The first thing I see is the photo of Tia. 'This is the one Mercy showed me. And it's the same one I got from Mercy's coat pocket in the cabin.'

'Were there any other photographs there?'

'Oh, yes,' I say, jumping forward. I'd almost forgotten about it. 'There was one of Mercy and Jamie, but of course *she* took that after she drugged me.'

Connie nods. 'Is it this one?' She takes a photo from the file she has, and holds it up.

'Yes! Oh my God, how have you got that? Did she bring it to you?'

'Yes.'

'What is going on here, Connie?' A hot ball grows in my stomach.

'Can you look at it for me. Closely please.'

I do as she asks. 'What the . . .?' I shake my head. 'No, no. This isn't the same one I saw.'

The photo Connie has given me is one of *me* and Jamie.

I look up at her, desperation pulling my brow so low her face blurs. 'I'm not going mad. I *know* what I saw. Clearly she's swapped them.'

'Why would she do that?' Connie asks, her voice still calm. My own ability to remain composed is reducing by the second.

'Obviously to make me out to be delusional.' I turn in my chair, look desperately to the door. Where is Jamie?

'How many times have you seen Mercy?'

'Eight, maybe more. I saw her at my house once, I'm sure. She's definitely been inside my home because she left her jacket in my wardrobe. I suspect because she wanted me to know about her and Jamie without having to directly tell me.'

'Has anyone else seen her enter your house?'

'Jean did. She's my neighbour – lives opposite us.' I don't mention that Jean could only tell by her walk. 'She had her grey coat on. The one we actually binned in Bateman's car park because I'd bought her the nice new one.' I tut and shake my head. 'I still can't believe that.' Somehow, my annoyance about that has grown.

'And did anyone see you with her on that occasion?'

My eyes widen as I think. 'Yes, actually, one of Jamie's colleagues saw us because I was worried she'd tell Jamie. You see, I told him I wouldn't go shopping on a Friday anymore. He was keen for me to avoid Mercy.' I snort air from my nose. 'And now I know why.'

'Anyone else?' Connie says. She seems to be ignoring my responses, continuing with her agenda.

'What is this?'

'It's important to get a full picture.'

'Yes, so you keep saying.' A niggling worry begins worming its way around my gut. 'I wondered if she'd been stalking me, actually – there was an odd moment where she mentioned my Instagram posts yet she was adamant she was "off-grid". And my account is about my IVF journey, my desperation to have a child. Did she target me, do you think? Or is it simply because of her link with Jamie?'

Connie scratches her neck, avoiding eye contact with me, which immediately heightens my sense of unease.

'Maybe you found each other,' Connie says, but before I can respond to that, she carries on. 'So, did others see Mercy approach you?'

I sigh and begin fidgeting with the cuff of my shirt sleeve. 'Yeah. Wes, the security guy. He turned out to be very helpful, actually, in the end. He got hold of some CCTV . . .' I trail off, not sure I should be disclosing this to Connie. I don't want to get Wes into trouble.

Connie looks at her watch. 'Right, I think we should move on.'

'Move on?' I put my hands out, palms up, and shoot her what I hope is an annoyed glance. Connie gets up and walks to her computer, swivelling the screen so I can see it, then after a few taps on her keyboard, the dark monitor springs into life.

'You've got the footage?' My jaw slackens. 'How?'

'We both have our means, Erica.' Connie smiles, then sits back down, a remote in her hand. 'I'd like you to watch a few of these.'

The words *Internal: Bateman's* are at the top of the screen, then it flickers and the picture settles as the video starts. It's the same footage Wes recorded on his phone for me, only this looks rather more official – the original, rather than a recording made on a mobile. I watch it, just as I did the first time and the many after that.

'What did you see?' Connie says.

'Nothing of note. You can't say for certain if there's a little girl in this CCTV.'

'But you can see the woman in the blue coat?'

'Yes, I assume that's Mercy. Although the coat looks blue, it's actually an insipid-looking grey thing – the CCTV must distort the colour.'

Connie sighs gently, the sound like a small hiss of air coming from a hole in a balloon, but it irks me.

'Is there a problem with that?' I say.

'Hang on, Erica.' Connie stands and goes to the door, opens it and says, 'You can come in now.' Jamie walks in, his eyes darting around the room as if he's expecting others. Connie waits for Jamie to be seated before taking her own again.

'I've got something I need to tell you,' Connie says, and I swear I catch a shake in her voice. She points to the paused recording on the screen. 'This isn't Mercy in this footage, Erica.'

'It doesn't matter if it is or isn't,' I say. 'I'm not even sure this CCTV is from the right day when Tia was taken. Wes is looking at outside footage for me—'

Connie and Jamie share a look that serves to paralyse my vocal cords and I stop speaking. Jamie places his hand over mine and I hear Connie take a deep breath.

'It's not Mercy in this footage,' she says. 'It's *you*, Erica.'

Chapter 55

Then

Some people don't deserve children. How is it that the ones who fall pregnant with ease are those who take their little ones for granted? Why must others suffer years of pain before the joy of parenthood? Worse still, why are some never even given the opportunity? Destined to be childless, living with a sense of failure and emptiness – their journey never to end with a precious bundle of love in their arms. Their life's purpose never truly fulfilled.

The little girl was so close. Within reach. She was going to be mine.

She didn't deserve her, that's for sure.

Chapter 56

Erica

'You think *I* was involved in Tia's disappearance?' I clutch my hand to my chest as it tightens, panic taking a hold, fear gripping my heart until I think it'll be squashed like a tomato. How can they think this? Connie stares at me, a sympathetic smile playing on her lips that I have the urge to wipe from her face. I turn to Jamie. His features are set – he casts his gaze downwards. He can't even look at me. 'What's going on?' I hear the wobble in my voice; the underlying certainty that everything is about to get worse.

'Come on, Erica,' Jamie coaxes. 'Think.'

'Think? I am so lost, I've no idea what the hell you've brought me here for. I thought it was so you could explain why you lied to me, kept the fact Tia was *your* child from me. Why you lied about Mercy. And where is she, anyway?' My cheeks are on fire. I swing around in the seat, checking the door, which remains stubbornly closed. 'You said she'd be here.'

'Erica,' Jamie says, finally looking at me. 'Just let Connie explain, eh?' He takes my hands in his; tiny electric shocks tingle up my arms.

I swallow hard. 'Okay.' My entire body begins to shake. 'But if you're about to say I was the one responsible for abducting a three-year-old child, you can fuck right off.'

Jamie's head drops.

Shit. That's *exactly* what they're about to suggest. Are they setting me up? Or is this because they think I'm so desperate for a child I'd take someone else's?

I'd never do that.

Would I?

The room begins to spin as my brain loses oxygen.

'Breathe, Erica. Breathe,' Jamie says, his own voice trembling. I take some big gulps of air, attempting to compose myself.

'Okay, okay. I'm fine,' I say.

Connie sits forward in her chair now and forces me to lock eyes with her. 'Do I look familiar to you?' she says.

'We've covered this. You're a colleague of Jamie's. I've obviously met you sometime before . . .'

Connie flicks her gaze to Jamie, then back to me. 'I left the prison service some years ago. I have my own practice that I run from home.'

'Yes, obviously. And my husband and Mercy have been coming to see you for couples' therapy or something.'

'No. I have been seeing Jamie, that's true. But not as a client.'

For a horrifying second I think I've got it all wrong. *Connie* has been seeing Jamie? Is it her he's having the affair with?

'Can you just say whatever it is, please. God, I feel like you're drip-feeding me information and, to be truthful,

314

it's getting on my wick now. Are you being paid by the hour? Is that why you're dragging this out?'

'*You're* my client, Erica,' Connie says, firmly.

'Don't be so ridiculous.' I shoot up from the chair, knocking the cardboard file to the floor. 'I've had as much as I can take of all this bullshit.' I stride towards the door. Jamie's arms are on me, pulling me back. 'Let me go,' I say. Tears sting my eyes. 'I want to go now.'

'It's not going to be easy to hear the truth, Erica. But I think you know it's time.' Connie's voice is strong, commanding, and for some reason I listen and go back to my seat like an obedient puppy. Connie bends to scoop up the contents of the file I scattered, then sits back down. 'You are the woman in the CCTV,' she says.

I look to the screen, at the flickering image Connie paused the recording on.

'I don't own a blue – *or* grey – coat,' I say with a defiant shrug. 'Next.' I raise my eyebrows, daring Connie to show me something else.

'Okay,' Connie says, tapping on the keyboard. Another recording pops up on the screen. 'This shows you talking to Wes, the security guard at the supermarket.'

'As I say, he's been really helpful.' And I mutter under my breath, 'Unlike you.'

'Do you remember this exchange?'

I tut, get up and move closer to the screen, narrowing my eyes as Connie unpauses it. I watch myself, white jeans, cropped jacket, shopping basket in hand, at the end of the counter. A security guard stands close by, who I take to be Wes.

'It looks like the day I met Mercy . . . but . . . keep it running,' I say. 'I think this is when Mercy shows me the photo.'

Connie clicks on the button. I watch and wait, but it's all wrong. 'Hang on, this isn't the right day. Not the same footage because Mercy's not there. Why are you showing me this?'

'The day is Friday – the first day you met Mercy. As you described earlier.'

'Well, keep it going then, she'll be visible in a minute,' I say, impatiently.

'Erica, Wes never saw anyone else with you that day.' Connie is calm; measured – the opposite to how I'm feeling.

'What? He's lying because he knows he's going to get in trouble for sharing the CCTV with me.' I wait for a nod of agreement from her – I'm flailing and in need of some kind of lifeline. My mind screams to be let out of this nightmare. There is no nod. Connie gives a sympathetic smile before delivering the next sting.

'He only ever saw you.'

Her words hurt me, like physical weapons pelting my body, and I stumble backwards.

'That's not right,' I say, a surge of panic rising as quickly as the confusion. 'He was the one Karen got to escort Mercy off the premises. He must remember her. We've *talked* about her.' *Haven't we?* I pull at my hair, frustration threatening to overcome me. 'Okay, well your colleague from the prison saw her too – Sita,' I say, looking desperately to Jamie.

'No,' he says. 'Just you.'

What they're saying is incomprehensible. Why is everyone lying?

'Why would I make up a person? I'm not six, I don't have imaginary bloody friends!' My phone pings, offering me respite from this madness. I pull it from my pocket and see I have a new message. From Wes.

'Oh, perfect timing,' I say, shooting both Connie and Jamie a smug look. 'It's Wes. I asked him to send me the external CCTV. This will prove to you I'm telling the truth about Mercy. I try to ignore the pitying glance from Connie as I open the message.

Almost showed you last night but wimped out cos I wasn't sure I should, the first line of Wes's text says.

But now I've spoken to your friend and she promised me it's OK, I've attached the footage you asked for. Hope I'm doing the right thing. I'm so sorry about all of this. Take care, Erica.

Wes x

There! He mentions my friend. He must mean Mercy. I give an internal whoop! This will wipe the self-righteous expressions from their faces.

'Here, look, see? I told you. You'll see this has nothing to do with me.' I open the file attached to the message and CCTV footage showing a girl wandering on her own outside the store begins playing. 'See, she's on her own. *I'm* not the one who took her. This is evidence of that. Happy? Can we move on now to why the hell I'm here?' I stop the video, slamming my phone down on the arm of the chair.

'Oh, love.' Jamie frowns. 'The friend Wes is referring to isn't Mercy,' he says.

'Stop, Jamie. Enough,' I say. But he's not listening.

'Connie has been going to the store with you sometimes, to try to get you to remember.' He's speaking to me like I'm a child. I shake my head, first gently, then with increasing violence until I feel Jamie's hands on me, stopping me.

317

'Why are you doing this to me, Jamie?' Hot tears sting my cheeks.

'We're trying to help you.'

'The photo of you and Jamie in the folder . . .' Connie says, picking it up. 'You found this at the cabin, yes?'

'Yes, Mercy's cabin,' I say, more calmly.

'It isn't Mercy's cabin. It's yours and Jamie's.'

'It's our holiday home, Erica,' Jamie cuts in. 'We used to go there to get away from the stresses of our jobs. You loved its remoteness, the fact no one could contact us, remember?'

I'm fighting the memories that are beginning to edge into my consciousness. I screw up my eyes, will them to fade into oblivion again.

'You think I stole Mercy's child and took her to the cabin,' I say, flatly, all emotion gone. 'What? Then I killed her? How can you even suggest that?' Visions of my nightmares flash in my mind. Tia in the woods, her top messy. Fire. *What did I do?*

'No, we're not suggesting that, Erica.' Connie slips off her chair and kneels in front of me, and suddenly I'm sobbing.

'No, no. Don't tell me. Please don't say it.' I hear my begging voice and, inside me, something breaks.

'Say what?' Connie places her hands over mine. They're cool, and goosebumps spread up my forearms. 'You say it, Erica.'

'I can't.'

Jamie holds the photo of the little girl in front of me. 'Who's this?' he says.

I look into the girl's blue eyes, smile at the pretty freckles across her perfect nose. I pull my hands from beneath

Connie's and touch the girl's soft honey-blonde hair, run my fingertips over the cupid's bow of her lips. Tears drop on her face. I turn to look at Jamie.

'This is Letitia. Our daughter.'

Chapter 57

Erica

Connie appears relieved, her face relaxing as she speaks to me. I've obviously said the right thing. But it has the opposite effect on me.

'You've been coming to see me regularly for almost a year, Erica. Every Wednesday we have sessions here, and occasionally on a Friday I've accompanied you to Bateman's, where some of the staff have tried to understand the result we were hoping to achieve. Some others . . . well, they were less open, or lacked understanding, and unfortunately sometimes only added to your confusion.' She looks to Jamie. 'We've been employing various therapies, strategies and techniques to assist your recovery. And due to our respective professional backgrounds, more recently Jamie and I have devised some . . . well, I guess you'd call them experiments.'

'You've been *experimenting* on me? Are we in the Dark Ages? Is that even legal? Did you perform electric shock therapy too? Maybe a lobotomy is next on the list?' I'm suddenly furious, but deep down I know I'm just trying to protect myself – my psyche – from the truth.

'Your reaction now is kind of what you went through when Letitia died,' Connie says. 'You didn't, couldn't, deal with it at the time and you managed through a process of denial. Which, of course, is a common stage of grieving. Only you never really moved out of that stage, instead pretending it didn't happen.'

'But why would I do that? *How?*'

'You were diagnosed with a mental health condition known as DID – dissociative identity disorder. Do you recall that?'

I shake my head.

'Okay, well, basically what that means is you've called upon another personality to manage what was, and remains, a traumatic event . . . It affects your ability to connect with reality and sometimes it can cause you to lose chunks of memory or even hallucinate. The manifestation of DID for you is somewhat rare – it's not often that dissociated personalities *meet*, as you and Mercy have. You've got distinct personalities. Mercy's almost an opposite to you in appearance – and she has different traits. Even to the outside world, the people who know you, like Jamie, myself, Wes and Jean – they actually *see* a distinct change when you're Mercy. Although, seemingly not as pronounced as those you see when you're interacting with her.'

Everything Connie is saying is confusing, yet at the same time makes perfect sense, and things begin to click together. I clench my fists. I don't *want* them to click. I want to avoid this discussion, go back to being mad at Jamie. But Connie is persistent. She's not letting me off the hook that easily. She's not going to stop; she's going to hammer this home.

'Mercy was a personality your brain created to step in to help you cope.'

'But I only recently met her,' I argue.

'You only *remember* meeting her recently. She's been in your life before. She's been here, too – I've met Mercy and we've had full sessions in the past. This time, you summoned her following a particular trigger.'

'The lost girl in the pink coat,' I whisper.

'Yes. Seeing her triggered your memory of Letitia. It was that supermarket you were shopping in when your daughter wandered away from you, so the similarity brought it all back. You did well to manage that situation, but a consequence of it was that you felt the need to step into Mercy's shoes. It seems that you needed Mercy to help manage what was the most traumatic day for you – Fridays – but not the other six days of the week. Your alter was mainly contained then.'

'But *she* had a missing child. How is that helpful to me?'

'A missing child, not a deceased child.'

I wince at Connie's choice of words.

'You see, on that awful day, by the time you realised Letitia was no longer at your side a number of minutes had already passed. And during that time you'd been in deep conversation with . . .'

'Wes,' I say, my heart dropping. I put my hands to my mouth, begin to rock.

'It's okay, Erica. It's not your fault,' Jamie says.

'But it was, wasn't it. I was flirting with the bloody security guard instead of keeping an eye on our daughter. Is that why you hate me?'

'I don't hate you.' Tears shine in his eyes. 'We've been through all of this. It's you who blames yourself. Not me.'

'It's not just me, though, is it?' A flash of memory – of the vile online theories, the shocking belief that I was lying or had something to do with my own daughter's disappearance – shoots through my mind.

'No,' Connie says, gently. 'Some of the immediate responses on social media were from people commenting on the mother's role in what happened, and you internalised this. It resulted in you mentally spiralling, taking yourself out of the public eye entirely and hiding yourself away. Jamie was the one who faced the media, to help shield you, but you were aware of what was being said. The backlash from the general public contributed to the fact you stopped going out, stopped working, stopped seeing family and friends.'

'But . . . but, I went to the police,' I say, my thoughts and questions twisting and turning in my head. 'They said there was no missing child.'

'They didn't have the details of the missing Tia – or Mercy Hamilton of course – but the detective you talked with, DS Offord, eventually realised you were the mother of Letitia, that you were suffering with a mental health condition. In your file, she found my number and called me to ask how she should react to your questions. That's why you didn't get information from them the day you visited the station.'

'But there was nothing online either.' A niggling doubt keeps popping up – one telling me they're trying to trick me, pull the wool over my eyes. An image bursts into my head and out again as quickly. A little girl in a bed surrounded by giraffes. Then, an image that makes my breath hitch. A tiny body on a mortuary table. With a blink, it's gone.

Connie is speaking. 'You had your own filter. You blocked any mention about your daughter in the media from your brain.' Jamie clears his throat.

'Not just that,' he says, glancing at Connie before looking at me again. 'I was worried about your recovery – wanted to protect you from the worst of it. So . . . I put a key word blocker extension on your search engine. Your phone too.' I stare at him, suddenly unsure who the hell this man is. 'I thought I was doing the right thing . . .' He looks haunted and I wonder if the cause is me more than what happened to our daughter.

'How did she die?' My words sound muffled. Did I even say them out loud?

'For a number of hours, then days, hope was alive; people were looking for Letitia. Then,' Connie takes a breath, 'a dog-walker found her . . .'

Oh God. I don't want to hear. I don't want to remember. Fresh tears run down my cheeks – the skin so hot and tight it feels like it might split.

'A mother is meant to protect her children and I failed. No wonder I was hated.'

'That's when the IVF cover story began,' Connie says. 'You plunged headlong into your new online persona where people gave you sympathy. You related to others' stories as they were all about longing and desire for a child, and it gave you meaning and a partial outlet for your grief.'

'But it wasn't enough,' I say. A sense of inevitability washes over me, my ability to fight what's being said lessening with each revelation. 'I needed a friend. Mercy. Someone I could help and who would help me.'

'Yes. Mercy's role seems to have been to give you strength to move on. But also she was there to help you work through

Letitia's death, come to terms with it in your own time and own way. By helping Mercy, your brain began to process what really happened. But you fought so hard against it.'

'I saw her here, though. With you and Jamie.' I give them both a questioning glance. 'I was right outside, looking in through that window . . .' I say, pointing to it. 'Why would I see her here?' Connie turns, then looks back at me, a thoughtful expression on her face.

'Firstly,' Connie says, 'I think maybe it was your reflection you were seeing in the windowpane, and in that moment, your mind conjured Mercy—'

'It just doesn't make sense I'd see her here at all,' I cut in. 'If I called upon her, or whatever you call it, to *help* me, why would I think she was having an affair with Jamie?'

'Secondly,' Connie continues as if I hadn't interrupted. 'As I said: Mercy's role was to help you move on.'

'Oh. Right,' I say, my body going limp with sudden dawning. 'You mean to leave Jamie.' Guilt surges through my veins as I catch a shift in Jamie's posture. But then he and Connie exchange an uneasy look. Now what did I miss? I hear Connie take a breath and my eyes widen as I sense her about to tell me something else I won't like.

'I think it was to make his wish to leave you more bearable,' she says.

The words hit me like a bolt of lightning. I feel physical pain in my stomach and lean forwards.

'I'm so sorry, Erica,' Jamie says now. 'Losing Letitia . . . it changed us both. We grew apart. You pushed me so far away, convinced you were at fault. Convinced I blamed you. Then, after trying for a baby and failing, it basically spelled the end for us. I tried to leave . . .' His voice breaks, emotion distorting his face. I look away.

'I thought I was trying to leave you,' I say, a short snap of laughter erupting from my mouth. 'I did such a good job of lying to myself. Why are you both so keen for me to remember? Aren't I better off living in my own world, the one where I don't have a dead daughter?'

'You've a lot of life left to live, Erica. You deserve to be happy. As does Jamie.'

'Yes.' I look to my husband. 'You do. I'm so very sorry. If I hadn't turned away – hadn't stopped to speak to Wes . . .'

Connie interrupts. 'Your attention was taken for such a short amount of time—'

'Two and a half minutes,' I finish. 'It took two and a half minutes to lose my child.'

Connie dips her head so her eyes meet mine and I immediately rephrase. 'It took two and a half minutes for someone to snatch my child.' I turn back to Jamie. 'Our child.'

Chapter 58

Dr Connie Summers

CCTV BATEMAN'S SUPERMARKET

EXTERNAL CAMERA 3

Child seen walking along the edge of the park within the grounds of Bateman's supermarket, adjacent to the car park. An unmarked vehicle pulls up in a blind spot, out of the security cameras field of view. Girl is seen to approach the gate leading out of the park on the far side. Trees block a clear sighting, but it appears a side door to the vehicle is opened, then closed within seconds. The vehicle drives off. There's no further sign of the girl.

EXTERNAL ENTRANCE CAMERA 1

Woman seen running from store. Looks around the immediate entrance before running down through walkway. Turns back, heads to park. Disappears from view for several seconds before reappearing at gate. Woman runs back to the entrance of the store.

INTERNAL CAMERA 1

Woman runs to staff, is seen going from one to another. Then woman approaches a customer as they pack their shopping. Moves on to the next. For several minutes woman is seen going to each customer before a Bateman's security guard guides her away from the area.

[POLICE CALLED]
[SEARCH COMMENCES]

Connie sits on the sofa, then reclines back. She sinks into the cushions, her body yearning for sleep. It's over. For now. The treatment plan was demanding. Stressful. She prays this time it's worked for good. But of course, can full closure ever really be gained when the police failed to bring anyone to justice? It's possible that the lack of having a person to lay the blame on means that Erica will always return to herself as the only one culpable.

If, when she sees Erica next, she is faced with denial and refusal to accept the situation as it is, Connie's afraid she will have to give up. She's never done that with a client, but then, she's never worked with someone with DID to this extreme. As Erica and Jamie left her house, she watched them walk to his car. Erica moved with a stoop, as if Connie had sucked some of the life from her. She supposes she did, really. That must be how it felt.

As Connie's eyelids grow heavy, she looks to the framed photo of Lindsay.

'Miss you, my darling.'

And as she drifts to sleep, her client's folder slipping to the floor, Connie wonders if she'll see Mercy again. Because she knows only too well how grief works.

Chapter 59

Then

It might've been easier to leave the tiny, lifeless body in the burning van. But the overwhelming guilt didn't allow it. With enormous effort, the corpse of Letitia Fielding was dragged to the edge of the trees, hidden in the long grass by the river. Of course, she'd be found, there was no doubt. And without the burning, DNA would be evident. There'd be evidence of foul play. Her delicate neck had snapped like a twig.

She'd been carefully laid. Her limp arms gently placed across her chest, her pretty blonde hair detangled with shaking fingers and arranged so it framed her pale face.

Angelic.

And now she was with the angels.

But that hadn't been the plan.

The child was meant to be nurtured, loved, cared for. She was meant to bring joy and life.

Instead, now all that remained was the stench of death.

An anguished cry echoed through the woodland, sending panicked birds flying from the nearby trees.

Chapter 60

Erica

We don't speak much on the way home; we're mostly lost in our own thoughts. Jamie's car had been fitted with new tyres by the time our 'session' with Connie finished. Or, that particular session – I've agreed to more although I don't think I'll keep to that agreement. Apparently, I've been here before – although involving Wes was a first – where I've almost, but not quite, accepted the truth. It's an effort to climb out from the car, every part of me hurts – physically and mentally. The hollowness inside me means I should feel light. But as I look up at our home, weights drag me down.

It's not a home though, is it.

It's an empty shell of what once was. A family home without a family.

Jamie reaches me, but I can't look at him otherwise the tears will start up again. Out the corner of my eye I see his hand hesitate in the air between us, then he withdraws it with a heavy sigh and moves away. As though I sense her eyes on me, I turn to see Jean in her window.

'Ah, look at Jean living her normal life with her cats and her knitting,' I say. Jamie stops at the front door and turns back to me, his expression weary. 'Or is she one of my imaginary friends too?' I add, sarcastically.

'Erica,' Jamie says, his tone sympathetic yet reprimanding. 'Don't do that. It's not a joke. She's been really helpful.'

'Yes. Of course.' My face flashes with heat. 'I'm just so confused about everything after what Connie revealed.'

'That's understandable. Come on, let's get you inside.'

'Perhaps we should just pop across. Let her know that . . . well, that I'm okay.'

'Wouldn't you rather wait until morning?'

'I am exhausted, but I think having a normal conversation with someone to remind me of real life might settle me a bit so that I'll actually sleep.'

Jamie pulls the key back out of the lock. 'You've been through a hell of an ordeal.' He tries to take my hand but I pull away. Yes, he's right about that. The life I thought I was living might not have been perfect, but it's a darn sight better than the one I now know is my reality. I blow air from my cheeks, feel my shoulders drop another inch.

'I'm sorry. I've caused all this . . . this pain,' I say. 'And sorry that you want to leave me.'

Jamie closes his eyes, takes a deep breath before opening them. 'Let's talk about all of that later. If you're sure you want to, we'll form a united front to go and speak to our neighbour, shall we?' He holds his hand out again and, after staring at it for a few seconds, I take it.

Jean sees us coming and springs from her chair, the cats scattering in different directions.

'Good to see you, Erica,' she says as she opens the door. Her voice uncertain. 'I'm so sorry about everything. I tried . . .' She puts her hands to her cheeks. 'Oh, my dear. You've been through so much.'

She ushers us both inside and I take my usual chair as she goes into the kitchen.

'I'll make us all a nice cup of tea,' Jean says, her voice shaking. 'Well, a coffee for you, Erica.'

I don't really want a drink – unless it's alcoholic – but nod. When Jean sets the tray down and sits opposite me, I stare at her for what feels like the longest time, trying to get it all straight. 'So, who am I to you?'

'I knew Mercy first, my dear. She's the one who introduced herself and would occasionally pop in. As it happens, that was where she chose to sit.' She points to the raggedy sofa. 'But then you knocked. I didn't realise at first, but I knew something was different – it was the way you walked. The clothes you were wearing – so different to when you were Mercy.' She smiles, her eyes tearing up again. 'You chose a different chair, drank a different drink. It was quite strange, how distinct you were from each other. It came as such a shock to all of us when you began speaking about Mercy – saying you'd *met* her.'

'All of us?' I look from her to Jamie, who, I note, hasn't taken a seat. It's like he's trying to stay out of it – remain on the periphery unless he's needed. This isn't quite how I envisaged a 'united front'. I sense he's pulling back, away from me now. Preparing me.

'Jamie, myself and your doctor, Connie.'

My focus flits back to Jean at the same time as Mercy's voice erupts in my mind: 'It's a conspiracy, don't listen to them.' I squeeze my eyes closed to block her out.

'In fact, you even saw her while you were here,' Jean says.

'Yes, I did. Clear as day.' This is the part I can't reconcile. If Mercy is an alternate personality, how did I see her? Hear her? Speak with her? Connie tried to explain, but everything was so confusing. I didn't, *couldn't*, take it all in.

'It was likely due to the new medication you were on,' Jamie pipes in. 'Hard sometimes to know if the hallucinations were due to your condition or the treatment of it.'

I suppose that makes sense. I'm lost for a second, deep in thought about reality – what actually exists and what is imagined – but Jean's voice brings me back.

'When you asked me about the little girl . . .' Jean dabs her nose with a scrunched-up tissue, then blows air from her mouth. 'Oh, deary me. Jamie was trying so hard, the doctor too – I wanted to do my bit. Be your friend, you understand? But I was so afraid of making everything worse. I know I said the wrong things sometimes – got myself into a right tizzy, even thought I should stop being friendly.'

'You have been wonderful, Jean,' Jamie says. 'Honestly, I couldn't have coped without you.'

I feel weirdly disjointed from this exchange; my head is light and nausea makes my mouth water. For me, I've only been talking to Jean for a month and a half, yet here they are, her and my husband, talking as though they've known each other – me – for years.

'Oh, really,' Jean blushes. 'It's been so lovely to have the company.'

'Two for the price of one,' I say, unable to prevent my sarcastic tone.

'I'm haunted by Letitia's darling little face, her waving hand the last day I saw her,' Jean says, her voice breaking.

My stomach tumbles at the mention of Letitia. I take a

sip of coffee, thinking that'll help settle it. But as I stare into the cup, at the milky-brown liquid swirling, the burning sensation of rising bile makes me gag. 'Can·I use your bathroom?'

'Of course. Straight up the stairs, dead ahead,' Jean says. I note her alarmed face as I leap up and as I dash up the stairs I wonder if it's because I'm about to throw up, or because she uttered the word 'dead'. I fall to my knees in front of the toilet and eject green liquid into the bowl. Each urge pulls at my stomach and I grip it, the memory transporting me to the time I was pregnant and suffering with morning – no – *all-day* sickness.

How have I denied Letitia's existence? According to Connie, it was to protect myself against the horror. The blame. I retch again as images of my daughter bombard my brain. Tears mix with snot as I wail and vomit. I don't care how Connie tries to frame it.

I lost my daughter.

It's *my* fault.

Chapter 61

Then

Friday

'Letitia, sweetheart, finish your Weetabix for Mummy.' I dart around the kitchen throwing open cupboards, making a note of what's needed, then moving to the fridge and ducking down to check what's left as she very slowly spoons the mushy food into her mouth. Breakfasts are a marathon unless I feed her myself. But she's now three years old, I need to encourage independence.

My mobile pings and I stop writing my list to read the notification.

Morning, gorgeous. I kissed you goodbye but you were soundo. About to go into work, so thought I'd let you know how much I love you both. Give my little Tishy-Tia a big kiss from Daddy. Have a good day. See you later babe x

I roll my eyes at the use of Jamie's nickname for Letitia – he knows it's a pet hate of mine and I always use her full name. I lean against the countertop and begin tapping out a reply, but another message pops up.

I'm suddenly aware of my own heartbeat, and a pang of nervous anticipation floods my body. Letitia is speaking to me, but I've no idea what she's saying, her little voice is drowned out by my own internal one screaming: 'Don't respond. Walk away!'

I've the perfect life; everything I want. Why am I even contemplating this flirtatious fling with a virtual stranger? The answer, that it's harmless fun and gives my ego a boost, isn't good enough. If it were Jamie doing this, I'd be furious. Hurt. I'd never think of it as harmless fun, that's for sure.

But, although Jamie loves me, physically I'm left wanting. Isn't that the real reason I'm looking forward to my Friday shopping trip? Not for the attention, the thrill of knowing I make another man hot with desire, but because of the promise of what it might become. For now, it's merely a physical attraction, not an emotional one. And it's not as if we can do anything about the sexual chemistry in the supermarket with my child in tow.

And maybe that's it. It's safe, in a sense. I can feel good, excited about what might happen, without ever breaching the barrier. If it's contained to flirting with each other, a few texts, then no harm is done.

'Mum-*mee*!' The sound of the spoon slamming onto the table brings me back to the moment and I put the phone down without responding to either message.

'You finished?' I sweep the bowl away, flinging it into the sink, then unstrap Letitia from the booster seat at the dining room table. 'Good girl.'

'Look,' Letitia says, her head low on her chest, her honey-blonde hair falling like strands of soft, golden thread. I follow her gaze.

'Oh dear. Never mind.' I snap a piece of kitchen roll off and rub at the wet, brown lumps of cereal on her stripey jumper, tutting when I make it worse. 'A quick change of clothes, then off to the shops!' I say, kissing her on her nose. I feel a surge of love as I look at the smattering of freckles across her nose, her wide, bright blue eyes and pouty lips. 'Such a serious expression,' I say, pouting back until she smiles. 'Right. Let's go!'

Letitia walks unhurriedly ahead of me, then pauses on each stair to turn and tell me the number. By the time we reach ten, she starts at one again and I smile. 'Clever girl,' I say, giving her a gentle nudge. Finally, she reaches the top and we go into her room.

'Can I wear the giraffe top?' She pulls at the middle drawer of the white chest of drawers.

'It's in the wash.'

She sighs.

'This is a pretty top,' I say, pulling the long-sleeved Peppa Pig one out.

'No. Not today,' she says, stomping over to the far wall and running her hands along the giraffe mural. 'I don't like pigs today. I like giraffes.' She turns, a shocked look on her face, then goes to her bed and pulls the duvet back. 'Where *is* Giraffe?'

I suppress an exasperated sigh as she begins rummaging around in her toybox. I am painfully aware she isn't going to find it there because I put it in the wash pile along with her top. I fear a tantrum coming on – either hers or mine.

'I think Giraffe might need a rest,' I say in my best negotiator's voice. 'He's been very busy going everywhere with you. Maybe we should give another toy the chance to go out?' She eyes me suspiciously.

I check the time. It's not as though I *have* to be at Bateman's for a specific time, but because he knows I'm usually there around nine, I'm aware that's when he'll be expecting me and he'll make sure, if he can, that he's near the entrance so we can have a quick chat without gaining too much attention. I've got ten minutes.

With some rapid negotiation involving ramming a large number of PAW Patrol figures into her carry case, I get her dressed in the Peppa Pig outfit, out of the front door and into her car seat in less than five minutes. As I drive away from the house, I check in the rear-view mirror and see Letitia waving out her window.

'Who are you waving at, sweetheart?'

'The cat lady,' she says, then turns her attention to her toys.

It's as though a murmuration of microscopic starlings have pervaded my insides, whirling and swooping as I park at Bateman's. I close my eyes and take some diaphragmatic breaths. I'm being ridiculous.

You're a married woman with a beautiful daughter. What the hell are you playing at?

'Leave those in here,' I say, reaching for the carry case bursting with figures. 'We don't want any to get lost in the shop, do we?'

'Okaaay,' Letitia says, despondently. 'Just one?' Her little voice pitches on 'one' and her pale eyebrows rise.

I look at the time on my mobile. 'Just one, then,' I say, giving in. I have to pick my battles, and now isn't the moment. 'Hold on tight to it.' After lifting her out of her car seat, I reach back in to grab the bundle of shopping bags, then take her hand as we walk towards the trolleys.

'I don't want to go in there.' Letitia gives a firm shake of her head and I rub my hands over my face. Why is she being so stubborn today?

'Fine,' I say, tugging one free of the row of trolleys. 'But I can't hold your hand at the same time as pushing this, so you'll have to hold on to the side.'

She does this for a second, then as a group of teenagers rush by us, she lets go. I manage to manoeuvre the trolley through the entrance, keeping an eye on Letitia who's right behind me, looking down at Skye, the pink PAW Patrol puppy in her hands. It's going to be one of those days.

As we bustle through the entrance, I spot him and my pulse takes a dive at the same time my stomach seems to first drop and then rise in a millisecond, making me light-headed. I smile as he approaches. He tries to make it look casual, like it's a coincidence he's chosen that moment to walk away from the service desk, but I'm sure it's obvious he's making a beeline for me.

'I thought you were gonna stand me up,' he says.

I really should've, I think, as he walks in the same direction as me but keeping some space between us. I check behind me, see that Letitia is a few steps back but happily talking to Skye, showing her the fruit.

'The two-metre rule isn't a thing anymore, you know that, right?' I say.

He smiles. 'Cheeky. You know I have to be careful. I'm pretty sure stalking a customer would be frowned upon.'

'Can you take a break in half an hour, say?' This is the first time I've suggested such a thing and my fingertips tingle, my body buzzing with adrenaline. I'm fully aware nothing can happen, but it would be good to talk to him away from the public gaze. His eyes widen and I see him take a sharp intake of breath.

'Absolutely! I'm at your mercy,' he says before turning and going back to the desk. I'm in the next aisle before I even realise I've walked that far, my face aching from grinning. I crouch to the lowest shelf and grab a packet of biscuits I don't even need and I'm about to turn to talk to Letitia when my phone pings. I instinctively know it's a message from him, so I stop, open the text.

Counting down the seconds, it reads, and my pulse pounds as I awkwardly tap out my reply with one hand.

It's just a bit of flirting. Isn't it? I pocket my phone.

'Okay, then. Let's get you your favourite magazine, shall we?' I say, turning to smile at Letitia.

But she's no longer behind me.

3 WEEKS LATER

Chapter 62

Erica

Once the last of my belongings are packed into the large cardboard box, I collapse down onto the bed and stare out of the window. I chose this Friday to do it because it felt right. In a minute, I'm making a trip. But not to the usual place. I won't be shopping at Bateman's on a Friday ever again. I don't think it'll be healthy being constantly reminded of where Letitia was last seen alive. And equally, seeing Wes will only cause my guilt to emerge.

Jean's yet to make an appearance at her window seat. Instead a single cat lies on the sill, stretched out, his tail looped in a C shape. Perfectly content, blissfully unaware of any of the events and drama of the past weeks. The past year.

'In my next life, I want to be a cat,' I say, looking skywards to make my wishes known to whoever may be listening.

I haven't really seen Jean since the evening I returned with Jamie from Connie's 'session'. She still keeps an eye on the goings-on, knitting while the cats climb over her, but I've been putting off popping in for a coffee. I feel a bit awkward now I know the full story – the fact she knew me as both Erica and Mercy. That all along she was aware my daughter was dead.

Plus, it's been a hectic few weeks with me and Jamie sorting out the cabin, stripping the giraffe wallpaper, repainting the room and putting the cabin up for sale. We haven't touched Letitia's room here, though. I think it'll be a while longer before we both feel capable of tackling that.

A shot of heat flares in my cheeks as the memory of accusing Jamie of having a child with Mercy flies into my mind. How I thought Mercy had stolen my nursery ideas from Instagram and copied them for Tia's room. All along it was Letitia's bedroom. Our cabin. He and Connie think 'Mercy' chose it as her place to live because it was similar enough to be comforting, but different enough to separate the two in *my* mind. I'm still grappling with the DID diagnosis. Despite now knowing I've been receiving treatment for almost a year, it's like the first time again for me, and there's a lot to take on board, so much information I need in order to fully understand it. Manage it. Connie assures me the hardest part is now over with.

I disagree.

The hardest part is getting up every single day knowing I was responsible for my daughter's death and that the person who took her – killed her – was never brought to justice. I have to learn to live with that; gaining full closure might never happen.

My phone pings. I glance at the screen, at the notifications notching up. Likes for my latest Instagram post on my new account. I deleted the **Erica_IVF_Journal** one, replacing it with my **Erica_workingthroughgrief_journal**. I'm slowly building a following and it's refreshing to be me – the mother of a child in heaven, as I like to think of it, although I'm not really religious. I get that believing in something like that offers a degree of comfort – maybe it will for me too one day. I've dropped the posing, attention-grabbing selfies, the person-who's-desperate-for-likes type of images in favour of simple, honest snapshots of my life at any given time. So, today's image was some boxes piled high and the caption simply stated: *Moving on.*

There's one more thing to do before I can fully immerse myself in achieving that goal. Jamie offered to accompany me, but I declined. He's done enough and I need to do this alone. He is helping me move into the flat I've rented on the edge of town over the weekend. After some soul-searching and a lot of talking, we both came to the agreement we'd eventually sell this house and split the proceeds. For now, he'll stay here.

One step at a time.

Automatically I go to wave up to Jean as I drive by, but she's not there. Jamie has since told me more about her involvement in the treatment plan Connie had devised and I'm grateful she put so much time and effort into helping me. I've learned that she was devastated when Letitia was found last year, she wanted to do everything she could to help ease our pain. Thinking about it, as she lives in that house all alone maybe it also gave her a sense of purpose. I should stop putting off seeing her.

This thought motivates me. I could grab some flowers at the supermarket and take them over. I'm sure seeing Jean – now I'm in a better frame of mind – I'll maybe gain closure of sorts. Plus, she'll be pleased to have some company again – Jamie said she loves her cats but misses human interaction since her husband passed not long after Letitia. She'd clearly been going through the grief process herself, which is likely why we connected. How she was able to understand what Mercy was experiencing. And why she took me, Erica the denier, under her wing.

The gravel crunches beneath the tyres, and the small stones press into the soles of my feet through the thin material of my pumps as I get out and begin walking to the entrance. Jamie gave me directions, but now I'm here, some kind of muscle memory takes over and I find myself heading straight to the right place.

I pass a number of large old headstones before spotting the one I'm looking for. Kneeling on the damp grass in front of the small marble-grey one, I run my fingers over the silver lettering of the inscription.

OUR ANGEL, LETITIA MAY FIELDING
BORN 4 JUNE 2019
FELL ASLEEP 16 SEPTEMBER 2022
MUMMY AND DADDY WILL ALWAYS LOVE YOU.

I place the cuddly giraffe down, leaning it up against the stone.

The day after we'd seen Connie, I asked Jamie where all of Letitia's things were. He explained how I'd begged him to pack everything up – every photo, trinket, toy and all of her clothes – and place them somewhere safe, away from my sight. Only some of the furniture in her room remained, and I managed to convince myself it was a nursery, that I'd prepared it in readiness for the new baby we would eventually have. Then, when I was ready, Jamie retrieved a photo album and some of Letitia's favourite toys from the space in the loft he'd created just for her. We talked about our little girl as we turned the pages of the album. It was the closest we've been, yet also the furthest apart; our grief processes polar opposites.

As I look at the headstone and read her name aloud, what I assume now to be grief seeps from every pore of my skin. My insides blaze with pain as if being tugged and squeezed, my heart yanked from its cage, ripped into bits and scattered on the earth. This is why I didn't come here, I realise. Why it was easier to deny my darling little girl's existence. Because the void she left is too unbearable.

The guilt, too damning.

I'm not sure how long I sit by her grave, crying.

The air has cooled around me. I shiver, and look up to see that the clouds have gathered overhead, blocking the sun. I struggle to get up, my bones creaking, pins and needles assaulting my feet as I stand.

'Sweet dreams, my little one.' I blow her a kiss, and then turn away. 'I'm so very sorry for letting you down.'

Chapter 63

Jean

From behind her lounge curtain, Jean watches Erica leave the house, then she steps over the cats and makes her way up the stairs. She's unusually out of puff by the time she reaches her bedroom and has to sit down. She places her palm flat against her chest, feeling the rapid beating of her heart. Once she regains her breath, she gets up and reaches into her wardrobe, retrieving a small, wooden chest. She lays it on the bed, then takes a silver key from her bedside table, unlocks it, lifting the lid gingerly as if afraid the contents might jump out at her.

'Oh, Frank,' she says, taking a photo out and running her fingertips over it. Tears cloud her vision before dropping in large blobs on the smiling image of her late husband. She puts it aside and reaches into the chest for something else. She grips the item in her hand the same time as a dull, crushing pain grips her heart.

'Not yet,' she says. 'Don't take me yet.'

Jean grasps on to the stair rail with one hand as she makes her way back down. Once in the lounge, she takes the letter she left on the table and props it up against the teapot to make sure it won't get missed. Then, instead of taking her usual chair in the window, she chooses Frank's and sits down heavily. The pain radiates to her neck, jaw and then her arm.

'Okay. Ready now.' She turns her head, gazing at the letter which she addressed to Erica. 'Forgive me, dear.'

Her heart feels like it's being squeezed between two strong hands. Her breathing shallows, each one now an enormous effort. Her grip weakens and the item she's been holding falls with a soft thud to the carpet as she takes her last breath.

All but one of the cats gather around her, like they know they've just lost their owner and are paying their respects. The remaining one is more interested in what Jean's dropped. He plays with it: pawing it, pouncing on it, until he knocks it underneath the sofa.

The pink PAW Patrol puppy is out of the cat's reach, and shortly, he loses interest.

Dear Erica,

I cannot express how deep my sorrow is for the death of Letitia. After you read this letter, you will have some long-awaited answers, but no doubt, additional questions, too. Ones I probably won't be able to answer. I apologise in advance for this, but I do hope the explanation I offer now is one that can give you closure. A similar letter to this has been given to the police – but that one merely states the facts, whereas this one intends to supply the psychology, if you will.

We share something, you and I – the scarring nature of loss, the soul-deep longing for a child, and the ability to deny the truth. And the truth of the matter here, I'm afraid, is that it's me, Jean Meneely, who is to blame for Letitia's death.

I watched you and Letitia over the months and years – thought at times you weren't the best mother. You neglected your child, put other things ahead of her wellbeing, working all the hours, leaving her care to others. I had all the time in the world and was willing to put my own life on hold to bring up a child, yet Frank and I remained childless, our attempts at conceiving futile. It was so unfair. I had so much love to give. We'd talked about adoption, but thought we were too old to be considered. How naive I was. You see, it'd actually been ruled out because of Frank's past – he'd been cautioned, put on the sex offenders' register for two years. It was an awful misunderstanding, but he admitted to the indecent exposure to prevent a prison sentence. That was the nail in the coffin. He knew he'd messed up our chances. Wanted to make it up to me.

Part of me was disgusted with myself when I began formulating an idea to take your child and start afresh in a town far away from here. Another part was excited. I tingled with adrenaline at the very thought of it. I planned everything; poor Frank was dragged along. I'm not sure he believed anything would come of my plan. Maybe he went along with my suggestions to appease me, thinking it wouldn't ever come to fruition.

Until that day Letitia waved to me as you left together in the car. Friday. Shopping day.

It was a sign.

This was the best chance I had, I felt it.

I immediately called Frank, putting in motion the

events that I'll forever regret, then I followed you to Bateman's. Your attention was elsewhere, as usual. You were always talking to someone, or on your stupid phone, ignoring your beautiful daughter. You made it ever so easy for me. Who would ever notice an old-looking lady entering a supermarket along with a group of teenagers and leaving moments later minus any shopping? I was hidden in plain sight. As I often am, sitting here in my window, literally on display, yet largely ignored. Just as I believed little Letitia was.

She also knew me as the cat lady – Jamie had often brought her across to stroke the cats. When she spotted me among the other customers that day, she smiled and held up her toy for me to see. You were too busy flirting with a security guard to know what she was doing. I beckoned her and she left your side. Just like that. Of course, so I wouldn't be caught with Letitia, I walked slowly out of the store before she reached me, knowing she was following. With my heart in my mouth, I walked towards the park and to avoid looking suspicious I carried right along the path then to exit the grounds. I hoped and prayed Letitia would carry on into the park believing that's where I was. It was a leap of faith, but I risked a look back and saw her near the park gate – where, on the opposite side, Frank's van was waiting. We knew it would be clocked on CCTV at some point, it was difficult avoiding all the cameras, so he was going to torch it once the deed was done.

The plan all went so horribly wrong, though. My heart breaks each time I'm forced to think about it. Frank was meant to go to an agreed location and I would follow on when safe to do so. That time never came. And this is where I, like you, chose to believe a different outcome because the real one was far too traumatic. My poor Frank. Poor little Letitia.

That day I was frantic as I awaited further instruction from Frank; the sign for me to join them at the rendezvous point. But long, torturous hours passed with no call. My mind grasped on to simple explanations, I convinced myself that he'd merely had to bide his time, lie low with Letitia for longer than we'd anticipated, or that it was too risky for him to contact me right away.

Hours turned into a day. I waited, in limbo, desperate to know what was going on, obsessively checking the local news. There was a search, a heavy police presence, and media speculation on what had happened to the missing three-year-old. I thought they were the worst days of my life. Until the body was found. Then, when police identified the little girl as Letitia, my entire world tumbled down around me.

I couldn't understand it and I was thrown into a state of panic but with no Frank here I was left alone to speculate and worry. Whatever had happened, though, I knew I was to blame. Two days later, Frank finally turned up and I learned the full horror. You see, neither of us had banked on such a little thing putting up a fight. Apparently Letitia kicked and she screamed and in the act of trying to restrain her, keep her quiet so as not to rouse attention, Frank accidentally killed her.

He was a broken man. He battled with his conscience and spoke of turning himself in. But in doing so, he knew he'd take me down with him. Even if he didn't divulge that he'd been doing it for me, he knew the police would be knocking on my door asking *uncomfortable questions. That attention would be drawn to me, too. We'd seen the public vitriol directed at you so what on earth would it be like if they knew who was responsible?*

On the Friday morning, the week following Letitia's death, I found Frank dead in his chair. He left a note explaining how he'd saved up some of his daily heart medication and taken them all at once. That he wanted it to look like natural causes to make sure no one would ever suspect two older people of abducting and killing a child. He was confident that a doctor would issue his death certificate without the need to report to a coroner because he'd seen the GP recently about his deteriorating heart condition. That's love, you see. I thought any threat of being found out was well and truly over after police failed to identify the van driver or any of the people captured on the supermarket CCTV. So when you asked me about the dead girl in the woods, I panicked. Thought you'd somehow worked it all out.

Please forgive me for what I did. I know that's a big ask. Having got to know you over the past months, I have come to realise I was wrong. I think maybe we all see what we want to see; the story that fits our narrative is the one we focus on to enable us to act in ways we know, deep down, are morally repugnant.

I hope you find peace, Erica dear.

With love,

Jean

MEETING 1

Épilogue

My mind is focused on my phone screen, on the shopping list in my smartshop app. It's easier shopping for one, but I still rely on the handy itemised nature of it and I've been experimenting with new recipes which require more than my usual ingredients. I don't want to forget anything vital. It's the first time I've shopped on a Friday at Bateman's after promising myself I wouldn't, and with the crowds of people now getting in my way, I'm regretting my transgression.

A high-pitched squeal tears through me, and I squint at the noise, turning sharply towards its origin. *Jeesus!* A child, no older than four, is standing in the centre of the aisle, screaming at the top of their lungs, face screwed up, mouth so wide I can see their tonsils. Where the hell are the parents? I'm not alone in craning my head, seeking an adult who will take responsibility for their child.

Then I freeze. Who am I to judge? I want to walk away, move as far from the child as possible. But if I do, who will make sure the child is okay? That they don't wander off and get lost entirely. I step forwards, ducking down in front of the still-screaming child. I'm sure she must be pretty, but right now her face is puce, all the blood rushing to her cheeks, and she resembles a beetroot.

'Hey,' I say. 'Please don't cry.' Her mouth snaps closed and for a split second I'm chuffed I've stopped the crying. But then something in her eyes tugs at my heart. Her big round eyes are filled with a sadness that shouldn't be possible at such a young age. 'Don't worry,' I say. 'I'll help you find your mummy.' I take her hand and head to the customer service desk, but a shout from behind me stops me in my tracks.

'Hey! Do you mind letting go of my daughter!' The woman storms towards me, snatches the girl's hand from mine and yanks the child back up the aisle in the opposite direction to me. I stand, my jaw slack, watching them.

'Rude,' I say, loud enough for her to hear. 'I was only trying to help. Maybe you should keep a closer eye on your kid!'

My pulse bangs in my neck as my anger surges. I fold my hands over my abdomen as a griping pain niggles at it. When they disappear around the end of the aisle, I turn and carry on with my shopping.

I'm at the end of the checkout when someone pulls at my arm. I suck in my breath as I turn to see a woman, dressed in an old-fashioned-looking grey coat. Distress is etched on the woman's face, her eyes are wide and imploring.

'Yes?' I ask.

'Have you seen her?' The single sentence sends a sliver of ice trickling down my back. I look down to her hand, where she grasps a photo. She pushes it in front of my face, too close for me to focus on it, but I can tell it's an image of a young girl.

'Is she lost in the store?' I ask.

'Someone took her, can you help me find her? Please! You're the only one who can.'

I'm lost for words, unsure what to do. No one else appears to be responding to this poor woman's desperate pleas. As I fumble with my shopping to take the photo of the little girl from her, I spot the security guard approaching.

'Erica?' he says, his voice soft. 'Everything okay?' My eyes are drawn to his shirt sleeves, which are so tight I can see his biceps straining against the material. Heat burns my cheeks and my breathing shallows as I turn my attention to his face. Something in his eyes makes my stomach lurch. I swallow hard. How does he know my name?

'Erm . . . I don't know . . . I'm not sure.' I stutter. I glance back at the woman. 'This woman,' I say. 'She's lost her child.'

The security guard takes a long breath in, then looks to where I'm pointing. He nods. He offers the woman a sad smile, then puts his arm out to her.

But it's me who feels the warmth of his palm on my shoulder.

'Come on,' he says. 'Let's see what I can do to help.'

THE END

Author note

If you haven't read *The Girl in The Photo* yet, please don't read on – it contains massive spoilers...

I hope you enjoyed reading *The Girl in The Photo* – it's been the most challenging to write of all my novels so far, not only due to the nature of the twist, but because I explore a number of sensitive topics, particularly relating to mental health.

According to the charity *Mind*, mental health problems affect around one in four people in any given year. One of the rarer of these is dissociative identity disorder (DID) which forms the basis of my book. I want to reiterate that *The Girl in The Photo* is a work of fiction, and as such, my portrayal of Erica's DID symptoms are extreme and not experienced in this way for the majority of those living with the condition. In Erica, I wanted to show how trauma was the trigger for her symptoms and her alter, Mercy, was her coping mechanism. I have tried to explore DID in a compassionate way, and not portrayed Erica as someone who is dangerous to others.

For further information, or support:

https://www.mind.org.uk

https://www.mind.org.uk/information-support/types-of-mental-health-problems/
dissociation-and-dissociative-disorders/useful-contacts/

Acknowledgements

The idea for this novel came to me over two years ago. It started with a vision of a woman showing a photograph of a girl to shoppers in a supermarket, asking: 'Have you seen her?' A productive brainstorming session followed (involving my trusty flip chart board together with my trusty friends, my husband, and some prosecco), which gave me the basis for what eventually became *The Girl in The Photo*. It took a while to come together, then the best part of a year re-writing, editing, re-shaping and further editing, tears and some hair-pulling, more editing and fine-tuning… But, I believe it was all worth it.

My huge thanks to J, San and Doug for their input and their unwavering belief in me that I'd be capable of pulling this idea off! Which I hope I have. Of course, this wouldn't have been achievable without the enormous patience and invaluable input from my editor, Elisha Lundin. I'm really proud of the finished result – thank you for all your hard work and for putting your trust in me. Massive thanks to the entire Avon team for everything that goes into making a book a success – so many people are behind the scenes, and I appreciate all you do.

Thank you to my family (and other animals) for your

constant support and encouragement. My gorgeous three children: Danika, Louis and Nathaniel – I couldn't be prouder of you all. And since my last book we've also welcomed a second grandchild and there's another on the way – I love being a Grammy so much to Isaac and Esther and look forward to meeting the third!

As ever, I owe a debt of gratitude to my agent, Anne Williams, who never fails to amaze me. Thank you for everything you've done for me during what I know has been a very challenging year. Your guidance, support and friendship mean such a lot and I'm extremely lucky to have you in my corner.

Writing can feel a little solitary, and so I'm especially thankful to have Carolyn, Libby and Caroline to talk to daily. The Fab Four are unstoppable! I really am grateful to have you as friends and confidantes. Special thanks to Libby for reading the first draft of this book and giving it the thumbs up. My thanks also to the many authors who I'm lucky enough to share the ups and downs of writing life with. You know who you are.

Following a Young Lives vs Cancer UK Good Books auction to name a character in The Girl in The Photo, the winning bidder was Christina Walker – thank you for supporting the charity. Christina wanted me to name a character after her gran, Jean Meneely. Given it's a psychological thriller, I guessed Christina wouldn't mind which character I chose to name Jean. I hope you are both happy with Jean's major role and enjoyed the book!

To my fabulous supporters and readers old and new. Thank you from the bottom of my heart.

Because this book has been a little longer in the making

than my others, I know I will undoubtedly miss thanking some people who have played a part in the process and my apologies if I've not mentioned you!

Other novels by Sam Carrington...

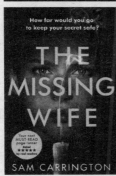